Accidental Birds
of the Carolinas

Stories by

Marjorie Hudson

Press 53
Winston-Salem

Press 53, LLC
PO Box 30314
Winston-Salem, NC 27130

First Edition

Cover art, "Birdhead," Copyright © 2011 by Emma Skurnick

Author photo (page 201) by Tracy Lynn

Author photo (back cover) by Steve Magnuson

Library of Congress Control Number: 2011904576

"Accidental Birds of the Carolinas" was published in *The Literarian*
at the Center for Fiction, Spring 2011.
"The Clearing" was published in *West Branch*, Fall 2002.
"New World Testament" was published in *Encore*, Summer 1997.
"Home" was published as "Almost Home" in *Story*, Winter 1993.

Printed on acid-free paper
ISBN 978-1-935708-30-8

for Sam

Up from the mystic play of shadows, twining and twisting as if they were alive,
Out from the patches of briers and blackberries,
From the memories of the bird that chanted to me,
From your memories, sad brother—from the fitful risings and fallings I heard,
From under that yellow half-moon, late-risen, and swollen as if with tears,
From those beginning notes of sickness and love, there in the transparent mist,
From the thousand responses of my heart, never to cease,
From the myriad thence-arous'd words,
From the word stronger and more delicious than any,
From such, as now they start, the scene revisiting,
As a flock, twittering, rising, or overhead passing,
Borne hither—

—Walt Whitman, "Out of the Cradle Endlessly Rocking,"
Leaves of Grass

CONTENTS

Accidental birds:
Birds found outside their normal range, breeding area, or migration path, arrived through storm, wind, or unusual weather.

THE CLEARING

THE FARMHOUSE SAT ON A RISE at the end of a long dirt road, in a clearing surrounded by fruit trees and ninety acres of pines. It was painted white, and peeling, and some former hippie tenant had scribed a mandala on the wall just inside the front door in fine-point Magic Marker. I painted over it, but it bled through again and again. I finally left it there, a pale and pastel version of itself, hanging ghostlike in the hall.

My first weeks here, wandering the neglected orchard, driving down dirt roads, walking to check my mail, it seemed that this part of the South was abandoned, left to the deer and wild persimmon tree, and what people remained lived solitary lives. The few I saw were isolated figures in a landscape—a man on a tractor across a field, an old woman bent over her garden.

I was the recluse, the woman with dark wild hair, the stranger in the house at the end of the road.

Chicken trucks and old Ford pickups were the norm on the two-lane, and none too many of those. One day I stood next to my mailbox and watched a truck hauling a circus ride rattle down the road. A boy inside lifted his hand in greeting. Did I know him? I raised my hand too, stood there, open-mouthed, as if some special message had been delivered. Then I walked the long dirt road back to my clearing and stayed there, where nobody knew me.

It takes no time at all to fall in love with such a place, if you are paying attention. All it takes is a Luna moth quivering on your porch light. A

newborn mantid's quick infant maw, attacking your little finger in the
grass. A strange throbbing from the shrubbery at dusk, mysterious
and sweet and insistent as sex: the call of a country bird, a whippoorwill.
All it takes is a particular scent, the breath of a place like a lover's
breath before a kiss, full of the richness of life, digestion, desire. The
breath of the clearing where I lived fell from pines and poplars, sweet
gum and oak. It fell from the mouths of neighbor cows rummaging
the apple tree and rose from the fermenting apples themselves.

It rose from the meadow grasses at evening, and settled into their
dry stems, humming, at noon. It sang from the creek, under rocks,
and from the pond, from the bellows of chilled, slow-moving frogs in
the cool of the evening.

How can I describe this place? It was rich as molecules. I knew the
microbes of the soil lifted to my tongue; sometimes rain fell, metallic
and dusty as a tin roof. I knew the smell of my own body—legs, breasts,
hair—inside the scent of the surrounding woods. All these things held
in the air like the gold must of evening or the pink chatter of dawn.

In those first weeks, I lay in my bed, heart pounding with yearning
for this place where I lived, my body infused with a delicious loneliness.
Mine, I mouthed to the glimmering dying day. I wanted to die, so I
could merge my molecules with that mungy ferment. I wanted to die
of happiness.

One day a neighbor came to claim a cow that had taken up residence
under my apple tree. Sarton Lee chugged right up to the house on his
old tractor, spread in his seat like a wrinkled toad, his nephew hanging
on behind. Sarton told me his legs didn't work worth a good gol-darn
because of arthritis. His nephew hopped down and walked around
the cow and began to wave his arms, slowly, like a swallowtail drying
its wings. "Hey, cow, ho cow," he sang. "Ho cow." The cow snatched
up another apple and jerked her huge bony pelvis down the path, away
from those long slow arms, up the road toward home.

Sarton watched them go, in no hurry to follow. He began to talk in
his pale husky voice, told me it was his pastures that spread out to
either side of my long dirt road, full of those low square cattle called
Angus, black against lush fescue. This was his milk cow, he explained.
His Irma. He had named it after his wife who'd passed seven years

before. He must have caught the look in my eye. "That might seem strange to you," he said. "You prob'ly never had a milk cow."

I nodded. I wanted him to go away. But he kept on. Milk cows were loyal, gentle, and completely predictable. They gave everything they had, their calves, their milk, and all they needed in exchange was a little grain now and then, some green grass in spring, good hay in winter. They had personalities, but what Sarton liked about them best was they were satisfied with the world. They knew how to hang on and wait for the good things in life.

His withered hands clutched the wheel; one groped, found the ignition key. Now he would leave. But no. He didn't grudge Irma an apple or two in the fall. He hoped I didn't mind. I shook my head. He looked up at the huge live oak spreading above our heads, listened to the choir of light breezes along its branches. "I planted this tree fifty years ago, for Irma's birthday," he said. "This was her home place." His crackled face stretched tight, looking up. I could see the soft place in the white fold under his chin, a place where the sun had not burned him dark and sere.

Early that fall the kitchen pipes froze. One of the charms of the South, I learned later, is that no one insulates their houses, believing in the immutability of warm weather. The plumber's name was Whiskey Collins, and he lived just down the road, in a tiny cinderblock house next to a collapsed barn covered in kudzu. I found him by asking the bleached blonde behind the counter at the Gas Mart. "Ever'body's pipes froze," she said, shaking her head. "He's fixed mine twice already."

I must have looked doubtful at this news. If he fixed it twice, didn't that mean he hadn't done it right the first time? "He's a friend of my cousin's," she explained, showing the gap between her front teeth. "The two of them were wild. He's settled down some, I guess." *People here want you to know their lives,* I thought, wonderingly.

I called Whiskey from the pay phone. "I'll come," he said, "but not till after supper. Everybody's pipes froze, you know." I knew, I assured him. He did show up after supper, and he worked into the night on the pipes in the wall behind my kitchen sink, humming tunelessly, his compact body contorted in the cabinet underneath, the smooth tread of his work boots sticking out, his monkey face popping up now and then with a screwdriver between his teeth. I found myself pacing, sitting on the front stoop, back to the kitchen, reheating my tea, watching him restlessly, hoping he would finish quickly. There were owl calls I liked to listen to this time of night. At least I thought they were owls. Whatever they were, I preferred their round, haunted notes immensely to human bluster.

But Whiskey took his time. He worked past midnight, and after he'd finished, run the tap for me a few times, and helped himself to some tea, he started telling me his life story, the way people seemed to like to do here. He was moonlighting, he told me, from his real work: monitoring pollution in the river, hoping to get a grant for a big study, studying biochemistry on his own. "I get books at the end of semester sales at the college," he told me. "Some of them are good." Whiskey's pale yellow eyes gleamed with earnestness. I imagined him studying by oil lamp, a room full of outdated textbooks. I could have named them: they were books I had long since thrown away.

"I gave up on graduate school," he said, looking at me curiously, inviting me to tell what I had given up on.

I had given up men and science. Science had been a kind of religion for me but I had lost the faith. It still showed up in my mailbox twice a month in the form of papers I would edit for a journal. Every formula needed checking. Some believe the weight of mankind's fate lies in such calculations. For many a year, in a faraway northern city, I had dedicated every waking hour and much of the night to such questions as: Would humanity die off from excess estrogens in plant foods? Would CFCs invade our pulmonary linings and make it impossible to breathe? Would electric fields cause brain cancer and miscarriage? How will science save us?

All these inquiries had once seemed essential. I worked weekends, nights, in a desperate battle to save the human race. Some winters I never saw the light of day. Suddenly, at thirty-one, it all made me tired. It seemed part of some relentless, self-perpetuating system, like the endless waves of cold air that blow across the Great Lakes from Canada, bringing blizzards, hailstorms, tornadoes, the mad acts of a vengeful God. For a time I amused myself by spinning lines for an article I would never write: "If You Focus on Destruction, Will It Come More

Quickly and in More Gruesome Forms?" I imagined I would sign it Elizabeth Enfield, not Liz, my old science journal name. I wanted to be strange and formal, even to myself.

One day, sitting at my office desk, struck dumb with the misery of it all, I remembered an ad from the back pages of *Nature* magazine. "Farmhouse with 20 acres land, 5 cleared, $12,000. Ambler County, NC." I had enough for a down payment. It seemed incredibly cheap. It sounded far away. I had no children; I had no obligations; my car was paid for; I had a small payout from my pension. And, after Robert, I had every reason to leave. I closed out my bank account, quit my job, packed the car, and left.

I planned to become lean, and hard, and strong. I wanted to be the stranger at the end of the long dirt road, with the mailbox, the science journals, my remaining link to the world. In October, I began to use the crisp vellum pages of outdated journals to light the evening fire.

When my pipes froze again, I considered abandoning the plumbing. It was too much trouble entertaining plumbers. I would use water directly from the pond. As the day warmed, however, and the pipes thawed, I heard the sound of water trickling, a gentle sound. When water began to pour down the wall onto the floor, I went for help.

Whiskey's door was bare in places, peeling silver paint like an aluminum bucket. I was lifting my hand to knock when it swung open. He saw the panic in my face and said, "I'm busy right now." I opened my mouth to protest, but he said, "Don't worry, a little water won't hurt that house. It's built solid." I forced myself to stay silent, to fit into the slow, dull etiquette of emergencies in this place, but I could feel my face pumping blood. He regarded me solemnly. "Since you're here, come on in," he said. "I'll show you my rig."

On a big oak table across the room, lit by shafts of sun through the single small window, was a gadget made out of test tubes and beakers and glass pipettes. I was amazed at how clean it all looked, how clear the distillate—like cold water from a good deep well. "Taste?" he said. I shook my head. He said he made the best white liquor in the county, and he sold it straight. Folks diluted it with corn syrup and cherry Kool-Aid, but that was just habit, he said. "It goes down smooth without all that."

The space around the still was slick and clean as a chemists' lab. The rest of the house was knee-deep in science magazines, books, and old clothes. There was no path through this detritus. You waded through it, like leaf litter on a forest path.

Whiskey wanted to save the river, which he said turned blue, green, and red with dye from the yarn mill upstream on Mondays, Thursdays, and Sunday mornings. Why don't you clean up your own house first, I wanted to say. "They flush it out Saturday night," he said. "They figure everyone's hung over, or in church, and nobody will notice."

I could see he was a believer, one of those who know the world is broken and can be fixed. It was a good thing, really, I mused, watching him work that night. The way the houses were built around here, no doubt my pipes would freeze and burst often. I would need him to keep believing in the healing power of fixing things.

Whiskey came again, many times, all through the cold season. He knew the secrets of well pumps, water heaters, electrical outlets that put out puffs of smoke and sparks. His eyes often looked tired behind his wire spectacles. He read too much, he said. Those worthless books, I thought. But he knew the oddball names of southern trees— "sourwood, that's for honeybees," and "sweetshrub, smells like licorice," and "redbud, also known as flowering Judas—you know, the tree Judas used to hang himself." I wondered at his story—could a grown man have hung himself from those spindly, brittle branches? Whiskey identified properly seasoned split oak by the smell—spiced apples—and could identify the former tenants of abandoned birds' nests by their linings: wren, goldfinch, hummingbird. "See the horsehair?" he said, holding one cupped in his hand, close to my face so I could see. A circlet of rough hair shone like silver wire. His fingers were long and perfectly formed. I drew back, expecting him to touch my face.

"Who has horses around here?" I said.

"Miss Irma used to." He made it sound like Miss Irma was alive, and I knew her.

The mailbox brought endless flows of pointless journal articles that I made fascinating, important-sounding. Late in January it brought a letter from Robert. I had sent him a printed card giving change of address, without a note of any kind, a way of saying, *I am gone too.* Robert had left me, saying he needed to be alone for a time. Robert, who made sure we had the right clothes, the right mountain bikes and espresso maker, the right friends and fashionable vacations. Now, he said, he was looking for the right life, a solitary one, as if that were the newest style. I was right not to believe him. Two weeks later he was with my best friend, who also happened to be my boss, who had been telling me for months, for years, that I shouldn't work so late, that saving the world could wait, and I ought to get out more on weekends.

I had burned an entire album of happy vacation photographs at Christmastime, some with Robert, some with other lovers, going back in time. Now I opened the letter. It was short. The subject of each sentence was himself. *Lizzie—I have been going through changes. I quit my job. I sold the car and went trekking in Nepal. I spent six weeks in a monastery there. I have found some peace. Write me.*

A laugh choked in my throat. A monastery. Robert, who thought of yoga as a way to scientifically increase the pleasure of sex. I could see the bristle of his cheek, his windburned jaw, in harsh Nepalese light. I wondered for an instant what he would find to satisfy him in that world. Then I burned the letter.

In February a front howled in from Canada and the pump froze solid. I did not know, in my city ignorance, that people ran light bulbs to their pump houses to keep them warm in winter. Whiskey worked late again, past midnight, his work shoes gleaming in the moonlight, stuck out from the little door in the well house in the yard. I stayed up reading my journal articles at the kitchen table. He staggered in past midnight, cheeks and hands red with cold, wire-rims steamed opaque with the sudden heat. He needed another tank for his torch. This was his night to check the river. "The Sissipahaw," he said, lingering on the esses, as if the word itself had power.

"The what?" I said.

"That's what it's called," he said. "Come with me. It's not far. You'll keep me awake."

I nodded. Whiskey, for all his books and wrench sense, couldn't keep the river from turning colors. There was something perversely satisfying in that. I wanted to see.

He drove his old Plymouth Duster, both headlights out, so that I recognized the road only by the crunch of gravel and washboard. He took a turn down a tangled path no wider than the car. Jostling over ruts and rocks, the car flung my body against the door, against Whiskey's shoulder. I pushed my feet to the floor, flattened my back against the seat. "Not far," he shouted over the spin of the tires.

At the river Whiskey grabbed his flashlight and shone it over the curvilinear water. The edges were velvety with ice, but the center of the stream flowed free. A smell like metal mixed with fabric softener filled my nostrils. The water bubbled bright magenta, foamy pink. Saturday night's color.

On the way back Whiskey stopped in an open place in the road. My skin prickled with how close he was, how his breathing warmed the air. I observed an animal reaction, the hairs standing up on my arms, an urge to make a guttural sound, something like a growl: *Don't get too close.*

Whiskey stuck his head and shoulders out the window. He was staring at the moon, so bright it lit the road. "I found a lump of iron in that field once," he said, happily, to the air. His neck stretched back so tight I could see the cords of his throat shining, blue-white and smooth, like some pure element extruded from his body. I watched his lungs expand and contract. "I had it checked at the college." His voice was squeaky with excitement. "It was a meteorite."

Whiskey slipped back behind the wheel. I became aware of his smell, like wool shirts and sweat and lichen. He tapped my shoulder, pointed out a planet through the windshield. "Mars, I think," he said, his exhalation warm and mossy on my neck. I edged to the window, stuck my head out, threw it back and looked straight up. Mars was a red and steady glow. The stars blazed a painful light. The world seemed upside down, ready to fly away. "Are you happy?" Whiskey whispered. He seemed to be speaking to the stars. They did not answer, nor did I.

That night I went to my warm bed and never slept for the tingling of my skin. I could hear Whiskey downstairs finishing his work, humming in his throat and clanging around till all hours. In the morning all the faucets worked fine and his teacup was washed and dry, placed upside down to drain on a clean hand towel. Looking at that cup, for just an instant, I could have died of loneliness. It's a cup on the counter, I told myself, it's not your *life*. I bundled up, went outside, headed for a protected nook I had discovered, out of the wind, sun in my face. I sat there, listening to the cold birds talking to each other, zooming above my head, for the rest of the day.

A few weeks later, Whiskey came to the door unbidden. "Why don't you help me," he said, "with the river?" I stared at him. He nodded at the stack of journals on the kitchen table. "You know your stuff. They would listen to you."

I shook my head. The prospect was repulsive. "You're the one who can make a difference," I lied. I tucked my hair behind my ears. "I'm no good at that."

Whiskey stared at me with his pale eyes. "You would be good at it," he said.

He was disappointed, I could see that. He would have to get over it. I closed the door. The dragging muffler on his Plymouth sounded like an accusation. *This is what it comes to,* I said to myself, *relying on people.*

The winter turned milder, everyone's pipes stayed intact for a time. I spent the remaining days of February tromping the fields, watching the slow daily progress and retreat of ice skinning across the surface of the pond, spying on winter birds in the thickets and vultures riding high thermals on thaw days, checking the bird book I got through the mail. Watching the clear blue sky for a shred of cloud. Chunking bricks of wood in the huge old potbellied stove. Finally getting the air mix right, learning the trick of the draft so the smoke didn't billow back, black and sooty, into the room. More and more I left my journals open on the kitchen table and wandered out into the clearing, forgetting to come back for hours.

At night I wrapped myself in quilts and lay in the north field, watching stars blaze like fire, listening to the owls—barred owls by their cry, *Who cooks for you?* Listening to the sounds wind made as it conversed with sleeping plants. Listening to my breath.

One cold morning after brief rain, frost came like quill feathers, stuck white and ribbed and random into the surface of the dirt road. I almost danced with the pleasure of it, its strangeness. Things were going to be different here, I was sure of it. The cold slapping my cheeks, the dazzle of each day, even my mastery of the wood stove were like promises of passage to a new world, crystalline and clean and solitary and safe. I did not miss people; the pain and marvel of cold air made good company.

When March came, full of endless pale blue days and dry burnt breezes, I planted peas, potatoes, spinach—my first garden. I had studied up: soil tests, manure, lime, crop yields, fresh seed. By the end of the season I would have everything required to last the winter. I watered once, and waited. I did not know, when nothing came up, that it needed rain. I thought it just needed time. I finally heard it on the radio. My perfect sky was a hundred-year drought. Corn was roasting in the soil. Crows were finding it by the cooked smell.

By early April the fires had started across the Piedmont, and the county lay under a haze of burnt soil, the microbes sizzling and ashes drifting onto cars, roads, porches. One day I lay naked in the yard, watching something like a gray feather float and sway, then land in my pale lap. Holes appeared in the laundry on the line. I couldn't keep the stoop swept clean of cinders. It was as if the whole world was a hearthstone, holding the ruin of chips and ash to its breast like evidence of a hidden source of heat.

I went to the Gas Mart for news. They knew me by then at the mart, where I went for gas and hoop cheese, cigarettes and RC Colas, and all I required of human contact, the old men's weather reports more accurate than any on the radio. When I got there, the usual crew was talking in slow, tense drawls about the fires and the weather and when it would rain—if ever again—and whether the wind had shifted from the big 300-acre tract still smoldering on Headon's Mountain. The prognosis, it seemed, was not good. There had been a brush fire at Sarton Lee's. Flames had raced across his back field and terrified his cows.

"I guess my trailer will be next," the bleached blonde, gap-toothed clerk said, shaking my cigarettes down into a paper sack. "Too bad I ain't got insurance."

"Maybe you still could," I said, knowing it was a lie, thinking how impossible it would be for me. I had not earned a penny in weeks. The broken-down house was not yet mine.

"Maybe you'll get a break," one of the men said. "Maybe the wind will change."

I paid for my gas, headed for the door just as a group of firefighters shouldered through. I found myself nose to nose with a man in a fire suit. He gripped my arms. "Stop," he said. "You can't go back." It was Whiskey Collins.

"What?" I said stupidly. "Why?"

"Fire jumped the line," he said. "Wind's picked up. We're moving Sarton's cows."

"Oh Lord," said the blonde behind the counter. "Oh my Lord."

"Jack's clearing out the trailer, Lucky," Whiskey said.

I'd never asked her name. It was Lucky. She had a boyfriend. He was Jack.

A laugh caught in my chest. My beautiful house, my Luna moth, my meadow. My safe place. My mandala, my home, my high soft bed. My precious loneliness.

"I have to go," I said. "I'm going."

My reputation as a crazy Yankee lady had by then been established, I learned later, by my refusal to attend church or cook in my kitchen. I lived off apples and air, people said. I kept my money under the stoop, they said. I was a lesbian, a drug dealer, a misfit. They had seen a picture of an African prince on my wall. I was married to a foreigner, I had mulatto children.

I did not know then that Southerners define a person by her people. Southerners, like nature, abhor a vacuum. I had no children. I had no people. For lack of evidence, they made up entire genealogies for me.

I turned to Whiskey that day and all I saw was the things I thought I owned—my orchard, my meadow. All I heard was the grass singing in the night.

Whiskey saw the wild light in my eye. He said, "I'll take you."

We banged and bumped down the road toward rolling muscles of smoke. The wind shifted again, long enough for the black cloud to ease out of the road, to swing away from Sarton's pastures. We made the clearing.

Sparks whipped up into a yellow sky behind dark pines. I opened the car door and stared. "Get what you need," Whiskey said. "Not what you want."

There was nothing in the house I needed: a bed, a lamp, a chair. I wanted to rip the sweet sun-dried sheets off the line. I wanted to dig the ghost mandala out of the wall and carry it away. I wanted to go to the smoky orchard, fling myself to the earth and hold on. "Give me a minute," I said. I strode into the yard and nosed the air for something I knew. I closed my eyes and saw morning light shining through the bare window onto the bare floor. I smelled the heat, building every day from the west, toward summer, and the melting tar and singed pine needles settling over my house and fields and apple trees and woods, like the hot breath of a charcoal grill.

The clear air collapsed and smoke filled it. Blind and choking, I ran for the car.

Whiskey took me to a friend's house in town, put me in the guest bed, and went out again to try to save the town. I lay there listening to the hungry wind tear at the windows.

Twenty hours later they sent him home, wind having shifted again, back-burning the blaze away from where most people lived. Lightning had finally come, starting new blazes and also bringing rain. I woke from uneasy sleep, heard Whiskey come in and settle on the couch, then dreamed I watched him dreaming, his pale eyes closed and sooty, twitching with visions of fire.

I heard him showering the next morning. He came and stood in the doorway, hips wrapped in a towel. Without his wire-rimmed glasses his eyes reflected many colors—they were not pale yellow at all, but hazel: blue, green, and gold. The line of his torso was angular and finely muscled and compact. His chest was deeply scarred on one side.

"Are you hungry?" he said. A woman came and stood behind him, a small bird of a woman with glossy red hair like fine silk cut short around her face.

"Hello," I said.

"I'll cook," she said, and looked at Whiskey, who did not look back. She walked away.

"Girlfriend?" I asked Whiskey.

He looked at me with his sad hazel eyes and shook his head. "Used to be," he said. "She's a good person."

It occurred to me then that Whiskey might be that impossible thing, a man who is at ease with love, who finds a way to love everyone he knows, and keeps loving them just for the pure hell of it. A man who makes friends of old lovers. A man whose former love will feed and shelter him, any anyone he brings, because her world is larger in his presence. For an instant, I envied her that easy connection with Whiskey's world, wondered what that could possibly be like.

Whiskey sat down with me for a breakfast of eggs and grits. The woman stood watching us, dressed in nurse's whites, then headed out for her weekend rotation, walking on silent shoes, closing the door softly as she went.

The rain sheeted down the windows, obscuring all but angry light. It had rained so hard last night, Whiskey told me, the water could not soak in, but flung itself across the scorched land and downhill toward any ditch. Ditches, streams, rivers were filled to overflowing. I washed the dishes while Whiskey made some calls. I listened to his crackling radio reports. Everything I had in the world was burned or drowned. I crawled back under the covers and stared at the window, unable to move.

Whiskey came and sat on the bed. He made a sound in his throat that was part song and part question. I looked up, face smeary with tears. He reached out with his long singed fingers and pushed the hair behind my ears, the gesture I know is my own habit, my own ritual of anxiety. I wondered if Whiskey thought he knew me well. Lovemaking would be an exquisite grief with such a man—shuddering, collapsing, helpless, sorrowful. I put my fingertips on his wispy beard. It was time to drown in sorrow.

I had never known a man who cried when he made love. Before Robert I had had six lovers, each of them, like Robert, businesslike and efficient, proud of his prowess, not prone to talk. Tears streamed out of Whiskey's eyes as he touched me. He pressed his wet face against mine, cried out when he came, shuddered and groaned in collapse as if in pain. He called my name as a kind of begging: *Elizabeth, Elizabeth.* I found myself touching him to comfort him, holding him as if he were a precious bird. I wanted to weep with him, but as if to refute his flood, my eyes became stingy with tears, squeezing them out, one at a time, tasting of bitter salt.

Sometimes a smile would spangle his face like sun and rain together. After a time, it was as if a layer of skin had burned off between us, leaving something clean and tender, smelling of pine and lichen and salt. We slept through the day, waking in the dusky light to eat and make love again. Whiskey told me about his scar—snakebite, copperhead—and asked me about my belly scar, appendicitis. He told me the story of his life, where he was born, how much he loved the people and the land and the river. I soaked his story in like rain, but could find little to say in return. Like the spangling light on Whiskey's tears, I knew this time would be gone soon, meant little. It was a comfort for two lost souls. It could not last. I had never known such a love to last.

"You are so quiet," he kept saying. "What secrets are you keeping, lovely Elizabeth?"

My house was half burned, the front porch and kitchen gone. The living room and the bedroom above had survived, but with one wall entirely consumed, leaving my four-poster exposed like a doll-house bed, safe and dry, on the second floor. The rain had turned the fire. The rain had saved it.

Whiskey poked around in the charred frame of the first floor, looked up at the floor joists of the bedroom. He began to list the kinds of things that needed to be done. I could see him picking up, one by one, and shouldering all the pieces of my life that were broken. I could see him thinking about the pleasures of repairing my life. I could see my life diminishing to something ordinary, involving serious plans and hardware stores and apartments in town. "You could—" he began.

"I'm staying," I interrupted.

Whiskey looked up and said, "Of course you're staying." He gave me a funny look. After a while he said, "I'll be back." I didn't watch him go.

I propped an orchard ladder against the blackened bones of the second floor and climbed to the bedroom. A few cinders had sizzled on the quilt; the small holes were deep, as if etched by acid. I pulled back the spread. The sheets were clean. I got in, fully clothed, and spread my arms and closed my eyes. A roasted smell rose from the beams of the room below. A wren darted in and out, making a frantic nest above the headboard.

I slept, waking to hear the night sounds from time to time: A mockingbird across the valley. The muttering of an owl. Wind clacking the charred limbs of trees together like bones. The wren's feathery snore above my head.

I didn't notice that Whiskey didn't come.

In the morning I looked out and saw that the rain had saved the huge live oak, the one Sarton planted for Miss Irma, and half my fifteen acres of woods. Blackened stumps steamed alongside a fringe of living pines. The orchard was gone.

The meadow sparkled in new light, black and singed green. I walked it in my white sneakers, and they turned black. The trunk of the old apple tree was scorched to a crumble on one side, its tender twigs crisp with heat. Charred branches scratched at the clapboard, scribbling messages in crazy ink.

I walked to the end of the road. Whiskey's cinder-block shack was smoke-blackened, but the trees enclosing it had somehow stayed green, branches lifting in a light breeze. His car was gone. I stood on his wood-chopping block and looked in the window. Someone had been cleaning up. Almost half the floor was clear down to linoleum, bags of trash piled up against the wall.

I kept walking. Passed Sarton's cows gathered on the green side of a rise, grasses burnt to cinders on the other side.

Up at the gas station my car had burned, frame twisted, roof blown off, tires melted to the ground. Lucky was down on her knees in the store's rubble, salvaging half-charred cartons of cigarettes. "Want some?" she said. "They're free."

I was hungry, chain-smoking Chesterfields and scrounging apples from the caved-in pantry, when Sarton Lee chugged by that evening with a box of food and an old Coleman stove and lantern. "You'll need this to tide you over. Don't thank me. We're neighbors." He tooled over to the charred remains of the house. Leaned and knocked on the support beam with his knuckle. "She'll stand," he said. "But I've got a spare room if you get tired of spiders in the sheets. Don't be shy to ask, now, girl."

I nodded. How had I missed how kind he was?

When Whiskey Collins came to check on me the next day, I was boiling an egg on the camp stove. "I'm fine," I said. "Sarton brought some food. I can walk to town if I have to."

Whiskey looked around with his multicolored eyes, pale as watered bourbon in the morning light. "Can we sit down a spell?" he said.

"All right," I said slowly. *Here it comes,* I thought, *the Where-do-we-go-from-here discussion.*

We sat on round sections of oak, the remains of my wood pile. He straddled his like a cowboy, picked up a stick, scratched lines in the cinders under his boots. "The thing is," he said, "I have something to tell you."

I had never known a man who articulated the color of my lips, the tender edge of my chin, my deep, deep eyes, my rampant hair. I always knew these things about myself by the way men held me in their beds, pushing and straining, going after some beautiful place they could claim, groaning with delight or shame. The fingers of faithless men had traced my lip, my ribs, my thighs and clutched at my heart. They had not sat across from me on a Southern spring morning and stammered out the words for loveliness as Whiskey did that day. "I love your eyes," he said. "I love your mouth," he said. "I love the shape of your lips. They are like apples. I love the way you talk and don't talk. I love how your ribs move when you breathe."

Hot tears sprang to my eyes. He looked at me, a pained expression on his face. "Oh, no," he said. "I meant to make you happy."

How do you say to a faithful man that true love is not what is needed in your life? What was needed was charred branches clacking, waking me from sleep; what was needed was tender morning light picking out each cell of devastation. What was needed was a way to shuck my cold, bitter husk, the hardened shell of someone I had been for a long time, who would share a bed without any faith or meaning.

Whiskey wrapped his arms around my shoulders and let me cry. He said he loved me anyway. "You are so alone," he said. For a moment—for half a second—I let myself think of him, his whiskery chin, his pale eyes, his neatly muscled arms and legs, his heart and gaze, in my high soft bed.

I made him promise to go away.

I stayed in my ruined house, open to the meadow on one side. A sheet of canvas kept the rain out, flapped like ship's sails in spring thunderstorms. After a week or so, my meadows sprung up such a green that it might be a new color in the universe. The green was so full of water, and sun, the sky's blue paled in comparison. On the charred side, the old apple tree erupted in new petals, defiant and rainwet against black branches. Tree leaves grew large and heavy with warm days and rainy nights.

The bank sent a letter forgiving mortgages for the next six months. I had a chance of staying. Cattle egrets came clattering across the roof the next day like a gift. They stepped high, bobbing heads and waving their sex-blushed wings in a slow dance. They mated for a day and then moved on.

The next week I turned my attention back to the garden. It was time to start over. I couldn't afford to make mistakes. I would grow my food, and preserve it, and save enough to rebuild. I planted every kind of seed I could scrounge from my shed, along with some tomato plants and onion sets from Sarton Lee. I studied old Home Ec books I found in his shed. I studied canning.

As I planted and hoed, I began to imagine the lives of the people who lived on this road, all engaged in this ritual of rebirth: Sarton in his kitchen, spooning grits, watching Dixie cups of watermelon seedlings grow on the windowsill; Lucky behind her trailer, coaxing tomatoes up a trellis; the old woman hoeing potatoes, picking beetles off fat green leaves and dropping them in jars of suds.

I could not imagine what Whiskey was doing.

One night in July the frogs stopped singing and in the silence there blew up such a storm that it ripped the canvas cover from the house. Rain flew sideways, drenching quilt, sheets, mattress, leaving me cold and shivering. Lightning struck the live oak and left a gash, oozing sap. In a lull, I crabbed down the ladder, ran and crouched in the dry corner of the shed, the only enclosed space I still owned. The earth breathed ozone under my feet, fear like aluminum on my tongue.

In the morning I slid the soggy mattress off the bed to prop it in the sun, but it slipped and tumbled out the second story to the ground. I headed to Sarton Lee's, thinking his tractor bucket might be able to scoop it back to the second floor.

At Whiskey's house there was a stranger's car. My god, I thought, he's gone. I hadn't thought about him in weeks. The idea of him leaving pierced me strangely. I edged around to the window, stepped up on the chopping block, and peered in. The floor was clean, shined and polished. There was a sofa with a bright new sheet thrown over, some colorful pillows. There was a rag rug in shades of blue and green. The still was gone. On the table in its place was a jar of flowers; there were place mats, plates, and silverware set for two.

There was a low murmur of voices. Two figures emerged from the bedroom door. I pulled back from the window, but not before I saw who it was: Whiskey, with his arm slung easy around a woman's shoulders. A small, birdlike woman with a flash of silky hair. His old lover. The nurse.

The light caught their faces: hers sleepy, smiling; his loving and protective. I'd seen this exact scene before, these same expressions: Robert and his new love, at my favorite breakfast place. Feeding each other bits of scone with their fingertips like courting bluebirds. I must have made a sound. Whiskey turned and saw me.

I stepped off the stump, twisted my ankle, fell into leaf litter.

"Elizabeth?" he called out. He rounded the corner, found me lying there clutching my ankle. "Oh, no, Elizabeth." Sorrow filled his monkey face, wrinkling his forehead like an animal's. The woman stood beside him, watching me. "Let me see," she said. She crouched beside me. "Go away," I said.

She regarded me with pity. "You were spying through the window," she said. "What do you think you saw?"

"We're fixing up for you, Elizabeth," Whiskey said, those pale eyes glinting. "She's helping me."

It was absurd. Why would they do that? And why would he think I would believe him?

He reached out his hands to pull me up.

"Go away," I choked. "Leave me alone." I pulled myself up, leaned on a tree to catch my breath. Then I ran.

"Wait," he called out. "Wait!"

"*Leave me alone!*" I screamed at him, running, running, every step a shooting pain, toward the safe kitchen of Sarton Lee. Whiskey did not follow.

Sarton nursed me for three days with comfrey tea and BC powder. He kept a Bible on his kitchen table and read from it each morning after milking Irma. Sometimes I listened while he whispered the words, murmurs of the fruitful earth, and the labors of man, manifest by fire. A heat wave had arrived, sneaking up on dry breezes, then sitting, like six tons of dead weight, on the shoulder of the land.

Heat pressed down on my body at night, drugged me to weariness in the morning.

On the third morning I was able to walk with no trouble. "I'm better," I announced at breakfast. Sarton handed me my coffee in a chipped teacup, loaded with sugar and milk, "Ladies style," as he called it.

"You can stay if you want," he said, looking down at his hands. I had a terrible feeling he was going to try to hug me.

"I'm fine," I said. "I should go." I watched one more time as he went through his lonesome morning rituals, his lips pursing at his coffee, forearm trembling to lift the frying pan, then out at the barn, head bent against the flank of his slow-moving milk cow, fingers squeezing the teats, still missing his Irma.

Outside, on Sarton's stoop, heat slammed into my face like the side of a shovel. For the first time, the company of summer seemed too much to bear. Sarton had made up a sack of things, some clean sheets and linens, a load of tomatoes to can, and a cold quart of buttermilk. I held the sack to my chest and asked, "Is it always like this? I've never been so hot in my life."

Sarton Lee nodded. "Like the plagues of Egypt around here, must seem to you. Fire, flood, lightning, heat wave. I'm expecting locusts."

I could feel the sweat trickling from my scalp, along the edge of my forehead.

Sarton looked at me seriously. "Barn gauge says eighty-six already," he said. "It's going to be a scorcher. Best take a break, cool off somehow." He paused, squinted up at the white sky, seemed to listen to a sound behind the whine of cicadas.

"Did you know he was married?" he said.

"Who?" I said.

"Whiskey Collins," he said. I shook my head. Sweat now trickling down my neck. "Wife run off on a day like today. For the longest time he thought she was coming back." He looked up at some far off shimmer of breeze and I glimpsed that white place under his chin.

Then he turned to me. "Irma used to say, 'Only the guilty run away. Only kindness makes you stay.'"

I nodded an agreeable way, wondering if he was as dotty as he sounded. On the walk home I got it. Whiskey, Sarton, all the people around here were the kind who stay. As far as running away, I didn't know if he meant Whiskey's wife, or Robert, whom he didn't even know, or Whiskey himself. It didn't occur to me until I was halfway down the road that he might have meant me. I was the kind who ran away.

If kindness is a part of love, Robert had never loved me. And I, in turn, had not loved him. I saw it then. Robert must have known it too. All the blame I'd held for him shuddered my chest, then hung there like shame, enclosed and beating.

When I got home, there were forty more pounds of ripe tomatoes hanging from the crusty vines. Four days later it was still blazing hot. The flame from the gas burner shimmered like a mirage; by two o'clock in the afternoon I'd burned my hand twice, forgetting that fire was hotter than the air and required special handling. My tee shirt reeked with sweat and tomato juice and seeds. I'd worn the same cutoffs for days, sitting in the dirt, grinding in the grime. My body smelled like cottage cheese gone pink with mold. The stink of my own body was making me sick.

I pumped some well water over my head, rinsed out my tee shirt in a bucket, wrung it out, and put it back on. I picked a fresh apron, the last one, from a pile of Miss Irma's linens. It smelled hot, like starch and sage. In one pocket was a folded page torn from a Bible; inside it was a twist of fine hair, like a baby's.

The verse was about a child who could not be healed.

It occurred to me then that I might be the only woman on earth who was so contained, as if sheltered inside a jar, through whose clear glass I could see life played out, but refuse its touch. I peered into the jars of whole tomatoes, suspended like peeled human hearts in clear plasma. Then I lowered them into boiling water.

After the allotted time, I lifted the rack, steam swirling around the jars, and set it too hard on the plank table. One jar exploded, spattering juice, scalding my leg, and sprinkling glass on my sneakers. I stared at the glass and red fleshy lumps of tomato, watched a swath of my thigh turn the color of rage. A car was coming down the drive. It was Whiskey, rumbling up slow in his Duster, raising great clouds of grit into the thick air, two others jammed into the front seat beside him. Whiskey pulled right up to where I stood in the yard, as if the world were one big road.

Before I could move, they tumbled out of the car. Lucky waved. "Hi," she said. "This is Jack. We came to rescue you." Jack looked at the mess at my feet and grinned. His face was leathery, like a work boot. "Looks like you need it," he said.

"You burned your leg," Whiskey said. White blisters had formed on a red patch of thigh.

"Are you okay?" Lucky said. She pulled an ice cube out of her Hardees cup, offered it on an outstretched palm.

I took the ice. It melted, popping the blisters and flattening the skin. "More?" Lucky said.

I nodded. Lucky's ice made an island of balm.

"Come see," Whiskey said. "Come see what we brought you."

In a Styrofoam cooler in the back seat was an ice cream churn filled with white froth and packed in ice and salt. "This man I know from the mountains brought blueberries," Whiskey said, in his excitable voice. "Wild ones. Sarton had cream. I had sugar. Lucky got ice up at the store. We just have to turn the handle."

"You mean you just make it? By turning the handle?" I said.

Jack guffawed. "Sure you make it," he said. "This is a city girl, all right."

The idea of ice cream took hold of me: more than anything I craved something cool and sweet, and lots of it. "Let me do it," I said.

They set the churn on the table and let me crank away.

By the time it hardened up we had each taken four turns and we were sweating from the effort, hotter than before. We ate blueberry ice cream until we were sick with it and our lips and tongues turned black from the berries.

It was still too hot to live.

"Feel your stomach," Whiskey said. He pulled up his shirt and laid his palm on his belly. Lucky did it. I did the same. "It's cold," I said.

"Not cold enough, though," he said. "Here." He grubbed some ice cubes out of the cooler, handed one to me, started rubbing the other on his forehead. Lucky grabbed a handful for herself and Jack. We lay on the ground, sated, sliding ice cubes up and down our arms and legs, all over our faces and the backs of our necks.

"I know this place on the river," Whiskey said, "where a spring comes up. The water's always fifty degrees."

"You measure it?" I said, skeptical.

"Naah, I just feel it," he said.

"That river is polluted as hell," Lucky said.

"Don't eat the fish," Jack said.

"This is different," Whiskey said. "Different water."

"Let's go," I said. I didn't care if he was making it up. I didn't care if it was polluted. It was too hot to live.

We were all wearing next to nothing. It would have been ridiculous to leave it on. We stripped, flinging our clothing on rocks and tree limbs, and jumped in the water. Whiskey had scooped out a deep basin and lined it with rocks, walling off the main flow of the river. The spring bubbled up from the gravel at our feet, cold and clear. I caught flashes of Lucky's breasts, white and bulbous, and the thick pubic thatches on the men. It occurred to me for an instant that it might be cruel for me to show myself in front of Whiskey. Then I plunged my head underwater and forgot everything.

There was splashing, and laughter, for a time, but then our movements became slow and luxurious. The water reflected opaque green and shifting blue from the trees and sky and hid our nakedness. We all settled into perches on submerged rocks, just our heads sticking out, dunking them too now and then, hair and river water streaming over our faces. Lucky sang songs, Jack chimed in with a resonant bass, Whiskey hummed tunelessly along, I applauded. It was like some wholesome summer camp I'd never been to.

Lucky and Jack sang in excellent harmony. "Do you play?" I said. Lucky giggled. "I mean, do you sing for people?"

"Just for Jack," Lucky said, making a kissy face at him, sucking air through that front tooth gap.

We floated together for what seemed like hours, the light slowly shifting lower in the trees, our voices dropping into silence. Lucky and Jack slipped off to the woods. I lay, half-dozing, in a shallow patch of sunset light with a rock under my skull, the delicious play of water and heat lapping my skin. Whiskey came and crouched beside my head, dripping water from his fingertips into my hair, onto my eyelids, then in my ears.

"Hey!" I said. "Cut that out." I shook my head and opened my eyes into the sun and saw my own body blaze before me, red and wavering in the water, the tips of my breasts floating at the surface, my pale hands and feet like fishes, submerged, lucent.

I saw then what Whiskey saw: I was beautiful.

My microbes shimmered. My molecules were forms of light. I fell in love with myself for an instant, and in that moment, opened my arms wide. Whiskey slipped into the water and glinted before me. A memory of tears shone on his face: river water, spangled with the colors of his green-gold eyes. I did what Judas did: I kissed him. I kissed him to tell him he was a good man and I was not worthy. I kissed his monkey face to be as beautiful as what he saw. I kissed his lips to drink the cooling water of his blessing, his steady faith. I kissed him, again and again, and did not stop, because I was a creature of this world, and like all living things, subject to the dizzying laws of nature.

Rapture

Here's how things started, or as near to the beginning as I can stand to say. (There's some things in this story I can't even think about.) This was way before that new girl come to live in the house at the end of the road. Before Miss Irma left this world. It starts with Wiener, my dog.

He was with me one night that fall, checking the east pasture fence, and I saw it clear. Smudged white across the tops of the apple tree branches like a silver cloud. A big old comet, just like they said in the paper, heading straight for that dust heap of stars, what my Daddy used to call Six Sisters and the Missing Girl Electra, because there are supposed to be seven and you can only see but six, and even with my glasses these days it's down to five to tell the truth. I started thinking, *What if it was some kind of force from the sky that lured my girl Trudy away? What if she's up there, passing by, in that silver cloud?*

Wiener put his big muddy paw on my shoe, looked up, eager, at the sky. He wagged his tail, and barked. The comet flared. No question. It flared. Then it happened again. Wiener barks, the comet flares, Wiener wags his tail. I got right spooked. That's when I thought it for the first time: *What if Wiener really is one of them star fellows in disguise?*

Wiener's a retriever—you know, that golden kind you see all over the place these days with moms and kids, hanging their floppy heads out the back windows of Jeeps. The most beautiful dog there is, in my opinion, and happy as a field of uncut wheat. Those dogs know how to be happy in ways I haven't even thought of. Some people (Ed, for instance) would say they was dumb, but some people don't know what they are talking about. You can be smart and pretty at the same time. That's what the women are always saying, ain't it? Anyhow, there are so many goldies now, it's like they all showed up overnight. They're on TV, in car ads, on the dog food cans. Seems like they took over the earth, or at least the good old U.S. of A., just in time for the new millennium. For a minute, standing there, I was sure that all those goldies—and Weiner too—were from a planet far far away.

Well, I sure as heck couldn't tell Irma that. If I wasn't careful, I'd start to sound like one of those Alabama boys that Ed Jones is always telling about, the ones that see swamp gas and cry *aliens*.

That night, in bed, I did tell Irma how the comet flared. She said, *Now, Sarton Lee, don't exaggerate.*

Couple of weeks later, Wiener didn't come back from his morning run. He'd never done that before. Irma called and called, standing out on the stoop in the wind, hollerin' up the hill, her white hair flying around, pin curls pulled out flat and pins scattering.

It was opening day of deer season but I didn't bring that up. Irma would have gotten all scary-hearted and made me tromp through the woods, looking for a dog's dead body, and that's a good way to get shot. Finally I had to go to town to get some feed and Irma had to drop off a casserole for old Miss Fearing so we left him a little food on the stoop and some water in the pen and the pen door open.

I put the casserole in the back seat, covered in towels so it wouldn't slide around or lose heat, then slipped into the driver's seat. Irma's got her hands folded in her lap, like she's in church. Didn't fool me a bit. When she's quiet it just means she's thinking about something. Thinking hard.

"He'll be okay," I said to Irma. "Don't ask me how I know, I just do."

Irma gave me her dark-eyed look and set her chin. Irma knows about my promises.

"You heard about George Howells, got his dogs tangled in a bobwire fence?" Old Ed Jones is leaning back in his chair, so far back it might tip over. This is how Ed gets folks to listen to him. He don't tell much of a story, but you can't help wanting to look and see if he will fall.

"I heard."

"Well, they done it again," says Ed. "Same fence."

"Some folks never learn," I say. My mind goes to some rusty bobwire that's been hung up for ages in the old poplar tree in the south woodlot. I've been meaning to cut it out. I'm hoping my dog is nowhere near it. Wire can cripple a dog. Get twisted around a foot or a joint and cut in and give blood poisoning.

I reach the pencil to sign for my feed and Ed has to clomp back down in his chair to put the slip in the till. We're all done and he's leaning back again, farther, farther, and I turn and say, "Hey! I forgot Irma wants some sorghum molasses." I did it just to see him jump. And he does.

"We're out," he says, feet flat on the floor.

I knew that.

I wished some of the others had been there, we would have looked around at each other and had a good laugh, and Ed's a pretty good sport, he would have joined in. Instead, I've just got old Ed irritated. Serves him right. I've got to heft fifty pounds of gol-darn feed myself, his boy has the day off to hunt.

When I got back home that night, old Wiener the Hotdog Eater was in his pen licking his chops and chomping his dry food. He had brambles and burrs and some funny white stuff stuck to his fur and face. I hunkered down and held his fur-face in my hands and looked him in the eye. "Wiener," I said, "you can't go running away like that." He just smiled and barked and licked my nose. The white stuff was sticky like marshmallows. It looked like it might glow in the dark, like those stars and moons young'uns put on their ceilings above their beds. I reached out a finger and took a pinch. Put it on my tongue. It was bitter to the taste.

Some of the gunk stuck on my sleeve and I showed it to Irma, just to see what she would say. Irma knows lots of things purely by women's intuition, things I don't get at all. But all she said was, "I'm just glad he's back."

I thought that was that.

I did notice that after I cleaned the gunk off him, the fur left behind had bleached out white. Wiener was now a golden-and-white retriever.

Winter passed. Spring flung blossoms on all the apple trees like popcorn. The stars shifted in the sky the way they do, like a big dizzy

Ferris wheel. Summer came, the comet came back, this time fanning its tail over the west pasture, just before sunset, and next thing you know Wiener is saving our lives right and left, just like one of those old Lassie shows. One Saturday I wake up four o'clock in the morning, Mr. Flufferbutt jabbing me with his nose. Irma's not in bed. She's in the bathroom, conked out cold on the floor in her pink quilted robe. Turns out she fell and cracked her head. I have to drag her to the car and drive her to the Emergency. Doctor says she's fine, just a little concussed is all. But if I had let her lie there all night . . . well.

I looked at Irma. Her eyes said, *Wiener*.

Irma didn't notice, but the fur on his feet and haunches got tinged white along the edges after that, like a silver lining on a cloud. Sometimes you could see it and sometimes you couldn't. In the dark, you could see his tail like a ghostly plume. I checked the white parts and there wasn't anything funny there. It was soft and fine as the rest. I figured he was getting old. They say big dogs get old fast.

The next week I'm mowing the back pasture, the part where it gets tricky down by the creek. Old stumps stick up and will crack the blade or turn you over if you don't watch where you're going. Noble Wiener rides on the back, on the grass blower. He likes how the blade flushes rats out from time to time. I hit a snag. We go tumbling. I see the blade whirring, could have sliced my head off I guess. Old Wiener jumps up and knocks me away and barks and barks, licking me, poking me, running to the house, grabbing Irma by the apron, just like she was June Lockhart and he was a famous TV collie dog who shall remain nameless. Irma comes running and I am trying like the devil to get out from under that blade without making it fall on my head, my leg trapped under one side, and a knot on my noggin the size and softness of a rotten peach. Blood everywhere. I thought my leg was cut off.

Turns out the blood was just one of those nick wounds that looks bad and bleeds hard. A bit of adhesive tape fixes it, pulls the skin back together so it will mend. Irma shuts the mower off, throws some creek water in my face and I get up and at 'em pretty fast. Walk up the hill on my own steam. Put some ice on that knot. Walk in the feed store next day all banged up, everybody's there. I have Wiener come in and sit-stay right next to me while I tell it. I admit, I up-play the Wiener part and down-play the fall-off-the-mower part.

Ed Jones waits till I'm done. Leans back a scootch more, till he's slam against the wall. Says, "I guess you would have pinned a medal on that dog if it wadn't for all that fur." Everybody laughs, and Wiener barks, and I laugh too but I can tell Ed isn't partial to pretty dogs. Give him an ugly old redbone hound any day.

I looked down then and saw it: Wiener's feet and ears were completely silver now, and there was a big saddle of silvery spots on his back, spreading. I reached down and smoothed his fur. "Good boy," I said. My hand on his back, spotted with freckles and scars and knobby and dark as a hickory stick. Wiener was getting old fast, and I wasn't feeling so hot myself.

That weekend Irma and I were pretty tuckered out from all the excitement. We hung around the house, didn't do much other than water the flower bed and read the *Ambler County Argosy*, all the news that fits, they print. I turned the page and there it was: a picture of little Eloise Wexworth and her big old golden retriever. The caption said she had been saved from drowning that week by her dog. Don't know if it was a trick of light or photography, but the durn dog had a kind of halo around its ears. The photo was perfectly clear. It was a goldie. Not a Lab, not a Chesapeake Bay, not a hound of any kind.

Bingo.

I thought about how pretty they look when they are running across a field. I thought about how this one, Wiener, come to us seven years ago in a basket from a neighbor—we never knew who—after our little grandbaby died of leukemia. Nancy. Seven years old. Light of our lives. Smart, too. Just about all our life got whomped out of us by that one.

They say the Lord giveth, and the Lord taketh away. Seems to me he's taken more than his share. Anyway, that one was a package deal. The Lord took Trudy. In the same breath, he giveth Nancy. And then he took her back again.

Back then I had blocked it all out what happened to Trudy, running away the way she did when she was just a young girl, getting messed up with all those hippies out west. Then eight years ago we got the call. They didn't come to the door like they do for soldiers. They called it in, like a medical report. *Overdose*, they said. They never said of what.

I was thinking, *She used to eat too much peanut butter and get sick.* I stood there with the phone heavy in my hand like it was a big block of pig iron, just couldn't get my mind wrapped around it. Then they said, "There is a child." *Of course there's a child,* I wanted to holler at them. *You just told me she was dead.*

I thought they meant my Trudy. They meant Trudy's baby, my granddaughter, big surprise, whose legal name they said was Smiling Buddha, but it seems had the nickname Buddy. She had grown up on a hippie commune, the lady's voice said cautiously into the phone, she was a little . . . *underdeveloped.* She kept going, talking about how they found her next to her mother's body, just sitting there, sucking her thumb, how it would be a real shock for a young child. My ears felt numb but still I could hear the lady's voice. I could see a skinny kid, like in India, wearing a toga and a wound-up sheet on her head. I could see a house littered with blankets and mattresses and beaded doorways and incense and beer bottles and who knows what and my Trudy's body strewn on the floor, face down, a child lifting her arm, dropping it, sucking her thumb and rocking. I shut it out. I had to shut it out.

When I told Irma in the kitchen I kept it simple. "It's Trudy," I said. "We lost her. A lady called. It was an overdose." I knew right away I should have softened the blow, led up to it somehow. My tone of voice sounded too calm, too sure of itself, to speak such a thing.

Irma gripped the kitchen sink, where she had been washing a chicken, pale rubbery skin, her knuckles as raw and pink as the bloody tips of the wings. She turned her head slowly and looked as if I had personally betrayed her, as if I had killed the girl myself. "How could you?" she gasped, blinking, understanding finally. *"How could you be so mean?"*

All that day and into the weeks that followed, I could see Irma making the effort to continue to stand being around me. I could see her putting aside a load of blame. I could see in her eyes the memory of me saying *don't worry, our Trudy will be back when she's good and ready.* I could see Irma remembering what I said one time: *You can just keep going if you go after that child.* I could see Irma tempted to go, even now.

Irma went to church a lot for a while. Prayed—mostly for me, I think. I could see she was trying to get strong for Trudy's child, who would be here soon. You muster yourself up for things like that, a three-year-old in your old age. We did not speak about it, but in the things we did, fixing up her room, pulling old storybooks out of the attic, painting her bed, it was clear we'd both decided, Irma and me, to take what life brought back to us.

Then she came. A black-haired girl with shy eyes, a big lady holding her hand, standing at the door. Irma's face said: *this is a gift from God.* We tried to call her Buddy, but it sounded like calling a dog, "Here Buddy, hey Buddy," and she didn't answer to it. So we called her Nancy, after Irma's mother.

From the beginning, when she was just a pair of big brown eyes and wouldn't say boo, I'd tell Nancy funny stories in hopes of seeing her dimples crinkle up and hearing her laugh. It took about three months before she would even look at me, but after that it was easy. "Itsy bitsy spider, went crawling up my nose," I sang one day, and she screeched in laughter: "That's not how it goes!" And she sang it right till I got it right. That was a miracle day.

She knew a few things. Nursery rhymes, love songs I never heard of, just a line or two, none of it made much sense. She liked to sing, "We will, we will, *rock you*," and clap and stamp her feet, just like they do at a baseball game. She had a cheek like a Virginia Beauty apple, white and red and plump, but sometimes I would catch her staring, her lips hanging open as if she might begin to drool. I sang and clapped with her, made her laugh, for the pure fun of it, but also, a little bit, to keep her mind off not having a mama. I could hold back the water in that dam, as long as Nancy laughed.

That lasted three years.

You watch a child for sickness. A sneeze turns to a cold. A cold turns to fever. You bundle a child up in blankets and wipe her down with alcohol and watch her looking at you, saying, *You will fix it won't you?* Then fever turns to something that eats at the bone and gnaws and chews until there is nothing left.

The good Lord in his wisdom dragged it out for a full year, that son of a bitch. The stars wheeled across the pasture sky and the doctors said this and the doctors said that, and the nurses changed her sheets and poked her arm and Irma held her hand and you could see through the skin to the bone, like we weren't feeding her enough.

You couldn't hold her at the end part, it hurt her too much. Those big brown peepers looking out at you, sickness squeezing the whole life of the body into the eyes. And then she was gone, turned into something limp and bruised and small, lying on that white hospital bed, so alone.

You are never so alone as when a child dies.

Ed Jones knows about that, he lost his oldest back in Vietnam and it busted him up bad. He was so proud of that boy, and turns out it was our own people shot him. Blew him to smithereens. Nothing left. A big mistake. I think that's why Ed tells his stories in that chair, leaning. Life for him is on the edge, something between a bad joke and disaster. I know that about him, though he is not the type to admit it. I know it because I been there. I seen what it took out of him. I seen how his eyes got hollowed out and his stories got more boring than ever. Nothing much ever happens in Ed's stories. He never gets down to the nitty gritty. Like whatever did happen to George's hounds? Did one of them lose a leg or an eye? Why won't he say so? Wonder why.

With our Nancy all I remember is I was the one who picked up her arm, checked the pulse, put it down, and knew that death had claimed the room. I remember going home late that night, getting in bed beside Irma, listening to her breathe. I listened hard, oh boy. Never moved. Careful not to touch her all night, and all the next day, and to the sad little wake and church funeral and finally burial in the family cemetery, on the north slope, and for weeks at a time afterwards. It seemed like, if either of us spoke, something might break.

Irma never slept either. Just lay there, listening, like me. She would get up first in the morning, not say a word till lunch, when she asked me did I want tuna or egg salad. Things went on that way for what seemed like years.

It seemed like every bad thing piled up on me after that. I even took the weather personally. When a late frost froze out the apple orchard, or hail bit holes in the early lettuce, or a new calf died in the birthing, I hunkered down into a bad mood. Didn't talk to Irma for days at a time.

Then one morning this little pup comes wiggling onto the front porch. I practically fell on my butt trying to get out the door. All during chores it was following me around, biting my shoestrings. People leave pups at the ends of country roads, I guess they reckon farm people are soft-hearted. But my paw taught us to drown the strays that weren't wanted. When it tried to come in the kitchen, I shoved the pup back outside with my boot.

Irma saw the look in my eyes. Turns out she'd been sneaking it biscuits for two days. She said, "Sarton Lee, listen to me: don't drown the puppy." She went back out to the stoop, picked him up, and put him in a basket by the stove. She gave him another one of my dinner biscuits to eat, with a pat of butter, and a bowl of milk. I guess I knew what the deal was then. Irma was keeping that pup. She kept him out of my way. She trained him to sit quiet. But she couldn't name him for the longest time.

One fine summer day I was about to grill us up a couple of hotdogs for supper. Irma had made a pie, her first in a while. I got back from the shed with the lighter fluid and saw that puppy sitting there, all pleased with himself. I looked around for the pack of hotdogs. He wagged his tail and barked. His golden fur shone around his head. Little belly sticking out like he'd swallowed a softball. That's when I saw the evidence, plastic lying in the grass around him in little pieces and big chunks. Not a hotdog in sight. I was too tired to get mad. "Well, Oscar," I said, "you wish hard enough and you'll turn into one."

That puppy just smiled, pieces of plastic hanging off his chin.

"He's not an Oscar," Irma said, "or a Mayer, either."

"That leaves one thing," I said. We both laughed. A short, hard laugh that sounded like a bark. We hadn't laughed in one heck of a long time, and it hurt something to do it. Like a muscle in your stomach you haven't used in a while, like it was scraping against bone.

I figured on getting smarter about love after Nancy. I figured you've got to love smart if it's going to work in this world. You can't go giving your whole heart away.

Trudy was the kind to love hard. She loved her dolls, it broke her child's heart when they got hurt in any small way. She loved her flock of chickens, she raised from chicks. She was tender-hearted about them, wouldn't let us touch them for meat, just eggs, and wouldn't eat the eggs herself. "My babies," she called them. She would only eat store-bought.

I guess she loved that motorcycle fellow she ran off with. She told Irma she would rather die than be without him. I can still see her, standing in the kitchen, halter top just covering her loose woman's breasts, haystack hair, angry eyes, and those dirty bare toes sticking out under her skirt, toes I used to tickle and call "crunchy peanuts" when she was just a small thing. I remember thinking, *Do I know this person? Have I even met this person?*

Sometimes these days I get an inkling of what it must have been like to be Trudy, to be a child who doesn't know her father wants to love her, a child who has to fly away and live somewhere completely different, thinking she'll find the world is good. I have to sit down hard to think about it. Wiener comes up to me then. He's looking a little rugged these days, the white fur has turned to something like dandelion fluff, puffing out of his head and flanks in patches. He's not so pretty any more. I just pat him and let the fluff fall where it may.

I never told Irma, but I see her from time to time, our Nancy, running across the lawn and behind the house, looking down out of a leafy tree. Sometimes I hear her talking in the corn. One time I even heard the way she used to call out a skip-rope song: *Teddy Bear, Teddy Bear, turn out the light!* For a time I thought I was tuning her in on my fillings, you know, the way crazy people can tune in radio stations. Then every once in a while I let myself think it: *Oh, Wiener, why did you come to us so late? Nancy would have loved you. Trudy would have loved you. She would have stayed.*

I can see the whole thing, how it could have been: Trudy sitting on the porch, little Nancy in her lap, corn tassels blowing, good crops for years on end, Wiener laying at her feet, protecting her babydolls. Heck, even Ed Jones' son comes back, marries my Trudy like he always wanted. Big wedding, Irma happy with tears, the way womenfolk like to be. Then I snap out of it. Wiener's just a dog. He might be psychic, and he might be from outer space, but here on earth he's just a dog. He can't take us back in time and make it right. All these visions are just a play-pretty paradise, sent to devil me.

Wiener must have thought I need to stop mooning around that day and go outside and do some hard work, so he leaned on that bad place in the pasture fence and knocked it down. He followed me around all morning, trying to get my attention, my forgiveness, pieces of silver fluff sailing off into the breeze like thistle seed. I thought for a minute he might be reseeding my field with his own kind, I might see them come spring, tiny goldies popping up amongst the green rye. Well, that just irked me more. When I came to the house for lunch, Irma took one look at me and started cutting apples for a pie. She made it. I ate it. It don't seem possible, but I managed to stay mad throughout the eating of three pieces of that pie, good as it was.

I spent the afternoon digging post holes by hand, chunking the digger blades in the dirt, flinging the hard clay aside, again and again and again, deeper. *It ain't ever going to be like that, it ain't, ain't, ain't.* The words got in my head each time I chunked. Wiener just lay there, watching, his brown nose worn pink with digging, his brown eyes steady in a cloud of thistle fur, looking like he knew a way to a world that was a better place, and if he watched long enough I might dig my way through.

Then he rises up, noses the ground with interest, and before I know it, he's digging too, and my hole gets bigger and deeper and it's the size of a suitcase, then the size of a traveling trunk, then the size of a grave, though not as deep. The soil is soft here and full of critters, beetles and worms, chewing at the earth and the roots of grasses. It looks so cool I drop down into it, lay out flat, and feel the dampness chill the backs of my legs, my shirt, my neck. Wiener sticks his head over the edge. I scooch over. He gets in too. We lie there, panting, looking up at the mystery of the square blue sky, wondering if what holds us down is as strong as what wants to take us up.

THE HIGH LIFE

DIP SLINGS HIS SNAKE-TATTOOED ARM up the side of the crank and chunks it down. The metal jolts and slips into place the same way his shoulder bone slips and shudders in the socket sometimes. Royal says he's too young to have that shit going on, but Royal doesn't know jack.

Day Two, the state fair.

Last week was West Virginia.

The week before, Georgia.

Today is—South Carolina. State capitol, Columbia. The freaking Palmetto Bug State. What a dog of a place to turn sixteen.

Dip shakes his head, rubs his shoulder, admires his tattoo, which is still a little scabby in the middle. Then he drops his head to check the motor. His curly red dreadlocks flop forward into his eyes as he bends to his work, the blue kerchief he has tied to hold them back isn't working. He can't see worth shit, so he feels around with his fingers.

He's been working on his dreads for a year now, and though he knows they make him look cool, they also make him nervous. Royal doesn't like them, calls him Shrub Head, that's a point in their favor. But they're long now and they get in the way.

Royal also says he looks like a girl.

"Have to tighten that nut, Royal!" he calls behind him. Royal hops up to the control booth, wavers, grabs a wrench, and hops back down on legs like bent wire. Drops the wrench.

Dip snatches it up, fits it around the nut with his long fingers, and gives a few turns, working sharp and quick by feel. Royal is getting on his nerves.

This is the time of day when Royal always says, "The fair is like a woman: all made up pretty in the morning—nasty at night." But this morning Royal is taking longer than usual to work up to his jag. Dip watches him hawk, spit, slurp his cup, held tight with both hands. Old man. Hands trembling. Ought to be ashamed. For the twenty-hundredth time, Royal has forgotten what he did the night before.

Last night, Day One, state fair, Columbia, South Carolina, Royal took off around four o'clock, in the middle of a fresh crowd, *Day One*, and never came back. Six o'clock, prime time, Friday night, Dip finally shut the ride down and went looking for him. Found him humping some woman behind the midway on the grass in plain view. Anybody could've seen them. Dip grabbed a bucket of water and dumped it on the two of them and they jumped up yowling, like dogs.

"Sonofabitch, boy, what the hell'd you do that for?" Royal's grayish hair strung down over his forehead and his ears, plastered close, making his head look small. That skimpy rattail in the back, tied with red thread. Had to be fifty years old, maybe older. Face like the bottom of a bucket. How in the hell did he get women to go with him?

The woman was shoving her skirt down and tucking her blouse in. One of her breasts hung free, the brown nipple dangling. She crammed it back in her bra. She hopped on one foot, grabbing for a sandal.

"Git," Dip said. She dropped the sandal and ran. Dip turned to Royal. "Put your pants on, man. You got a job to do if I have to tie you to the crank."

Royal followed him back to the midway like a puppydog, did his job the rest of the night. Around nine he got the shakes so bad Dip had to tie his hand to the crank with an old red bandanna, like he's had to do before, so he wouldn't jerk it into "high speed" or "off" by mistake and throw people out of the seats like rag dolls. Royal lasted till eleven, finally passed out in the ticket booth. He woke up this morning hungover and jagged as a broken beer bottle.

Looking at Royal, Dip wonders: How did you ever think this man was the epitome of cool?

"There'll be some honeys tonight," says Royal. He sets his cup down, fumbling inside his vest with one hand.

Dip mutters, "Give it a rest," but not loud enough so Royal can hear.

"I know when they like me, Dip, and I always get my woman ripe and ready." Royal's found the flask, works the top with his teeth.

Dip stares at a clot of color down the midway. There's a person. There's a dog. The colored flags of the Sno-Cone booth whip and snap. He squints and waits. This time of day, before the crowds show up, everything looks new. The flattened grass has sprung back up, green and bristling, even the yellow dust smells sharp and cool. Maybe somebody he doesn't know will turn the corner between the Ferris wheel and the Headless Woman's tent and come this way. Something in the distance might shift, take shape, into something new. Something good.

Dip hasn't seen anything really good since south Georgia. There was this crippled guy in a wheelchair who shot out a paper star with his left hand, while his right hand hung in his sleeve like a dead thing, all shriveled. What was so amazing was the expression on this guy's face when he won. He didn't look happy, exactly. He looked like he was high, like he might be about to spin out of control, jump the fence, like he was gathering his legs under him like the ratty old lion that escaped from some pitiful county fair in North Carolina and hid, crouching, behind the popcorn stand. The man's eyes shone in the red and yellow light, like lion's eyes.

The lion was still on the loose when they left that fair.

Royal tops off his coffee cup from the flask and drinks. He looks at Dip, changes his tack. "These Columbia broads, they're all fat, and they got too much pancake on."

"Fat," Dip says. He squints his eyes. The colors merge, blues and greens and yellows and reds, summer colors, fair colors. The colors shift, the first hot wind of the day rising, kicking up a little dust, rustling the awnings and flags and cellophane and trees.

Royal sets his cup down and says, "Dip, you ought to get you some girl tonight. You know it's easy. They go with you, you shoot a few ducks down, win a damn Bart Simpson or Pokemon and bring em back here on the ride."

"Mmmhmm." Just that one red flag.

Royal's fingers clench around the cup and he holds it steady against his vest. "Then I crank it up for you so she'll slide over on you." He sucks the cup dry, tosses it on the grass. "She can't get away! She'll be on top of you! She'll love it!" Royal has hit his stride, voice rising, hands moving as he speaks, liquid smooth.

Dip looks away, dreads flopping over his forehead, pretends to check the midway behind them. *Something good*, he says to himself in a kind of desperation.

Royal looks him over, kicks his cup. "I know what's wrong with you," he says. "You need to get laid." Royal pokes Dip hard to knock him off balance, but Dip rocks back, easy. The midway springs back to its natural shapes, boring, predictable.

Dip exhales and grinds out his butt with his heel. "Don't you got something to *do?*"

They have a full count. Royal is switching the lever to ON, warming her up, just like right. It's nine-thirty Saturday morning and people are coming straight for the Slider. The name painted on the side is "Alpine Flier," but Royal always calls it the Slider and Dip calls it that too. It's one of these rides where the music blasts while cars go around and around, skim the back wall, rock over a couple of humps, nothing much for a track. It's not a thrill ride like the Thunderbust. But people like it, it's fast and loud.

Dip has rigged up a sound system with a Peavey amp and Bose speakers and he can drown out any ride on the midway. All of Royal's old favorites, on ratty bootleg tapes. Jimi Hendrix. The Doors. Ten Years After. What his dad used to call "Woodstock shit."

When he was little, Dip and his dad's girlfriend used to listen to this music on the sly. One day she taught Dip how to slow dance in the kitchen, with Clapton crooning Layla on the record player. He held her respectfully, an arm's length away, looking down at his feet instead of straight ahead at her chest. Dip was staring at the black and white squares on the floor, trying to count, when he saw spots of wetness appear on the tile between them. She rested her head on his. She was crying. "He's so fucked up," she kept saying. "And you're so sweet."

Dip considers the tapes in the shoebox. Hendrix. What the hell. His dad *really* hated Hendrix. He takes the tickets, watching for phonies and stubs, says, "Around to the top" until the top cars fill on down to the bottom. Then he says, "Next ride, five minutes," and pulls the chain in front of three bored-looking girls. He flicks a switch and Hendrix blasts out so loud it shakes the steel under his feet. He signals Royal to put it in gear, hears the gears clunk into place. The cars slowly begin to turn. Royal looks all right now. He might slide through morning on that one flask and make it to afternoon.

Dip picks up the microphone. *Boys and girls, moms and dads, cool dudes and hot chicks, welcome to the fabulous Alpine Flier, it's a hot hot morning in Columbia South Carolina and the sky is blue and we got some tunes for you. . . .* He boogies in place a little, shaking his legs into his sneakers. Dip wears loose Indian cotton baggies that whip and fly in the breeze made by the passing cars, and make him look like he's jitterbugging even when he stands still. His voice booms out of the speakers, a trick, like ventriloquism, something that starts in his throat and tumbles out of the speakers all down the midway. Royal taught him that voice. It sounds just like a professional DJ.

The faces passing by are easy, laughing, round and soft. He signals Royal to crank it up. Dip shakes his hair back from his eyes and sings along with Jimi, howling it out, *"Scuze me while I kiss the sky . . ."*

The sixth graders are jabbing each other with their elbows as the ride's force begins to slide them into each other. Pretty soon they'll be sitting practically in each other's laps, calling each other homos. Dip picks up the mike again, *"Faster, faster round and round, we like to boogie to the sound."* Two of the girls are laughing and pointing at him as they sling past. Royal cranks it up. The eighth graders are hanging on to each other for dear life. Two little kids look scared. An old guy by himself still looks bored. Royal cranks it up again. Dip turns and lights a cigarette, then lets it burn fast between his teeth in the whipping wind. He hisses between his lips, *"Put your hands up over your head and come around the bend, up to the top you'll never stop, shake your hands and SCREEEEE-UUUMMMM . . ."*

They scream. All their faces seem flattened now, wedged in, mouths open and teeth showing like animals. Dip nods to Royal and Royal slows it a notch. Then a notch more. Heading for the stop. On the last turn, Dip runs the ramp around, cigarette dangling, his long sinewy arm clicking the safety gates open, one after another. The ride stops, he crushes the butt under his sneaker and kicks it under the track. *All safety rules enforced, never an ash on a client's lap,* said the guy who sold them the ride. *That's the key to success.* Man wanted out of this life, wanted to get married, have a family. Dip never thinks about that. He's had a family. A mother who got sick and went away when he was little and never came back. A father who hated everything Dip did after that, from eating his dinner too slow to walking across a room too fast. When his father caught Dip touching himself and watching through the crack in the bedroom door, watching as his father screwed his freckled girlfriend, the way he grabbed tight to both her breasts and held on, it was all over. No more family. His dad jumped out of bed, tossed Dip's clothes in a trash bag and called him a little bastard. He shoved him out the door and hissed, "You're not even mine, you little freak. Come back and I'll cut your dick off."

Dip doesn't want a family. But today, for the first time, he wonders if there's something else you can have, not a father yelling at you, but not this high life shit with Royal either.

Royal has been his partner for two years—two years to the day since his father threw him out. Royal picked him up hitchhiking on the Lake Road in the rain that day in October, said, "Hop on in, bro. Man, you look like a drowned rat." Looked at the plastic bag on Dip's shoulder, muttered something sounded like, "Who threw you out with the trash?" Royal looked him over, head to toe, and Dip prayed the rain on his face covered up the fact he had been crying. Royal pulled into a truckstop, bought him an egg sandwich and a cup of coffee and told him he needed a partner.

Sitting across from him in that booth, Royal had looked like an old greaser, hard lines like calluses bit into the sides of his mouth and eyes. But he had a little slick ponytail wrapped with a red thread at the back of his neck, done up in a loop. Dip watched him closely, holding completely still, knowing he couldn't squirm every time a cold slick of rain slid out of his thick hair and down his back.

"You lucked out," Royal said, cracking some pistachios with his side teeth, spitting the shells into his left palm, dumping the wet red hulls in the ashtray. "Opportunity of a lifetime. I happen to have an opening in my company. Royal's Rides. Operation, maintenance, and repair."

Dip watched his small hard mouth working the nuts, a little red juice wetting his lips when he talked. This guy was not a queer. Definitely.

Dip had never been to a state fair—never even been to a circus. His mother tried to sneak him to one once when he was little, but his dad had caught them. Stood in the driveway blocking the car. He was always doing stuff like that. Dip was glad to be out of there. Royal looked cool. Running rides sounded cool. It would probably be a little like motorcycle mechanics, which he always thought he might like. "Yeah," he said, "I could do that."

"Deal?" Royal put out his hand, the tips of all the fingers stained pink.

"Deal," Dip said, and shook it. The hand felt strangely soft. Like it didn't belong to this person Royal. Like there was some mistake. Dip shrugged and flipped his hair back. He was going to grow it long now. He was going to twist it up into dreads and be a freak with all the other freaks. He was going to travel all over the country and have a job too. "When do I start?"

That first summer in Florida, Dip rode every ride he'd ever heard of and more, ate every carnival food there was. He would sneak off and ride The Swings—that ride where you feel about two years old, till the thing cranks up and your feet fly in the air and you realize the only thing to keep you from being flung into the sky are two skinny, rusted chains. Dip would hold his arm out to the side, watch how the warm sticky wind lifted his hand, then made it dip down, shaking the hairs on his forearm. The air felt like a breast in his hand.

Royal caught him on the ride one time, started calling him *Dip* for the way he did his arm like that. His dad had called him Steven. He forgot that name somewhere up in the air, looking out at the flat scrub below, thinking how different Florida looked, how warm it felt, and how his life was completely free and good, with Michigan far away.

Living with Royal was nothing like living with his father. Royal shaved on Tuesdays and Saturdays and was careful about cleaning the sink. Royal knew how to catch a snake with a propped milk crate and a live mouse on a string. Royal knew how to get the best noon spot, on the shady side, for the ride when it was slam dark at four in the morning.

And when he wasn't teaching him Devil's Solitaire and Queens in the Middle and diesel engine mechanics, Royal told Dip everything he knew about women. Including the difference between PMS and just plain bitch, how to say thank you after a blow job (you returned the favor, Dip is still not exactly sure how), and to never, ever mess with somebody's mama.

Royal taught him how to play poker and win, how to drink beer and hold it, how to piss out the window on the same spot for two weeks till the grass came up thick and green. Royal crunched his Cheerios dry, with beer on the side, every morning for breakfast, and mixed Schlitz with V-8 when he felt a need for more vegetables in his diet. Royal knew how to cook on a hot plate with whatever could be scrounged from the midway, including coffee and blue spun sugar, which he mixed together for a jolt in the morning. The first meal he made for Dip was melted cheese sandwiches, which he toasted over the glowing eye on a wire shelf taken from the refrigerator, and served on a paper plate with sliced candy apples on the side. "Apple a day," he said, crunching, like this was some kind of Holy Rule of the High Life.

Most of all, day by day, month by year, Royal taught Dip about all the "regulars" who come to fairs—the fat moms and screaming kids, the Army guys in gangs, the young honeys looking for trouble, the old guys that looked like his dad, with their brush cuts and bitter eyes. Royal said they all came to get jolted out of being so boring, to get so scared they got sick, to play at living high. They want the high life, he would say, but that wasn't living high. "This is the high life," Royal would say, and pop a fresh can of beer, crunch a few more pistachios. Dip used to agree, but now it bored him. He watched the women for a couple of years, thinking about what Royal said, and after a while decided that some of them were pretty, and sweet but, unlike TV women, they all had at least one thing wrong with them. A funny lip. A fat ankle. A mean expression. These days, every once in a while, he cranks the ride up to the limit, just to see the candy smiles turn to fear and all that moussed-up hair turn flat and hard as a plate of day-old spaghetti.

Sheila was different. Royal's girlfriend a year ago. Royal told Dip he'd hung out with her longer than anybody, said she wanted to leave the show, settle down. Little skinny blonde, hair like cotton candy, Royal said it even smelled sweet. Royal would fluff it with his fingertips, and sniff the ends.

Sheila worked the Sno-Cone booth with Ricky. She was still a kid herself, barely eighteen, but she always called Dip "The Kid" and gave him free Sno-Cones. Sometimes she cheated at cards in his favor. Sometimes she would stand up for him when he won and Royal wanted to fight about it. But god, after what happened, she was gone.

It was Dip's birthday, his fifteenth. They were playing five card stud, twos and sixes wild, and Dip was winning. Or, rather, Royal was losing. He was hitting it pretty hard. Feeding Sheila shots of tequila spiked with lime Sno-Cone syrup. He'd given his birthday speech, the one he gave every time somebody had one: "Birth Day. You know what that means, don't you? The day you slide out of your mother's slit into the cold world, screaming, covered in blood and cheesy stuff."

Sheila was so drunk she laughed. Royal perked up, dragged her out of there, and disappeared for about twenty minutes. Came back and pulled Dip out of the game, saying something about a present. When they got to the trailer, Sheila was lying on Dip's sheets, passed out drunk, the Indian bedspread pulled up to her mouth, sucking on it in her sleep, her bare white body exposed from the waist all the way down to her painted toes.

"It's okay," Royal kept saying, his blurry eyes wild and unfocused, his hand shaking the girl's shoulder to wake her up, "I got her all warmed up for you. Time you learned what it's all about. Go ahead and do it. She don't care. We're family."

Dip stared at the patch of yellow-brown crotch hair, dried and crusty-looking, just hanging out. He stared at her thin pale legs and lumpy white knees. Her toenails looked like those pistachio shells Royal was always crunching—they were too long, and oval, and red.

Royal pushed, and Dip lost his balance and fell across the bed onto the soft yielding body of Sheila. Her hair smelled like candy and booze. Her breasts were pointy and thin under the blanket. She groaned. Dip slid away from her, pushed off the mattress, and turned toward Royal. "That's *Sheila*," he said in a ragged voice, "what are you *doing*?" He shoved Royal into the wall, once, twice. Royal's body slid sideways, like a sack of rocks. Dip heard Sheila stir behind him, saw her open her eyes.

"Damn," she said, staring at the two of them.

"Sugar cone, Dip wants a piece of your tiny fine little ass," Royal slurred. "You don't mind a bit, do you? You *like* Dip."

Sheila tried to focus on Royal, then on Dip. She opened her mouth, as if she had something important to say, but what came out was a glistening green slick, all over the bedspread and down her belly. Dip shoved his way out the door and upchucked in the yard. He could hear Royal inside trying to clean up the mess, saying, "It's okay, baby, it's okay," and he could hear Sheila's voice through the screen door, asking, "What's going on, *what's going on?*" Dip ran across the midway to the Slider, climbed into one of the tufted vinyl seats, closed the safety chain, curled up and stayed there all night, hunched into his leather jacket.

He should have left then, but he didn't. He had no place to go. When he and Royal drove to the next town, Dip stared out the window, looking for something in the fields and yards they passed by. Somewhere in North Carolina, there was a lady by the side of a country road, standing at her mailbox, her crazy black hair up around her head like magic fingers lifted it. Dip had his hand out the window, floating on air. The lady raised her hand as they drove past, like she recognized him, like maybe they were related. He knew it was crazy, but he wondered if she was a long-lost aunt or somebody who knew his mother. He watched her turning away in the sideview mirror, *Objects in the mirror are closer than they appear,* and when he looked up, the sign by the side of the road said, "You are leaving Ambler County."

Dip is coming back from his dinner break and he slows down because there is this woman. He stops. He stands completely still. Even his baggies hold position.

She is maybe five-foot-one and skinny and tan. The backs of her legs rise out of her alligator boots like tight ropes, backs of her knees twitching a little as she moves to the music, cutoffs just covering her ass. Her halter top just skims over her waist, and her black hair hangs in gentle ripples, longest hair he's ever seen.

She's got an armful of toys and prizes and she's grinning at someone across the crowd, somebody on the ride. She waves her arm up for a minute and calls out, "Hey, Mike, hey, Brian!" She's waving to her *kids.* She doesn't look old enough to have kids. She's got on a huge silver and turquoise bracelet, the real thing, Navajo or some shit.

She reaches her stringy brown arm down to the pocket of her cutoffs and pulls out a pack of smokes, tamps them, then pulls one out and lights it. She stands with her cigarette held low between her long fingers, just letting it burn.

His eyes follow the smoke as it curls around her hand, dips, and runs down the side of her leg. That's when he sees the scars. All up and down the inside of her left thigh, the skin is crumpled and twisted under the surface. The skin on top is smooth and brown, it's an old scar. What in hell would make a scar like that? Car wreck. Burn. Knife. Boyfriend.

The woman is laughing now, her head held forward on her long neck, her eyes eager and shining in the warm light of the late afternoon. Moving that one foot to the beat, the muscles in her leg pumping a little as she moves. Tight. That's the word to describe her. Dip can't stop looking at her, and he can't move.

She turns to check her bag sitting on the ground beside her, glances up and looks directly into his face, catches him watching. Her eyes look surprised, then hard, then her wide mouth opens as if she might speak but instead she smiles, a funny kind of smile. She looks like she knows him through and through, but knows better than to talk to him.

She pushes her bag closer with one toe of her boot, crosses one arm over her chest, and, finally, takes a good long drag off her Marlboro. She scans the cars again for her kids. Then she kind of shakes herself and laughs, grinding the cigarette into the soft earth with her heel until it is a faint smudge in the grass.

The ride's over. It's his turn to spell Royal. He's late. He can see Royal looking out over the heads of the kids on the ramp, looking pissed. She's running up to her boys. Dip loses her in the crowd. Then he sees her bag still lying in the damp grass, people stepping over it, stepping on it. Dip jams through the crowd and grabs it up and looks around for her again, but she is gone. Royal is waiting.

The weight of the bag feels familiar and warm against his ribs as he squats under the rail and clicks the exit ramp shut. He reaches around Royal and opens the gate. He barely notices Royal muttering, "Bout time you got here," doesn't even see him split. He is standing at the gate, kids in line staring at him, some woman's baggy purse hanging on his shoulder, heart pounding.

"Hey, mister, c'mon," a kid is saying. "Yeah, let us on, buddy," his friend says. Dip goes on automatic, fingers taking tickets, pointing the way. Halfway through loading up, Dip pushes the hair from his eyes and looks out into the crowd. Maybe he can still find her. He's got her purse, could check her wallet, find her address. Hell, he could find her right now if he wanted to. Go to the kiddie rides, track down her kids. Win a bear for—what was his name?—Brian. Buy a motorcycle—why not?—take her for rides, teach the kids to ride. He wonders if Royal would miss him. He touches the wad of cash in his back pocket from last night's tickets.

The Slider has started and he doesn't remember turning it on. He doesn't remember clicking the safety gates. He's got the mike in his hand but can't think of anything to say. His stomach twists inside him so hard it hurts. He touches the silver knob on the mixer and flips the sound up so high that you can hear the beat all the way down the midway. He looks at all the people whizzing around, laughing, getting their taste of the high life, and he can't stand it. He moves the lever back, faster than he should, to Stop. The people stop laughing. "Hey!" someone yells. "What the hell!"

Dip unsnaps the chain, flicks back his hair, and walks away into the crowd.

It's getting dark on the midway and the crowd has gotten louder, rougher. He sees her right away. Her face is like a lean animal in the yellow-red light. She's standing with both her kids in front of the milk bottle stand, watching one of them—Brian?—throw baseballs that will never score. Some brush-head guys from Fort Jackson are drinking beer and cussing every time they miss.

Then he sees Royal. Royal is watching her, licking the corner of his mouth with his dry turtle tongue, spitting red shells.

Dip pushes to the front of the crowd and wedges in beside her. "They're magnetized," he says, in a whisper. "He'll never win."

The woman draws back and turns to look at him. "Fuck off," she says, and turns back to the game.

Dip swallows. "I mean, I didn't mean. . . . I got your purse. From the ride. Where you left it."

She looks at him again, spies her purse on his shoulder and puts her hands on her hips. She knows him now. Maybe. She's got a look in her eye that makes him almost piss his pants. Is she going to even take it? Is she going to grab her kids by the hand and walk away? "What the shit," she says, "are you doing with my purse?"

Dip blinks. His hands jerk out and lift the bag off his shoulder and hold it out, a gift. "I brought it," he says. "You left it."

The woman reaches out one long stringy arm and picks up her bag by the strap like it's a snake. She jams her fingers inside, rummages, finds the wallet, flicks it open, checks the bills, the credit cards, then just holds it cocked in her hand for a minute.

Dip can tell Royal is watching but he doesn't care.

"What do you want?" she says. "You want a damn reward?" The kid Brian is turning around now, to see what's going on.

"No!" Dip says, desperate now to say the right thing, to find the rap that works. "I mean, I just . . ." he looks at Brian. "I just want to do this thing." He starts to talk faster, like it's his rap, like it's somebody else talking he's never heard of before, saying something so stupid, so much like a kid, that it almost makes him want to blush: "I want to do this thing for my birthday because it's my birthday today and I just got this idea it would be fun to do something with a kid, like just a little kid, not even a bunch of kids, maybe just one, or even two—you've got two—and we could go, like, on a ride. There's this great ride. A kid ride. I used to go on but it's really just for kids." The woman is looking at him like he must be insane. Like he wants to rape her kids. Or knife them. Cut up their legs with scars.

He can hear Royal laughing behind him, doubling over, laughing that loud *haw haw* that you can hear even over top of all the people calling and yelling and cussing and breathing along the midway, bumping into him, elbowing each other, stepping on the backs of his sneakers.

The woman sees Royal. Royal sees her looking. He chokes it out, between coughing and laughing and doubling over, "You goddamn stupid kid think you gonna pick up a woman like that you dumb mother—Oww!" Royal looks up real fast. The woman gets in his face, says, "Buzz off, asshole," then turns back to Dip.

Dip is not sure what has happened. But Royal is hopping on one leg, clutching at the other, an aggrieved look on his face. "You crazy little—" Royal looks around, aware that people have turned to stare at him. "Bitch," he says. "That crazy little bitch kicked me, for no reason, just out of the blue." There is a wheedling tone in his voice, the tone he uses when he's calling out his ride, gathering a crowd, talking up the honeys, getting everyone to see things his way. But it's not working with this crowd.

In the yellow light, Dip can see the familiar face of the man who runs the booth. Man's mouth is starting to twitch. One of the soldiers calls out, "You can take her, man, she's about as big as a minute." Royal looks like he wants to. But then someone starts to laugh. Others join in.

The woman leans down to one of her boys so he can whisper in her ear. When she stands back up she shakes her head, a grin twists her mouth to one side. She reaches one of those claws towards Dip and grips his wrist to pull him closer, around the jostling crowd. Her smile curls around her perfect, sharp teeth and she hisses in his ear: "He says, 'Don't kick the big one, I want to go on the ride.'"

Dip dimly hears someone ask, "What did she say, what did she say?"

The woman turns, veers out of the light and down the midway, two boys hanging on her belt loops at either side, and above the crowd he hears a thin high note: her laughter; and again, like a mockingbird.

Dip runs across the damp, flat turf into the dark field between the games and the kiddie rides. He follows the leather smell of her, the silver of her arms, and when he finally glimpses her again she is standing in the blue light of the Tilt-A-Whirl, her face lit with love and trepidation, that jiggling leg, that cigarette held in readiness like a weapon, watching her boys' small bodies leap into the world.

Dip wants to hurt her. Dip wants to be her family. If only he can take her far away from where he is now.

PROVIDENCE

AFTER TYLER KNOCKED ME DOWN that spring and I got so scared, and there was nobody I could talk to about any of it, one day there was a Voice inside me telling me what I had to do. "Make Tyler some noodles with meatballs," it would say. I'd do it, and he would like it, and we'd get a break from him being so mental for a while. "Wear the red shoes," it would say, and I'd do it, and Tyler would like it, or I'd feel happier, and I'd feel like I could do something right after all.

Tyler had stopped telling me what to do all the time, "Nina do this and Nina do that," like he used to do, and now this Voice took over. I don't know if it was God, but that's what I thought at the time. Why not? God had better ideas than Tyler ever did.

After that there wasn't any of that asking my girlfriends what they think or doing the Tarot or wondering if my mom had been wrong about how I should marry the soldier before he went to war. I hadn't been sure then, but it had made him so happy, and Tyler was such a sweet boy back then, like a fifth grader at heart, with his brush cut and his fast car and his text message love.

When he came back I tried to help. Played his music loud, drank beer with him, let him hang with the buddies and drive around town skidding tires, like he still had some kind of Hummer and was gunning down I-Rocks right and left, on an as-needed basis.

There was nothing wrong with him. He still had his arms and legs. But they had discharged him and didn't plan to call him back.

I was glad at first.

And then I wasn't.

One night he was drunk and couldn't sleep. Sitting on the edge of the bed, groaning, his head in his hands. What's wrong, baby? I said, tickling his back the way he used to like, but he slammed me to the floor before I knew what was what, and then he's lying on top of me punching my ribs until they start to crack, one-two-three, and then the choking and the banging of heads and god I guess he saw my tatt shine out in a little patch of moonlight, the *Baby T* just on my shoulder bone, with a heart and an arrow and a sunburst, his choice, and he fell back on his knees and saw what he had done. I give him credit for this: he picked me up and put me in the car and drove me to the hospital. But he left me there and went driving around and rammed the Viper into a brick wall. No more fast car.

My girlfriends said stop being such a drama queen. Everybody's got problems. My mom said find a way. He's a good boy at heart.

But that was just the start of it.

I tried to help him, and he told me some of it, how they made him torture people with electricity just like in that movie *Three Kings*, you do it until people start cracking their own teeth and spitting them out—not that I believed that, but I know they made him do something horrible for him to make that up. And this was a guy who used to want to raise golden retrievers, NOT pit bulls, before he went over to that hell pit. After that I knew what he saw under his eyelids when he slept, those eyes roving back and forth, back and forth, I was afraid to be in the same bed with him. I could smell something bad in his sweat, something like evil, old chewing gum, blue jeans left in the washer damp for three days. I could almost hear the gunfire sounds and screaming and things blowing up like they do in the movies, but he could hear it for real. For him it was real. He was sour with fear, and his arms and legs looked like snakes rippling and writhing in the sheets.

I couldn't sleep in that bed. I lay there awake. The only way he could go to sleep was wrapping his arms around me, hanging on for dear life. If I got up, it woke him up too and he would start to yell. His new medication made him even more touchy than before. One night I was lying there, still as possible, trying not to breathe too much air because the ribs still hurt and Tyler was clutching them tight. I started to panic and I knew I would die if I stayed here. I knew Tyler would squeeze the air out of me and I would die. I hadn't heard the Voice in a while, so I figured it was my turn to talk to it. I made a little bargain. "You tell me what to do, one more time, and I'll do it." That calmed me a little. Somewhere in the night Tyler eased his grip on my ribs and I began to breathe, then sleep.

I woke up that fine spring morning to silence in the house and Tyler gone, not even the spooky sound of him smoking: *Suck it in. Hiss out. Ahhh.*

"Get in the car, Nina," the Voice said. "Take your stuff."

I dragged everything I owned out to the ratty old Mustang, which Tyler loved, he called it the Bitch 'Stang, and which he was someday going to fix up but now was the only car we had that worked. It started on the first crank. I blew out of Detroit so fast, heading south, that I left my iPod in the charger and my cell phone on the kitchen counter. North was Canada. South would have green leaves, not snow, in April. I didn't need The Voice to tell me that. I figured that out on my own.

Around Pennsylvania the car radio went out. All I could hear after that was static, and the hum of the tires on asphalt, that one bad tire going *shush, shush, shush.* About three hours past the North Carolina state line, when God told me I was about to run out of gas and money, I checked the gauge and my purse. God was right. I could not believe the price of gas that spring. (The war did that too.) I pulled off the interstate and went looking for a gas station; but that Voice said, "Turn Here." I looked. There in the middle of a cow pasture was a big sign that said, "Providence."

Ha ha, I said. Very funny, Mister Voice.

Of course it was only a Baptist church. It wasn't like God was painting signs now. I wasn't *that* crazy, not yet. The road passed the church and ended by the river at a washed-out bridge.

"Don't cross that bridge till you come to it," I heard a voice say. It wasn't God, this time. It was me.

I got out of the car. I looked around. This was a place I'd been looking for my whole life. There didn't seem to be any people in it.

The river was wild and brown, running over rocks, and purple vines were growing over everything. Together, the river and vines smelled like grape jelly and mud. Somebody's sneakers were hanging in a tree over the water. Next to the river was an old stone building with the roof caved in. On the other side of the river was a long low red brick building, with tall chimneys and broken out windows. I already loved it.

"Looks like the end of the road," I heard my own voice say. Yes, I was already talking to myself, an early sign of madness, my mother used to say.

I turned around and looked back up the hill. There was an old whitewashed store with a tin roof that was caved in a little on one side. I got in the Bitch 'Stang and rumbled back up the hill, running on fumes.

It was only April, and it was already hot. A trickle of sweat slipped down my scalp, onto my neck.

The store had a big sign on the front, not as clean and new as the Baptist church sign, but faded and peeling and with a word that looked like "Mississippi" on it, only with the "Miss" part missing and the end screwed up:

SISSIPAHAW, NC
POP. 41

A square little American flag, hanging off a pole. A soda bottle rack out front. Some crates of potatoes and onions. This place was just like the movies where you see old Southern guys spitting tobacco and dusting off moldy hams hanging from the rafters and playing banjo. But it was deserted. Nobody on the porch. I cupped my eyes against the window. Dark inside. Cooler, maybe. Was it even open? Damn, I hoped so. I needed gas.

I didn't hear any Voice saying "This Is It" or "Yes it's open." I went in anyway.

The screen door creaked. It was too dark to see much of anything. Just a long row of dusty cans and a soda cooler, the kind that looks like a box freezer with its own bottle opener set into the side. Way in the back, something moved. Something was coming out from behind a counter and heading my way.

"Hep you?" a squeaky little Southern lady voice said. A face popped out at me like a tiny Cabbage Patch doll.

I almost ran.

Instead, I said, "I want a Diet Coke and a place to live. Cheap."

"We got RC," she said, and shuffled back to the cooler to pull one out for me. It wasn't Diet, it wasn't even in a can. It was in a chipped up old bottle like they had in the fifties. It had ice on the outside. I took a swig. Cold. Sweet. I missed the chemical taste of Diet, the way it sizzles on your teeth like it's zapping the enamel.

I paid her for the RC and she said, "Place to live? They's an empty house for every one's got people in it here. I know one you could have. Fifty dollars a month." She said it like fifty dollars was too much. Like it was a lot of money. Like she was trying to get away with something, hoping to. "It's got furniture already in it," she added.

She didn't even come up to my shoulder, and I am none too tall. She kept clicking her dentures, big yellow teeth. But she had sharp blue eyes. She was looking me over like I was some kind of unusual beetle that just crawled out from under a rock. Staring at my arm band tattoo and my hand tattoo and the white place where my wedding band used to be—I'd long since put it in the ashtray. She stared at my bra straps sticking out and ear studs, *Okay, I have multiple piercings, want to see my belly button?*

The Voice said, Rent the House.

"Sold," I said. I went out and pumped some gas. She watched me from the porch. Making sure I wasn't going to run out without paying. Looking hard at the "New York" under the mud on the license plate, not knowing that for me, that meant Utica.

What the hell was I doing in the South? It was all crazy rednecks here and little old ladies and banjo pickers. I was thinking this was all a mistake, but then I remembered the Voice was in charge and I got my confidence back.

I flipped my hair so the cracker lady could see just how dark the roots were and how cheap my earrings were. She looked. I reached behind the front seat and pulled out six ten-dollar bills. Went up to her and put it in her hand. She took it. Yankee or no Yankee, my cash was good.

She smiled. Stretched those lips wide enough to see all those teeth and bright pink fake gums at once. "It's just up the main road and take the left fork at the river. Second house on the left. They's a dog likes to sit on the porch. They ain't no lock on the door, but I can put you a padlock on it if you want." She looked out the window and then back at me. "Looks like you come a long ways in that car of yours," she said.

"Yeah," I said, sucking down the cold sweet pop. "About a thousand miles." I slipped that old chipped-up bottle that must have been around since 1959 into the wooden case of empties on the porch.

"You got a dime coming to you," she said.

I took it. No point wasting dimes.

I got the 'Stang to chug up that road to the house. I knew which one it was right away. White paint, green shutters, screen door hanging open. Scarred-up, three-legged dog blocking the door, but nobody home.

The dog thunked his tail and hunched over to the side to let me pass. This was his porch, apparently. I was just visiting.

Inside, slat wood walls had gaps between them that looked like they were filled with dirt. One room on the right, and one room on the left. Kitchen in back. The floor boards had places where knots had fallen out and bugs could crawl in. Maybe snakes. Spiders had made a web all across one of the windows. It shone like silver hair in the sun. I walked to the back door. Flung it open.

You could see the river shining down there, through all the purple vines. It was such a high, rushing sound I thought airplanes were going over at first. But it kept going, changing key sometimes, but playing mostly the same tune. You could hear it all through the house with the door open. It was a lonely sound.

"This is It, Nina," I said out loud. "This is the Place."

I had never been in a place like this before, that felt like someplace you loved when you were two years old, too young to really remember anything but how it sounded, how it smelled. Dirt and mud and grapes and old paper. It smelled musty and old and sweet. My shoes felt good on the floorboards.

I was getting used to lonesome.

"Wonder what Tyler's doing now?" I said out loud. "I bet he's pissed." I said it like it was a joke, like I had gotten away with something. But then I felt an awful twinge. I had done something terrible. I had run away from Tyler, stolen his Bitch 'Stang, and left him to die in his own private hell.

All the way down here, I'd put off thinking about it. Every time it came up that I had screwed him, I would listen, and the Voice would say, "Keep driving." But now that I was holding still it caught up with me. I could see him sitting on our bed, crying, making phone calls, going into the closet for his gun, putting it against his head. He used to talk about that being the way to go. He used to talk about how we could go together that way. One after the other. Right there on the bed.

"Go," the Voice said now. Only one thing to do. Walk to the river through the bushes and trees just to get away. I wasn't far enough yet. *Many rivers to cross*, Jimmy Cliff used to sing, *can't find my way over.* Yeah, fellah, I know what you mean.

The weeds slapped my jeans, I stumbled over hidden rocks and stumps, got caught in brambles until they held me, completely stuck, in one place. Just when I was about to give up and start to cry, I saw a path. A path like deer would make, or Indians. Just wide enough for one foot at a time. The brambles gave way. I stepped down the path and followed it all the way to the side of the river, rested my hand on the trunk of a huge old tree with white bark. The trunk of the tree rose up above my head like a long, smooth, white muscle, with scars where someone had carved a heart and initials in the skin. Below, the river was ridged and riffling. Were there alligators in rivers like this? I had no idea. The water made a chattering sound, like waitresses gossiping in a coffee shop. I couldn't tell what they were talking about, but I listened anyway. It made the vision of Tyler dead go away.

There's one thing I'm good at, besides running away, and that's cleaning up. That house needed cleaning and I went crazy doing it. I cleaned the petrified mice out from behind the stove. I cleaned the toilet ring with a pumice stone from my nail kit. I swept off the front porch. Somebody across the street opened a curtain and peered out. I swept off the back stoop. I could hear a TV talking next door and saw some laundry hanging that hadn't been there before. I had neighbors. They were so close by they could watch my every move. It creeped me out. I wanted to be alone, just me and my Voice, dammit. I had come all this way to get away from people.

I went back inside and sat on the chair. There was one stuffed chair, two straight-backs, a small table, and a bed with a bare mattress, crackling plastic cover on top. "What are you doing, Nina?" I said to myself. "Did you come all this way to hide inside your house?"

I answered my own question: "Yes. Yes I did. That's exactly what I plan to do."

I took the plastic off and slept on the bare mattress that night, blue ticking lines like shadows across the musty cloth and hard buttons. I had run away without bringing any sheets. I curled up under my jean jacket. One of those buttons kept digging into my ribs. I tossed and turned. Dreaming about Tyler. Tyler had caught up with me.

I dreamed about Tyler smoking, his face gray and dead. I dreamed about our wedding day, his face pink and eager at the end of the aisle. I dreamed about his kiss, his tongue, frantic in my mouth as if he had something to say that he could never quite get out. I dreamed about the time he went with me to my parents' house in Fairfield, and how he held on to me in that little bed they gave us while I cried and cried, hating them for who they are, for getting old and staying the same, for making me just like them, old fuddy duddy boring Nina. How he brushed his hand up and down my spine, kept whispering, "Nina, Nina, you're not that bad. Not that bad."

I woke up with the moonlight spangled all over my legs and arms. There were strange sounds in the night, frogs and howling dogs, and something that might have been a lion's roar. Or was it the river? A hoot owl called, then stopped. I listened for it. But it was done calling.

That morning I opened my eyes and remembered that somebody said, the week before I left, they saw him with that bartender chick, a brunette.

Let her get her ribs crunched.

Let her play possum and feel like dying. See how long that lasts.

I took all the old newspapers out from the cracks around the windows. Started a list of things to get: Caulk. Mister Clean. The paper came out in bits and pieces, yellow crackling wads. I read some of them. People dying in 1917. Refugees escaping Europe. I put the papers in the wood stove and lit a match, and just as it flared, a flock of black birds flew down the chimney into my face and tore around the room. Black ashes and wing marks all over the walls, my shirt, my face. Finally one of them found the open door and the rest followed. I stood there, mouth open, tasting cinders. "Watch what you do here, Nina," I said out loud. "There are live things in the chimneys."

I went to the board wall and listened. Things were living in there too, I was sure of it. It was humming.

Nobody knew I was here. Girlfriends, mom, Tyler, nobody. I would sell the car on eBay as soon as I could, keep the cops from tracking it. I would sell the ring, six diamond chips and a sapphire, worth maybe a hundred bucks. I was going to start over. Just then a bird sang on the back porch. It sounded so happy.

I sat down on the floor and cried my eyes out.

After a while I went out and sat on the back stoop. My face felt like the balled up Kleenex in my hand, dried into a hard crust. The three-legged dog came hunching around the side of the house, hopped up and sat next to me. I wanted to kick him but I was too tired. Then I saw it. Somebody had left a note under a plate of pie on the top step:

> I come by to see if you wanted some strawberry pie but you cudn't hear me with yr TV on I guess. – Yr. nebor Ruby.
> P.S. Dont mind my dog Roger, he likes yr. porch better than mine.

My next door neighbor's name was Ruby. The dog's name was Roger. I was sitting on a porch that belonged to a dog.

Anybody with any sense would have known that wasn't a TV.

And what in the hell is strawberry pie? In Utica, we had blueberries and lemon pie and apple pie. I've never seen a ripe strawberry there before June. But this was a wedge of red whole berries, some kind of clear glaze on top, toasted crust underneath. I picked a fat red berry off the top and popped it in my mouth. Such sweetness, melting on my tongue. I hadn't eaten dinner the night before, or breakfast this morning. I guess I was on a starvation diet, trying to disappear. But suddenly I was hungry.

I picked the pie off the plate and shoveled it in. Crumbs falling down my shirt, red glaze dripping. The dog, Roger, wagged his tail, raised his head, and sniffed. I gave him the last bite. "Well, Roger, I guess we both like it," I said.

He licked his chops and grinned.

I was finally talking to an actual living thing who lived on the material plane. I said, "If I talk to a dog, I'm not crazy, right?"

Roger nodded.

I didn't need the Voice to tell me what to do. You eat somebody's pie, you've got to thank them.

I went over and knocked on the door. Roger stood there beside me, wagging. It didn't seem like he had any trouble getting around with only three legs. He was happy just to be alive and visiting with the living. I could hear somebody coming. I took in a breath, felt my ribs expand. The door opened. The cracker lady stood there smiling, her pink gums shining.

I could not speak, but then a voice came and finally said, "Hello."

New World Testament

MY NAME IS CHRISTIAN JACK OF THE HAW TRIBE, *and I write this in the Year of Our Lord 1720, as a Record of my time and my Father's time and that of my People, whose Time is ended here, at the end of Wars.*

My Father told me This as he lay dying. He charged me to write it down in the style of the English, as John Lawson taught me, but when I write these words they cry out to me to be lifted up from these pages and to fly like the talking hands of my father's People, before the English came.

My father had a great belief in the power of the written word. He had seen John Lawson use the words of his Holy Book and make miracles occur. My father had no need of miracles but he needed the story of his friendship to be told. I think he knew that soon his People and their way of speaking with gestures and gentle sounds would be gone, and that the only way to tell his story would soon be John Lawson's way. I watched him lying there, his head propped on soft deerskin, his eyes like wet black rocks in the light of the fire, drawing himself up into the posture of a leader, a man who tells A True Story. As is tradition with my people, he began by giving his name, his People, and his place in the world. For these are the things that my People count most precious, and the first words of any story are the most generous gift the teller can give, the gift that makes the ending possible. These were his words.

My name is Enoe-Will, and I was John Lawson's friend.

I follow the ways and teachings of my eagle father and my river mother, and the nations of the Sissipahaw follow my ways and teachings, and the land my ancestors blessed is called The Land Between Three Rivers. The English call it the Great Valley of the Cape Fear.

John Lawson came to my village one day just as the light of winter fires rose in the gathering places beside the many huts of my people. He stood before me and the sun-glow disappeared, giving the gift of brighter light to our cook fires. His hair shone like the sun fading, and the firelight in his eyes welcomed me in my own land and made me want to rest there for a while.

John Lawson made his sign, his hands flying like the wings of small birds who know the mysteries of air and he spoke my language to me, a language of gentle sounds and motions, and asked for my friendship, first of all.

I say first of all because it is my knowledge now after many years that this request comes much later for most English in their relations with each other. It is as if they hunt each other like lone eagles from far away for a long time, looking with sharp eyes for all the ways they will not be friends, then after a long time they might open their hands and welcome a new friend, but their hands are so curved inward with the holding of this knowledge that they can open them only so far by then. Such a friendship, in knowing the ways they will not be friends, is a very small thing.

John Lawson opened his hands like birds jumping from the nest, like firesparks rising in the sky on hot winds. I embraced him and we were brothers of the sky, wind, fire. We would become brothers of the earth, forest, river. But everything is possible with a man who opens his hands first.

John Lawson asked me would I come with him and show him the way to the English who live across three rivers and I said Of course. He asked me if I would show him the ways of my people and the beasts of the forest and the birds of the air and the sacred plants and spirit trees and I said Yes. He asked me if I would accept gifts for traveling with him and I said Who knows? For I was embarrassed that he would mention a gift to a friend.

His understanding glowed like fire inside his eyes, brighter now that sun-glow was pale as first stars on the horizon.

We left at first sun, three fine braves with us, for the place known as Roanok. We traveled across the river mother which passes

Achoneechee, and the little calling creek of small trout, past the place where rocks sing to each other in the sun, along the creekbed that is dry except in first rain, all sisters to the mother river, the one John Lawson called the Cape Fear.

By late that morning, my new friend John Lawson fell far behind my braves and I stayed with him. I saw his shoes were hard against the earth and did not know how to lean against the mother's rocks and rivers as she pushed against his feet. He smiled at me but the way he walked was like a deer who has been dishonored by an arrow in her haunch instead of her heart.

But he said nothing of this and I kept beside him, wondering at his strange ways.

We sat and drank at a fine small creek and continued on our way, he still walking in his English way, only more so, until I realized he was trying to follow our ways of walking without understanding our ways of walking. I asked him with my hands if my friend would stop for I was tired. "Honest Will," he said, "you have the graciousness of royalty, and much more common sense."

From then on he called me Honest Will, which I am to understand is like having the title of a chief or king in the land of English.

I motioned for him to take off his shoes, which he did gladly, and I could see where they had rubbed his ankles and heels raw as where a dog chews at its fleas. And he suffered me to place upon them cool leaves and a little mud from the home of the wasp who lives in the ground, and place upon his feet the moccasins I wore, more broken in and soft than any I could have made from my leggings, and he looked at me with love and surprise and asked me, "But how will you walk?" and I showed him how my two feet know the earth and her ways as well as the deer with her four feet. And he nodded and saw the sense of it and followed along, dancing a little when we went to cross the small river whose water smells sweet with pine.

He exclaimed to me, "Honest Will, these things are a blessing to my soul. Never will I wear an English shoe again!" And he did not, not for all the while he traveled with me.

John Lawson woke every morning and took a sharp knife in his hand and scraped it against his face. In the light of early day his cheek sparkled with tiny red hairs and the backs of his hands shone with red hairs too and I wondered whether these strange things might make him soft to touch like the pelt of a living fox. Sometimes he made the sharp blade cut his skin and he would call out the name of his gods and dedicate this sacrifice to them. Again, I wondered at the strange ways of these English.

We traveled for many days across the land of my people. I showed him the tracks of our buffalo and bear, and he made his markings of their tracks and their bodies in his records. I showed him the willow oak and the water oak, and he made them appear in pictures just as they grew by the sides of the river mother.

John Lawson exclaimed in wonderment at each new animal, each new leaf or bird. One day he stood next to a great oak tree and called out in the voice of the tow-hee bird and many birds came to the branches above him and spoke back to him. He kept still except to smile at me and wink one eye, and I thought, Here is a friend who knows my ways and the ways of my gods. And I was content.

While we traveled I saw that John Lawson prized above all else one item he called the Holy Book and every night as sun-glow left the sky and came into our campfire he would inspect the Holy Book closely, turning the pages quickly like many leaves falling at the same time from one tree, then stopping for a while at one page and making a sound with his lips like many wasps who live in the ground while they sleep.

I asked John Lawson about the Holy Book and wondered if he would use it as a tool in his own land of English, as I would use the seeds inside the Holy Gourd to make a sound while I sing the story of my ancestors. "Honest Will," he said, "you are wiser than Solomon. That is just how I use my book."

Then I could see the fires in his eyes turn inward as he thought. "Will," he said, "would you like to learn the ways of the Holy Book?" I said I would. He handed it to me in open hands and the Holy Book itself had open hands, as it offered friendship to any who would hold it with open hands just as John Lawson did.

And so I held it and looked and looked at the markings black and lumpy as the twigs of witch hazel in winter just before they bloom. Then John Lawson laughed and reached out both of his hands and turned the page and the markings changed to something so completely different that I dropped the book and it fell to the earth and the earth pressed against the book and told it to close itself. But my friend John Lawson laughed and brushed the earth from its covers, then opened it again and held it before me and I could see suddenly what it was.

It was a man. Inside the Holy Book was a man.

The man wore the color of the sky and was killing a cougar with his hands but there was a fawn lying on the rocks and the rocks were sipping the blood from the fawn where the claw of the cougar had held the fawn.

John Lawson said to me, "David." And I said the English word back to him, "David."

And John Lawson taught me the words of the English and the sacred stories of the Holy Book and the men inside it. He told to me the story of a man named Moses who was a great leader who traveled across many lands and years. He told me the story of a man named Abraham who had many wives and children. He told me the story of a man named Jesus who had made a great sacrifice for his people. And we sat together at the campfire after the sun-glow had gone from the sky, making the sound of flies on wasted meat with our lips.

"Thus sayeth the Lord," John Lawson would say. "Thus sayeth the Lord," I would say to my friend. "He leadeth me beside still waters," John Lawson would say. "He leadeth me beside still waters," I would say to my friend and think of my river mother. "Our father, which art in heaven," John Lawson would say. "Our father, which art in heaven" I would say to my friend. And I would think of my father eagle and I would smile and John Lawson would smile.

It seemed that besides my moccasins, and the many creeks with cool water, and besides my people's rivers and trees and sacred beasts, this book was what made my friend John Lawson the happiest of all.

John Lawson told me that his god was in this Holy Book. I told him that my gods were in my earth and my trees and the sky before sun-glow, but that my own special gods were in the eagle father and the river mother. And he said his own special god was in the Jesus son.

And because we are brothers, he told me his god was also my god. And because we are brothers, I told him that my gods also protected him. And then he told me that his god said he could not have any other gods, and that his god wanted me to give up my gods.

And I looked at my friend John Lawson and I was sad. I said to him in my new English language that I could not, that I belonged to my eagle father and river mother and that they had taught me how to live and how to die and that only my children who had not yet learned their true names could have new gods. John Lawson closed the book and sat next to the fire and finally he said, "I understand."

But I do not think he did.

For I know from what he read to me that the English choose their gods. Some of the ancient English, the tribes of Israel, would choose wrongly and anger the god they did not choose. And some of the disciple English would choose to betray their Jesus god. I told my friend John Lawson I did not choose my gods. My gods chose me.

I told him that for many days I fasted and waited for my gods to reveal themselves to me. And when my eagle father called to me, and when my river mother called my name, I became theirs. How would I choose what I belong to? Who can claim the rivers or the sky? To choose my gods would make them, like friendship among the English, a very small thing.

John Lawson looked at me sadly and said once more, "I understand."

Maybe he did.

We did not speak the words of the English for many days. My mother river rose up into the sky and for four days she wept and cried and told me the story of her ways which were the ways that kept me safe in the land between three rivers. There was no other talking.

Now the English who live at the other side of three rivers are mostly the kind who stay in one place, not like my John Lawson, and my people do not understand their ways. But they are across the three rivers and that land has different spirits and those are the ancestors of the Tuskarora people, who cannot be trusted.

Many years ago we were in alliance with these Tuskarora but even before the English known as Smith settled on their ancestors' lands and cut open the breast of their mother to bleed her for silver coins and fire water and huts that do not let in the smell of earth, they had become strange to us. When they spoke to us it was with fists and sounds, their hands closed like rocks that live away from water.

One day we came to a place where three Tuskarora warriors stood, burning the first of the ten birds they called to their arrows for their god, and I cried out because I saw the bird whose feathers singed the air in my nostrils was my father eagle and his feathers and wings are sacred spirits to me.

John Lawson made the hand sign and sound and fists for the Tuskarora warriors to leave this place and this fire, and I saw the surprise and fear in their eyes and they gathered their bows and quivers and birds and pouches and slipped away, grumbling like rocks in a flooded creek. John Lawson looked at me and sadness filled his eyes and then he turned away and stood staring at the sky while I gathered my father eagle into my arms and sang to him his eagle song of soaring.

That night I thought I heard John Lawson make the sound of hummingbirds with his lips as he lay in the darkness by the camp fire.

John Lawson was still my friend but his hands were curling up and making our friendship smaller. His hands curled closer to his chest like birds who could not fly easily, birds who had been wounded in their wings.

I asked my eagle father how I could help my friend John Lawson and my eagle father sent me a vision. In my vision, my eldest son was traveling with John Lawson to the land of the English and learning the ways of making paper speak and the ways of the god of the Holy Book and John Lawson was happy again.

Now, I love my son the way John Lawson loves his book—above all else. And what should I do for my friend John Lawson who has offered me what he loves above all else? And when we came to the end of the land between three rivers, to the place where the English called Smith live, I went to John Lawson and told him that my son would learn his ways and travel with him and follow his god.

And John Lawson smiled greatly so that the light of sun-glow that came into his eyes leaked to his cheeks as well. And his hands opened up to me like young eagles eager to fly in their first season. And my heart was mixed with sorrow and great joy because I had done what no man can do: please two gods at once.

My son traveled with John Lawson for many years. One day my son returned to me and fell at my feet and told me my friend had perished. The Tuskarora had tied my friend John Lawson to a tree and stuck his pale skin all over with splinters from the pitch pine and set those splinters afire so that the sun-glow in my friend's eyes was dimmed by the glow from this fire and he cried out the names of all his gods and then my name. And when I heard this I cried, Why, why, but my son who loved John Lawson like a father said he did not know. But that John Lawson's hands had leaped like birds in flight, like lions, and like small deer, all dancing at once inside the fire, gathering around him in the flames, flying into the sky on clouds of thunder and turning into rain.

HOME

WE'VE BEEN MARRIED A MONTH NOW, and everything is finally in its place. My books squeezed next to Carter's on his rows of oak shelves; my favorite chair settled in next to the fire.

The two-lane leading out of town to Carter's farm has become a familiar path with revelations at every turn; plowed fields sculpted as a Japanese garden, deep pine woods, pastures dotted with round bundles of hay that hold the light and cast long shadows like living things. When I was in college at UVA, I used to escape, drive out into the hills, and dream of living on some curving two-lane, the kind of road that twists and turns and opens to light slanting across fields and hills, flickering through low branches, shimmering leaves. Now I live on just such a road, in Ambler County, North Carolina.

One day last week I came around the curve and saw the Hillyard's field had turned bright green—acres of it spreading out on either side of the road like spilled paint. I lost a box of kitchen things off the back of the truck, staring at all that green. A bump, then the crunch of gravel under the right front tire, a cardboard box flipping into the air in the rearview, then exploding, ladles and spatulas and tin measuring cups fanning out onto the road behind me, glinting like treasure in the afternoon light. It took a while to pick them all up. I'm still missing my favorite ladle.

Another week and the boy will be here.

"Sometimes it's like walking over hot coals just to move through the day." My mother whacks her trowel against a clay pot, while I sit perched on her kitchen stool. "Doesn't surprise me a bit that you'd run off the road looking at some grass or a sunset or even a cloud. You weren't paying attention. As usual."

My mother talks at the pot, not at me, but I know she sees me stubborn as fired clay before her, the girl she shaped and reshaped for years before I slipped away into myself. Now she's saying how hard her life is these days, how she knows I'll never come help around the house like I used to now that I'm married. She doesn't understand why I even came here; I should be home tending to Carter. "Yes, Ma," I say, looking out the window to the neighbor's yard and beyond to the line of trees.

I don't tell her why I came. I don't know how to be a mother.

Carter is off at work the day I find them in the closet. Boxes of photos from before his divorce. Polaroids, three-by-fives, wedding portraits, slides, all jumbled together with birthday cards, child's drawings, paper cutouts of snowflakes and hearts, a valentine that says *Mama* in big yellow Crayola letters, the *a*'s predictably backwards. Between a snowflake and a heart, my fingers grip something hard and slick and pull it out: a square of petrified American cheese still in its wrapper, cracked as old soap, scabbed with gray mold. I stick it back in place.

I spend hours going through them, one by one, over and over. They look so happy. In one, the boy is caught between them on the sofa. Carter looks straight into the camera eye. She moves her head to look off-camera, laughing, blurring, the moment the shutter clicked.

I bring a sandwich back upstairs, spill some mustard in a card, try to wipe it off but it smear her words instead. *I love you, darling. Happy Anniversary.* I pack the boxes up and put them in the attic, in the farthest corner I can find where the starlings have got in and left white droppings crusted over a wad of sticks and leaves.

The boy arrives tomorrow. I have cleaned his room twice. I have looked at pictures of him as a baby, as a toddler, at four. I have asked Carter his favorite food, his favorite color, his favorite bedtime story. Many things Cater says he just doesn't know. But I can't hold back the eagerness, almost panic, spreading into my hands as they move from the sink to the counter to the stove, and finally, to the back of Carter's chair.

I drive to the store one more time after supper—chocolate ice cream.

The boy has been here six days now. When he wakes up each morning, the air is charged with his energy like clouds at the edge of a spring rain. He runs down the stairs to his daddy. He comes to sit in my lap. He eats his Cheerios, then he wants me to come outside and play. "Watch!" he says, then he runs, whooping and flapping like a bird across the yard. When he falls and cuts his knee on a rock, I come to comfort him but he pulls away, screaming, "No! I want Mama!" and runs inside, pounding up the stairs to his room, slamming the door, now making a high-pitched, keening sound.

I stand outside his door, my arms hanging loose, my body flooded with a strange dread.

"Let him cry," Carter says, looking at me and leaning against the doorjamb. "Give him time." He goes to the medicine cabinet and picks out a box of Flintstone Band-Aids.

I walk back down the stairs and stare out the window at the bird feeding there, wishing I knew how to open that door.

The boy will be gone tomorrow.

The deer are wandering across the county roads in broad daylight now—does careening into cars, bucks standing still, then tossing back their crowns of horns and leaping in pursuit. Bucks scraping the bare saplings in the orchard, does nibbling the tips, leaving flirting scents all across the pastures in a pilgrimage to the old persimmon tree.

Carter and I go to check the fruit, popping the skin open with our thumbs. We taste the yellow flesh with the tips of our tongues, pulling away bits of flesh that start out sweet, but then turn prickly. I cough out the stinging pulp, laughing, let my saliva rinse at least part of the taste away. Carter chases me, grabs for a kiss, and we tumble down onto that damp floor of rotted fruit, spitting and giggling until we fall silent and finally hear them, rustling toward us from the power line.

Carter flings a persimmon. The deer crash away through the underbrush, clumsy as drunks.

On the walk back, a buck stands in the middle of the dirt road, staring us down. I wonder that we don't catch them in the midst of their scrabbled mating, hunched and lunging, whenever we walk the edges of these woods.

In the old days, my mother and father and I used to sit on our porch after supper, staring at the deep woods, waiting for deer to emerge from the shadows and step into the fields. Straining to make them out in the mist that gathered in the low places, we focused our eyes in the unseen, a faith redeemed each time they materialized like unexpected rain from a single cloud.

I remember the scent of the creeping mist, the deer stepping, one by one, into the field, the fine hairs on their back legs lit up in the fading sun. The light would flood my eyes, making me squint until they hurt before I would look away.

My mother would sit quiet with her beet-colored lips in a dark straight line. My father would stand up, whisper, *Look at them*, his body rigid and alert. They would slip into the woods so fast I wasn't sure they'd ever been there except for that odd sensation that the air was heavier now, laden with a new smell like damp moss. My breath would flicker, then would follow the leaping bodies back into the woods a little ways.

Winter has passed in a strange, jolting rhythm. There is the heart-plucking sound of the phone ringing upstairs on Sunday nights to let us know she's on her way. Her angry face at the door. Sometimes she appears without warning to argue with Carter, carrying the boy into the night, leaving Carter with a stunned look on his face. The boy comes. The boy stays. The boy goes. We're beginning to get used to each other.

Now he is here again, and every day we put on our boots and clomp along the berm, slicking a muddy path to the top of the hill. The boy lifts his yellow boots high and stomps, spattering mud all up his corduroys.

The March sky polishes our cheeks smooth and tight with cold. We walk, spying out the place in the field where the turf is soggy under the tender grass, where the delicate, wedge-shaped hooves have cut so deep in so many circles that this dance becomes an endless, fathomless formation that draws us into itself. Carter and the boy and I join hands, fall into step, laugh, and circle round.

Carter points out tufts of fur stuck in the rusty barbed wire, black deer pellets stuffed with persimmon seed, tracks ahead on the path. They dance at night, the boy says, grave-faced, and we nod. Carter says the boy's mother told him that.

I can see her standing in this field, small, dark, solemn, making incantations to call them up from mist. She is a dove-gray shadowy thing that slips along beside us.

June. We're bringing the boy home from his mother's. It's a long drive. The sun fades behind a hill and lightning bugs gather in the humid air above the road and smear onto the windshield in curlicues like gold leaf. The boy slouches in my lap, his sleepy weight still warm with afternoon sun, my arms easy around him. Looking down at his dropping head, I notice that his small ears are sessile, like the leaves on certain plants, the lobed part indistinct, almost webbed at the base. I have never seen ears like this before. He does not get them from his father.

"Mama," he says in a dreamy voice, "sing me that song." He's never called me that before. I wonder if I should let him. I sing the only song I can think of, a drinking song about gamblers and ramblers a long way from home.

And if moonshine don't kill me I'll live till I die, I croon in his ear.

"Where are we?" he says sleepily.

"Almost home," I say.

The boy is playing a game he's made up out of rocks and sticks placed in patterns in the dirt. "This is the house," he says, placing four sticks to make a square. "And here is Daddy and Mama, and here is you." He puts two rocks together on one side, then one over to the other side. "This is me." He puts his rock in the middle. "I have a special room all to myself," he says and places four smaller sticks around his rock in a square.

I see it now. We all live together. I live way over to one side. He lives in a cramped and secret place between us.

His mother is not gone.

August. She's come to pick him up, for a whole month this time. Carter says it's fine, they've had a talk, the boy will be back right on schedule.

As he closes the door behind her, a kind of relief sweeps over me like waves of just myself, just Carter, spreading into the corners of the house, clearing out the boy's trucks and blocks and dolls on the floor, his broken Big Wheels in the corner, his T-shirt crusty with SpaghettiOs, the smell of rotten bananas I haven't had time to throw out.

Carter kisses me, holds me for a moment, then goes outside to mow the yard. I begin to gather up the boy's things in my arms, to store them away for a while, but when I glance out the window, there is her dented-up blue car, turning past the far line of cedar trees, taking with her his favorite teddy, his sleepers that smell like wet spaniels, his fat, sweet arms. I squat against the door, gripping his flabby stuffed rabbit against my belly until the hollow feeling goes away.

My mother looks me over like an antique dealer pricing a pewter cup, shakes her head, chucks her trowel onto the clipped front lawn.

"Don't you know by now?" she says. She laughs, a short bitter laugh. "He'll never belong to you. Children only belong to themselves. And maybe to the place they grow up in."

I see the worry lines etched around her eyes, the furrows where I left my mark. I see the pain in her expression I must have molded there with no idea my thumbs could press into her so hard.

October. The fields smell of must and hay, the gum tree leaves like red stars shot with light. I hold the boy's hand in mine, way out in the middle of the pasture, watching for his father to come driving around the bend.

"When I grow up," the boy says, "I want us all to live here on the farm." His round face sweaty with the pride of possession: fresh-cut fields, autumn woods, me, his mother, Carter. Everything I've imagined about the boy's first family rises like bile: his father grumbling, hoeing potatoes; his mother sunning her white breasts on the slope of the back pasture, planting these trees, painting this fence. She and Carter making love in our bed. The boy, two years old, stumbling around the yard, walking into dogs, gripping their ears, then sliding onto the wet grass and laughing. Then at four, when things began to fall apart: running on stout legs from one parent to the other, bringing dandelion heads squashed in his damp fingers, pencil drawings of spiders with hairy legs.

I look down at his wheat-straw hair, still swirled around the crown like a baby's and rub my thumb against the scar I know is there across his knuckle. Who wouldn't want to return to the place they first saw the night stars, first heard their mother cry, first cut through their own pliant skin to the red flesh of a knuckle or knee, almost to the bone?

The boy smiles. This is his place by right of birth and memory. He belongs here, and he does not belong to me.

I'm coming around the curve at the Hillyard dairy, driving way too fast, away from my home, my almost-child back there, the image of his stubborn face claiming me, owning all of us the way land owns its own shape. *When I grow up, I want us all to live here on the farm.* There is no escaping her in this place. She clings to us like cockleburs twisting into our skin just where we can't get at them, coming loose to seed new fields.

Around the curve, in the cone of my headlights, is a shape I know from dreams, standing perfect and still and dove-gray at the edge of the road and then gathering its legs beneath and—an incredible thing—now hurling itself toward my car. A thud and crunch against the hood, the tinkle of glass, my foot jams the brake pedal to the floor. My shoulder twists forward, bounces off the steering wheel. The car stops, settles on its shocks. I lift my head and look. Blood spatters drip skinny black lines across the windshield. I pat one hand over my face and chest, feeling for the wetness. I place my palms on the curving glass, but it is dry.

The deer hit hard across its chest, hard enough to cut through the fur, the tough skin underneath, jam bone and muscle toward the heart, some soft place spurting red juice, legs and hooves a tangle. Somehow it has leaped clear and disappeared. Into the ditch? Into the woods?

The deer is gone.

I sit in the dark, gripping the wheel. I start to shake. Minutes accumulate like shadows in the corners of the car. The wet autumn forest watches me and waits.

I lift one hand, shift into gear, turn the car around and creep back onto the road, the strength returning slowly to my legs.

One headlight is out, but I hold the image of Carter's face before me framed in a square of yellow light. It's as if he's looking out our attic window across the valley, pulling me through the dark toward some place deep and unknowable as the braided paths in autumn woods, all the way home.

ACCIDENTAL BIRDS
OF THE CAROLINAS

1

COL. RANDOLPH JEFFERSON LEE, retired Army, prepares for his daily run, which he's lied about for months, telling Anne he will stay in the neighborhood, he will call her on the cell if he gets in trouble, and he will keep it down to a stroll, a slow walk, no running.

The cardiologist insisted on daily walks. Slow walks. But, by god, if a man can't run up a hill, what the hell good is he? So over the months he's slipped away from the curling asphalt paths of Stonehaven Downs Retirement Village to a place where he won't be spied on.

Now he is finally running again. A halting, gimpy jog, maybe, but you could call it running.

Rand glances guiltily at Anne sitting at the kitchen table, her fluffy, just-washed white-blonde hair, her head tilted that funny way of hers, peering through her fancy multicolor reading glasses at the paper. The lovebirds chatter in their cage next to the window. Anne's deep into her morning routine. Good.

She's finally stopped fussing over his every move when he goes out. What she doesn't know won't hurt her. But thank God for the Gooley Ridge, that patch of enormous pines across the highway that nobody seems to own. Once he crosses over the old railroad bridge none of the Stonehaven gossips can see him and report back that he is overdoing it again.

He slurps coffee, steals another look at her. Is she snubbing him, after their dustup last night? She asked him to come with her to some crazy Spring Gala where all the ladies are supposed to wear sundresses and the men are supposed to wear straw hats. Croquet is involved, she said, or cricket, she wasn't sure which, and vodka-spiked lemonade, and it is all supposed to celebrate the first day of the Stonehaven Farmers' Market.

"What does farming have to do with croquet?" he'd asked her. "It's the dumbest thing I ever heard." He is sure any respectable farmer would laugh up his sleeve at such doings. Why in God's name does this place inspire such silliness in his wife, who's been a sensible, intelligent woman for all their forty years together, the kind of woman who makes wry cracks under her breath to make him smile.

The social program here seems modeled after a summer camp for Southern debutantes. Tea and crumpets. Balls and juleps. My god, last April—when they were still new here, before he'd figured out their game—they'd bussed the newcomers down to some coastal plantation for a party with hoop skirts and a Rhett Butler lookalike. Rand stood, cringing, in a corner, getting drunk as fast as possible.

Anne ate it up. Laughing, asking to see the elaborate pantaloons under those skirts, even dancing with the Rhett character, who was paunchy and fortyish up close and, from what Rand could tell, knew only one dance step. The man led Anne in an endless backward circle till they were both dizzy and had to sit down.

Rand avoided dancing. But he remembers a ridiculous twinge of jealousy about that Rhett character spending so much time touching his wife. Anne seemed to be enjoying that a little too much.

To be fair, Anne had agreed later that having the black serving staff sing "Dixie" for them had been in terrible taste. "Maybe they were being ironic," she said, with her wry grin. "God, I hope so."

Since then, Rand has picked and chosen his social events carefully. These days Anne goes to most of them alone or with her new friends Reese and George.

Rand finishes his ration of half a cup of black coffee, turns to the kitchen window, where he can just see the crowns of the Gooley pines across the highway, lit by the early slanting light. Strange gurgling sounds emerge from his gut. He ignores them, glugs bottled water at the counter, stretches his calves, aware that his once taut body is not taking punishment well these days, not well at all.

Anne comes up behind him, rests her fingertips on his biceps and peers out the window, over his shoulder, her small breasts brushing against his back. All is forgiven. Her hair tickles his neck. It smells faintly sugary, like strawberries, with a sharper scent underneath, some new perfume. He feels a stirring in his groin, which quickly fades. Old soldiers never die, they just get soft.

"Look at that light!" she exclaims. "It's positively—" she searches for the right word— "positively Roman," she decides. "That lovely slant and glimmer. Well, I guess Michelangelo could have painted those trees, they're old enough. What a painting he would have made!"

"I don't think he made it here in his travels," Rand says, "and if he had, the ones you see now would have been knee-high. Do the math, dear." He hears the sharp tone in his voice, but he can't help it. Anne is always getting her facts wrong. The life span of a white pine is only about 400 years. The oldest one in Virginia is 450. These can't possibly be any older.

He feels Anne's fingertips withdraw and smells her faint coffee breath as she turns away. There is no reproach, just a separation between them descending like a thin glass panel. "I'm just remembering Rome," she says, a little sadly.

"Ah, Roma," he says. They had both been entranced by Rome. He's the one who'd made sure they flew via Rome and paused a few days there whenever they had home leave. That was a long time ago. Since then they'd raised kids, moved stateside, sold the house on Long Island, and just two years ago retired South, to this place that Anne loves and he—after giving it chance after chance—truly despises.

Only the running is keeping him sane now. That, and coming up with new ways to avoid Anne's nutty social plans. Other entertainments have faded.

Now she's opened the birdcage, has one of them in her hand, stroking it, humming a little song, peering at it over her glasses while it pecks seed from her palm. Still a damn good-looking woman after all these years. Strangely, lately she seems to be getting younger.

She catches him looking at her. "Going for your walk, dear?" she says.

"Right."

"I'm off to tennis."

So. She is skipping the Spring Gala after all. Good. The Cutest Farmers Market in the World can start without them.

"Okay." Rand pulls his watch cap over his bristly military cut.

"Be safe," she calls after him. "And listen to the birds!"

"I will," he says.

Anne's lips curl in the slightest of wry grins from behind her coffee mug. Forgiven again. Anne keeps lovebirds in the breakfast nook and a pair of cockatiels in the den, presents to him for some anniversary or another over the years. They've had them for ages. She's fond of them, she feeds them and cares for them, but she keeps them mostly for him. He is, as she is wont to say, a bird fanatic.

She knows he misses his jungle birds, his Asiatic migrations, his forays to look for Birds of Paradise, those extraordinary tufted, decorated, strange-plumed fowl of the tropics. He lets the cockatiels out sometimes when she's not around. Lets them walk up his outstretched arms and peck his hair. Lets them fly around the room. Like a damn kid, being bad. He always wipes off the furniture, as needed, before she gets back, and she's never said a word about it, although by glances and lifted eyebrows he knows she knows.

He leans in to kiss her good-bye, an old habit that still suffices to warm him. She turns her head slightly. "Lipstick," she says. She knows he hates the feel of it on his lips. He gives her a peck on the cheek. That cheek his whole life has been soft, powdered, and gardenia-scented, confined as she was, by protocol and safety concerns, behind the compound walls of overseas military housing. In those days Anne dressed in modest clothing, covered up in all public places, hatted and scarved against the harsh tropic sun and the harsher judgments of the natives. Now her cheek is lean and brown and salty, like a tomboy's, playing all that tennis through the mild winter. And under that fruity shampoo, there's that new scent, a whiff of lemon, again.

Rand opens the door, steps outside, and lets the fine April day enter his lungs. It is, after all, the one beautiful time of year around here. He might see that Pileated woodpecker, find its roost. He looks up, sees the pines glowing on the ridge like a promise, and sets off down the asphalt path, watching his feet, one of which drags a little when he tries to go faster.

As his blood begins to warm and move into his arms and legs, discomfiting thoughts crowd his brain, the facts of his new life in this strange little Southern town. It is a toy village, plotted and planned on a looping swirl of roads over the abandoned tobacco fields of what had been a large plantation in the nineteenth century, long since grown over in pines. Now the woods sport faux-Anglo street names and half-timber architecture, as if Queen Elizabeth has begun colonizing anew.

Rand turns down Sir Walter Raleigh Lane, feels the ache in his calves and that one place in his left knee that catches and makes a clicking sound. He is "run walking" now, pumping his arms, letting his hips slide side to side in that peculiar-looking way. It gets the heart rate up. But none of Anne's spies will mistake it for running. He slips his hand surreptitiously into his pocket, turns off his phone. There are many spots in this new neighborhood where coverage fades out. That's what he tells Anne anyway. What he really hates is the feel of something alive and demanding on his person, tracking his every move. He doesn't like the hard bounce of it in his pocket, either, and he's thought about "losing" it in a pile of pine straw in the woods, but she would just get him another.

He puts one foot after the other, taking his mind elsewhere, letting the pain in his hips, knees, and thighs float a few layers beneath conscious thought. By the time he's done, the body's aches will have floated away. Running is as good as morphine. God, he loves it—when it's over.

His first year here he simply pretended it wasn't happening again, all the signs floating below consciousness like some watery checklist for drowning: shortness of breath, the lead weight in his legs when he tried to run, worse every morning instead of better. Finally, the sweating collapse six months ago on the pale blue living room carpet. Anne had been lunching with her new friend Reese. He'd managed to call 911 himself, crush some aspirin between his molars, and hang on. The EMTs arrived in due time, brought him back.

But what the doctor told him, and he hasn't told Anne, is that if he doesn't go into an extensive rehab program, chances are he won't last more than a year or two, and even then rehab won't make much difference. Surgery won't help.

"It's in the genes, I'm afraid, Colonel," the doctor said, cheerfully, as if he were pleased to be exonerated from responsibility for Rand's health troubles. "Not a good candidate for transplant, I don't think, but we can send you home with a defrib pack. Let's get your wife in here and we'll show her how to use it."

Rand put it in the trunk of his car and left it there. Anne has been living with the possibility of a recurrence since the first heart attack in Singapore twelve years ago. Now she's restricted his diet to Grape Nuts and skinless chicken and salmon without sauce. No need to scare her further.

This is his rehab. He'll either get better or he'll die trying. Meanwhile, he is getting his papers in order, checking off the duty roster—will signed and notarized, stock portfolio rebalanced, pension papers in files, life insurance on auto-pay—aware that somehow fate has decreed that his last days will be spent in a place he loathes. He gets his papers together and watches as Anne falls in love—blatantly, shamelessly, besottedly in love—with Stonehaven Downs.

She is in love with the commons—gated and picketed to keep in some rare and exceptionally cute form of sheep, cropping away, as tourists snap photos. She is in love with the expensive little shops in the village square, the ladies-for-lunch café, the cappuccino wagon— the first, no doubt, in this dusty, hazy, forgotten scrap of the rural South, and one that attracts more flies than clientele on August afternoons. Anne is even in love with the flock of Pilgrim geese, herded by the property manager's not-quite-bright little daughter—more often than not, they herd the girl, until she gets wise, or gets tired, and whangs at them with her stick.

On their brief visit to the new house last Christmas, the kids, Carrie and Jeff, who never used to agree on anything, looked around, looked at each other, and gave their approval to the move. Carrie, squinting through her fashionable L.A. catwoman glasses at the furniture, the sheep, the neighbors, saw the sense of the move. Jeff, sitting unshaven at the kitchen table in a ripped sweatshirt from the University of New Mexico Archeology Department, dicing celery for the stuffing, saw that his mother was happy. Still, neither one of them could figure out why anyone would want to live in the South.

"It's weird here," Carrie said, twirling her wispy hair around a pencil. "I mean, at the Gas Mart these guys were picking the filters off their Winstons and smoking up the whole room, talking about NASCAR and chewing on Slim Jims and drinking RC Cola. It's like that old TV show on Nickelodeon, what is it? Where the sheriff goes fishing with Opie?"

"Andy Griffith," Jeff said. He lined his celery up and eased the blade through the ribs in straight lines. Then made careful cuts crosswise.

"Yeah. It's like that. A time warp, nineteen-fifties Southern Cracker Land. "

"The South will rise again," Jeff says, his lip curled in a half-grin, half-challenge. "Isn't that what they say?"

"This isn't the South," Rand told them. "This is Stonehaven Downs, a world unto itself."

Anne gave him a look. "We love it here," she said, turning to smile brightly at the kids. "It's perfect."

Rand turns down Queen of Scots Way. Now he remembers. No wonder Anne was happy this morning. He finally gave in last night and promised her a dinner party next week, for sixteen. She will at long last get to use her mother's ancient dining room table with matching chairs in mahogany and chintz, plus silver settings and individual crystal salt bowls with tiny individual salt spoons. She's been wanting to do that ever since she got here.

He has not yet figured out a way to get out of it. Maybe he'll get the flu or have another heart attack. Dinner with seven self-satisfied Connecticut couples, all strangers, is his idea of hell.

The inane chatter, the sloppy drinking, the inevitable social climbing and one-up-manship. Civilians are just as bad as mid-rank military. They like to brag, while pretending not to. Here they brag about their kids and grandkids, their furniture and collections, their former lives. She can do that kind of thing without him all she wants soon enough.

After the heart attack, all her new cronies took Anne aside and instructed her on how to manage a bearish retired husband. It was just after Kip Larsen went to the hospital, and the Stonehaven ladies were already on high alert.

The first rule: get him on a schedule. Well, he is on a schedule now. The second rule: get him out of the house. Well, he was out of the house. Third rule: watch his every move. When he came home from his walks the first few weeks, she made sure she was there to the hail the conquering hero, Gatorade or iced tea in hand, looking him over carefully, surreptitiously, for signs of wear.

One day when he breezed into the kitchen, having experimented with a new route home, he found her on the phone, looking worried, then guilty. She hung up quickly, saying, "*There* you are!" That happened often enough that it became clear she had some lady spies along his route, calling in reports of his progress or lack thereof. She gave him a GPS phone and made him promise to use it. Now, after six months, she's finally lost that vigilant look of wives who watch their husbands for signs of artery blockage. She's taken on a few more tennis lessons and let him go his way.

For his part, when he got home from the doctor he had been terrified for the first time in his life—not about death, old friend, but that Anne might find him when the next one came. He who had faced off with four-star generals and Asian dictators and Korean battalions couldn't stand the idea of her finding him helpless on the floor. And what would happen after.

She would call 911, they would bring him back, and he would live as a vegetable, lingering for months, years, unable to move. She has signed the DNR order he placed before her, but he knows she won't, can't follow through when the time comes. Her heart is too soft. Hard cheek, muscled lean arms, brown legs, snapping blue eyes, she will cave in the instant she sees him face down in the pale blue pile. She will call.

It happened this way to Kip, who now lives an underwater life of breathing machines and slow drip feeding, his face floating and bloated in the blue light of his nursing home room, the whoosh of oxygen into his lungs sounding just like Darth Vader's labored breathing. Kip, the most cheerful soldier/sailor Rand has ever known. Look at him now.

Kip's wife Adelle lost the house. She is lucky some other coma-widow with more resources has taken her in. He sees her from time to time, hunted and pale, fingering the budget bin steaks at the grocery store. No, not that way for Anne.

They went to see Kip, sat beside him for an hour, watching the machine shove air through his hollow lungs. Saw the nose pinched with prolonged death agony, eyes sunken and dry under tissue-thin lids. He turned to Anne. "Promise me—" he said.

"Who says you're going first?" she said, her blue eyes sharp, cheek flushed.

In that moment he saw it clear: He would not allow this to happen to them, to him, to her. He began to make a plan to be far away from rescue when he dropped. Never again the dusty chemical smell, the prickly feel of recently vacuumed carpet on his cheek while he lay gutshot, a ball of pain radiating out from his core, the taste of raw aspirin and bile in the back of his throat. Never again the carefully orchestrated rescue, an entire battalion just to save one wounded soldier.

Never that again. He has a plan.

Every day he goes off the asphalt onto a path that is a faint track in pine needles, a path that leads to an abandoned train trestle that crosses the highway and ends on the high ridge, in the midst of the great towering Gooley pines. There is one other person who goes into those woods at 0900, with clockwork regularity. He has planned it so that he goes an hour before, with the GPS as backup so she'll know where to find him.

Rand crosses Lady Jane Gray Way, breath coming a bit ragged now. Now he passes a gaggle of garden ladies, all done up in grass hats and latex-dipped gloves, planting petunias. They wave. He nods, knowing they'll report any sign of weakness to Anne. He knows he looks more fit than their husbands, which makes him suck in his gut, which throws off his stride and, before he can catch himself, he trips on a chunk of asphalt—the new roads in this place are already dissolving—twists his knee, stumbles, bounces off the heel of one hand and recovers.

The ladies call out, " Oh, Colonel, are you okay, Colonel? " They are coming this way. Crap. A new, hot nerve shoots pain from knee to ankle. He waves the ladies away, keeps going, waits till they are out of view to stop and pick the asphalt out of his palm.

All the women here seem to be gardeners. All the men talk investments and real estate and golf. No question this place is a great investment. The houses here cost less than half the price of the one he and Anne owned for years on Long Island. Here, three universities and major hospitals lie within an hour's drive, yet virtually no traffic passes on the main highway, save an occasional tractor or chicken truck.

The local grocery store is big on pimento cheese and wilted iceberg lettuce, but the Southern Foods truck delivers steaks and such to individual homes in Stonehaven Downs, everything you might need, frozen. Stonehaven has not yet been discovered by the rest of the world, but it will be soon. After they put in the new bridge to Chapel Hill, property values will soar.

Rand turns down Dover Beach Road, elbows pumping, breathing hard. Almost there. Three new houses for sale on this block. He pauses to check a house description and price in the Realtor's tube: 2 bedrooms, office, den, $325,000. Still cheap as hell, but rising. "Extra one for investment, Colonel?" He looks up. Some friend of Anne's.

"Sure," he wheezes, "why not?" Keeps going.

Two years ago Rand and Anne found, made an offer, and closed on a house in less than ten days, then put Anne's mother's rambling old Long Island house up for sale, made rather a killing on it. It had been a sound business decision. Living here would keep them from starving on his early retirement military pension and leave Anne with a nice nest egg when he was gone. He could live out his days without worrying about the neighbor's loud rap music or the call to some sticky foreign clime, or what would happen to Anne after his heart, old ticker, gave out. Time had spied on his plans, caught up with him, forced a change in strategy. But he still has his morning run, his *Times* on Sunday, his birds, his routine. Until last winter, he'd had runs and chess games with the Navy man down the block. Poor Kip.

Unlike Kip, he has a plan. He can do his short time.

On the far edge of the Downs, the World's Cutest Sheep huddle and baa for some visiting relatives with young kids in tow. The big thing around here is to come see the sheep when the grandkids visit. He has to admit the lambs are funny. Leaping straight into the air sometimes, as if someone pinched them. Once in a while some idle grandparent lets a six-year-old get too close to the electric wire carefully concealed behind the quaint pickets, and loud crying ensues.

Today the young rams are trying out their new toys. Two of them keep hunching the backsides of their sister ewes, who respond by kicking them. Take it easy, fellas, he wants to tell them, it takes practice. The real ram here is a magnificent old stud with shaggy black fleece and curling horns and a baleful eye. He's not on display today. They've got him shut up someplace. Too bad. Kip loved that ram. Ever since they paused here one day on their run, watched him copulating with one ewe after the other. Kip said, "So that's the secret. A harem. Have to try that. Bet it keeps the juices flowing."

"Think you could keep up with that, old man? Anyway, I hear in the Navy it's all rams, no ewes." Rand liked to needle a Navy man. It was a kind of routine with them.

"You heard wrong, Colonel. The way I heard it, the one-stars in the Army like to screw a roomful of full-bird colonels."

God he misses Kip. Man had it right about the one-stars. Kip liked to talk, but he knew how to shut up and run too, and when Rand put on the speed, he always rallied to keep up. He was an adequate chess player. A good man, for a Navy man. Truth to tell, if there was going to be only one other retired military in this damn place, he'd been glad it wasn't an Army man. He is tired of Army talk, Army rank, Army orders. He got tired of that a long time ago.

Kip liked to talk about his grandkids. That was the closest thing he came to one-up-manship. A sprint always shut him up if he rattled on too long.

Well, he's shut up now, hasn't he? Kip's face, flaccid and pale in the hospital lights, a crust of drool at the edge of his mouth. Nobody there to wipe it clean. Machines pushing air into dead lungs. Damn, don't think about that.

Rand notices he's almost stopped, he's walking so slow. Breath coming in ragged rasps.

Time to get moving. That's the way. One foot in front of the other.

Rand wonders why his own children haven't made any cute grandkids for Anne. Neither one has married. They are certainly old enough—Jeff must be a couple of years past thirty. And Carrie is—twenty-nine? Yes. Her next birthday will be what she calls the big three-oh. The children of his middle age. He and Anne had put off children, so many other things to worry about overseas. These days, Anne certainly talks about it enough, to him. "We shouldn't have waited so long," she says. "I hate waiting for grandkids." She's never dared bring it up to Jeff or Carrie. "I wouldn't presume," she always says.

The familiar hitch in his side starts now, just under his arm and down the ribs to the gut. It makes him gasp for breath; it makes him want to stop.

He keeps going.

There's some kind of warbler in the woods ahead. Fifty, maybe a hundred, from the sound of them. Getting closer, now, to the Gooley pines. It's late in the migration season for warblers, maybe these got lost. In February, yellow warblers, magnolia warblers, and pine warblers all came fluttering through the neighborhood at once, hidden in the thickets. He identified them by standing under a holly tree, completely still, for twenty minutes, while they gobbled berries and shouted above him. He stood there memorizing their marks, then went straight home to look them up.

When they first moved here, Anne set up feeders in the back yard and called out the names of all the new birds she saw—plus the familiars. Cardinals, jays, sparrows. She set up a pair of Adirondack chairs so they could watch together, but they never did. He hated sitting still, getting bit by mosquitoes. But he did watch from the kitchen window. That's where he sighted his first accidental.

After a fierce rainstorm, there'd been a harvest of pinecones in the yard and a tiny bird alighted in the midst of them, brilliantly colored as a circus wagon. Bright blue head. Green back—not just any green— parrot green. Vermillion chest. When Anne got him the glasses, he could see bright red circles around its black eyes. Anne paged frantically in her *Peterson's*. "Could be a pet store bird, you know, an escapee." She paused. "Well, we *are* in the Carolinas—" There was a note of wonder in her voice "—could it be? I never heard of—oh. Extinct. Jesus. Rand, give me those glasses."

He handed them over, looked at the page. "It's *not* a Carolina parakeet," he said. "Is that what you thought?"

"No," she said. "Hoped. But it sure is . . . *colorful*." She was paging again. "Here, after the warblers, yes. A painted bunting." She handed Rand the guide. "Proof."

"Okay," he said. It seemed to be the one. Such a tropical-looking bird, more like what they'd seen in Malaysia or the Philippines. "Do they live here year-round?" he asked.

"Let's check the map. No, no. This one is out of its range, which is more along the coast. Maybe the storm last night blew it here. They call it an 'accidental.' Why, Rand, it's just a wayfaring stranger, like you."

She grinned. She called him that, from time to time, especially on their foreign travels—it was a tribute to his Appalachian roots, and a kind of statement about the blues he would get in the first weeks at a new post. She would even sing the old gospel tune sometimes in her quavering contralto, when he needed cheering. *I am a poooooor wayfaring strangerrrrr, wanderin' throooooough this world of wooooe.*

"I've never seen one of these before," she said, excited, staring at the bunting. "I'll have to add it to the Life List."

He started his own sublist then. Accidental Birds of the Carolinas. First accidental: Painted bunting. A bird that didn't belong here.

It's funny, Anne's the one who got him interested in birds in the first place. She'd taught him the identifying signs: feet, beak, wing, markings. She'd made him listen to the call-and-response, the living world of bird communication woven into the air around him. She'd thought she could convert him into one of those doddering birders who travel in a pack, doing their Christmas counts and Audubon surveys. He tried that once or twice and hated it. Now he's the one who heads out alone and spies on birds, part of his "walking therapy," and she tromps out with a cast of thousands, scaring them all off.

"You make everything into a party," he once said to her, complaining.

"And you pick the solitary sports," she'd said. "Running, for instance."

That was not true, of course. He ran with Kip Larsen for two years and enjoyed the company thoroughly.

She was always a people person, but now she's such a social butterfly, doing her volunteer work at that school for retarded kids, lunching with ladies, hosting a tea for the library. She's become more confident. He finds it attractive, but unsettling, and a little lonely, as if he's suddenly bunking with an unpredictable younger woman.

He once saw in her something of his own adaptability, his own cheerful fortitude as they forayed to one station after another overseas. Korea, Cairo, Philippines, Singapore. All that was over. She, who spent her whole life making one temporary nest after another, is now making a home. The fierce joy with which she commandeers the plumbers, tile-setters, painters, and bricklayers, it frightens him a little. Where had that joy been hidden all these years? In the East, her attitude had been more like grim determination.

Now she seems so happy that he is sure, on some level, that she will be fine without him. He feels a twinge near his heart. The thought of her carrying on, feeding the lovebirds, having dinner parties, dancing with strange men, floods his belly with sorrow, weights his legs, makes him veer toward the edge of the asphalt.

He rights himself, keeps going.

Rand takes a furtive look around, no gardeners out in their yards, no passing cars. He ducks down the dirt path that leads across the abandoned railroad bridge. He crosses, steps carefully off the ties, and looks up. The crowns of the Gooley pines blaze with light. He has timed it perfectly. If a heart attack does take him, it will take him there, in the sharp-scented woods, birds calling overhead, cheek resting on clean pine needles. If it happens there, he will make sure it's fast. Running can be a trigger. Running uphill . . . well, that could finish things quite nicely. After fifteen minutes without oxygen, the brain has virtually no chance of working again. After an hour, the blood begins to cool. After two hours rigor mortis sets in. No EMT in the world will attempt resuscitation.

There is a section of this path where he can get up speed, run full tilt for 50 yards. Sometimes Rand sprints so hard, he throws up the pint of water he swallowed in the kitchen. The sprints will do it, if not today, someday soon. Those sprints, and the sausage-and-egg biscuits he sneaks afterwards at the Sunrise Market and Gas down the road, a place no self-respecting Stonehaven man ever goes—except Kip, he remembers with a guilty twinge. They used to sneak there together.

Now he leans against one of those sharp-scented pine trunks, gasping, coughing, resting for the sprint.

He will practice it till he gets it right.

She can kiss his cheek good-bye after it is cool, she won't even see him until after the death certificate has been signed. That's the way it worked for their neighbor Horace, who keeled over in the backyard while no one else was home, and that will be the way it works for him. There will be no enormous medical bills. No fuss. No regrets.

Now he finds the pine needle path, faint among the enormous trees, and sucks in breath for the run to the top. One Mississippi, two Mississippi, go.

Rand is breathing hard, forehead pressed against the bark of a behemoth pine, pulse pounding in his ears, when he hears the sirens winding down Route 177 from Quarryville, faintly at first, then whooping faster and closer as they round the bend and cross the Sissipahaw River Bridge. His heart skips a few beats. For an instant he thinks they are coming for him. He has imagined it so many times. He listens with dread, till he hears the ambulance turn in at Stonehaven, mute its sirens, and go about its business. It is not coming up the ridge to the Gooley pines. He is not having a heart attack. He is not dead.

Ten minutes later, on his walk down the hill toward home, he sees it heading north, toward the hospital, no siren, no big hurry. *Another man bites the dust*, Rand thinks. Not me. Not yet. He has to admit that he is greatly relieved.

When Rand gets home, their neighbor George is sitting on the kitchen stoop, head resting on his crossed arms, arms around his knees. Napping? Or drunk on gin and tonic, more likely, even at this hour. George is a party man from Connecticut. He drinks gin and scotch interchangeably, it seems, without seeming to care which, but it's always the good stuff, none of that Army-issue in plastic gallon jugs. His wife Reese is Anne's best friend, her most loyal tennis partner and lunch companion. Maybe George is going to invite him to lunch again, or for a round of bad golf. He thought George had finally given up on him. He had *hoped.*

Rand approaches, wheezing a bit, trying to control his breath, mute it. Anybody could tell he hasn't been just walking.

George looks up. It is the strangest thing. His face is red and splotched. His eyes are bloodshot. His shoulders shake. There is no mistaking it. He isn't drunk. He's crying.

That siren. That slow-moving ambulance.

"What happened, man?" Rand calls out, breaking into a jog. "Is it Reese?"

George shakes his head, miserable. Rand watches him try to stand. Watches George's hand reach out, a trembling, old man's hand. Feels George's fingers grip his arm. His chest goes numb.

There is only one other person it could be.

2

After the first jolt, like an electric shock to the heart, Rand pushes George away, charges into the house, and shouts her name, expecting to find her on the floor. When he doesn't find her, he charges back into the kitchen and demands to know where she is. George swallows his drink, sets down his glass, tells him the facts. "It was on the tennis court, old man. She just went down. She's at the hospital now. Reese is there. Waiting for us. Buddy, there was nothing they could do."

Rand picks up the phone. "What hospital?" His voice is hoarse.

"Quarryville. I've got the number. We should go. But before we do—" he hands Rand a glass filled to the brim with Scotch. Rand drinks it down. He stares at George with loathing. Then he dials the number. A voice mail system answers, "Thank you for calling Quarryville Hospital. If this is an Emergency, please hang up and dial 911. If you wish to speak with someone, please stay on the line and listen for your choice of options. . . . Press One for the Emergency Room, Two for Visitor Services . . ." Rand almost throws the phone across the room.

He gets in George's car, phone glued to his ear, until the river bridge, where the signal dies out. He redials, no answer. Redials, no answer. He shouts at George to drive faster, though George is already speeding and weaving all over the road.

There has to be something they can do. There is always something they can do.

It turns out Anne registered her own DNR order with all the local hospitals. When she didn't respond to twenty minutes of a tennis court geezer's rickety CPR, when it took the ambulance another 40 minutes to get there, the EMTs declared her DOA. It is incomprehensible. Everyone knows EMTs always hook you up and resuscitate you even if you've been dead for an hour. At the hospital, they took her straight to the morgue.

Someone takes him to her. Someone lifts the cover on her body.

Anne is not Anne. Here is a stranger with waxy skin, sagging mouth, a crust of spittle. He reaches out to wipe it away. His beautiful Anne. Her blue eyes sealed under pale freckled lids. A whiff of lemon under the hospital disinfectant and the faint sweet scent of spoiling flesh.

Death squeezes Rand's heart till he cannot breathe, then settles around his shoulders like a numbing shroud.

Someone puts a hand on his arm, guides him away.

Someone fills out forms, hands him a pen.

Someone sits him down with a Styrofoam cup of coffee, but he waves it away.

Someone drives him home.

Someone makes him a cup of tea with lemon. He hates lemon, but he drinks it dutifully like a refugee in a camp. He knows he is in shock. Sustenance shall not be refused. Your duty is to survive.

Someone makes phone calls in the background. The thought of her in the hospital, cold, fills him with dread, then rage. Reese's hand floats into his line of vision, takes his teacup, fills it with some steamy brew that smells of oranges. He turns to her, croaks, "I'll sue the bastards. I want to call my lawyer." Reese fends him off, tells him they need to keep the lines clear, waiting for callbacks from his kids. The kids. Christ, the kids. Rand completely loses his courage at the thought of telling them. Someone else will tell them.

Someone finds him asleep in the recliner in the den and takes off his shoes, covers him with a blanket. He wakes in the dark with a jerk. What is he doing here? Another spat with Anne? He makes it halfway down the hall to the bedroom before he remembers. No Anne there. No Anne at all. He turns and goes to the kitchen and pours himself a bourbon. Wishes he had a cigarette. Thinks there might be one in a drawer somewhere, though it's been twelve years since he quit. Why is the phone ringing at this hour? He can't stand it. He yanks the cord out of the wall. In the morning, Reese finds him asleep at the kitchen

table, his head resting on one arm, all the drawers in the kitchen pulled
out and their contents scattered.

Reese makes coffee and pours him some, pulls him to the sofa to
sit for a while, explains that the kids have been trying to reach him.
She has plugged the phone back in. More people come and go, handing
him phones, making phone calls, putting him into cars, driving him
places, giving him more forms to sign, putting food out and pouring
coffee. He has a dim sense of George hovering in corners, exuding a
ginny smell, and Reese constantly at his elbow.

He doesn't remember eating. He won't sleep in that bed. Again he
wakes up in his office chair, wanders into the kitchen, sees the light is
on and there are familiar kitchen noises. Anne? Not Anne. Reese is
setting up filter, coffee, and water, and swearing at the button that sets
the auto switch for morning. "What are you doing here?" he says,
befuddled. "Oh, Rand," Reese says, her face collapsing in a puddle of
tears.

Somehow Carrie and Jeff are notified, picked up at airports, and
brought to the front door. Somehow he endures their stricken faces,
Carrie's desperate hug, Jeff's awkward clutch-and-pat. Carrie makes
sure all Anne's relations are notified. She gets his dress uniform quick-
cleaned for the funeral, sets out a dark suit for the wake. All is arranged.
The women do it all.

The wake is brutal. Anne's face horribly alive in the casket, the
mortician's tricks at work. Was it some kind of tasteless Southern
tradition? They have dressed her in a blue flounced party dress, tan
shoulders exposed, hair frosted and sprayed, gardenia on her breast,
eyes closed with a dusting of blue shadow, as if she were taking a short
nap before heading out—alone—to a fancy ball. Reese must have handled
it. Damn her. What was she thinking?

And the flowers. Someone has sent lilies, reeking of death, and an
arrangement of roses shaped like an enormous halter as if Anne had
just won a horse race, but the worst are the spring flowers. People
somehow knew which ones were her all-time favorites: white daisies
and blue larkspur. They are everywhere.

He had forgotten her love for these particular flowers until he
overhears a complete stranger whispering to another: *There was a*

field behind her childhood home—on Long Island—and when she was a girl, she told me she used to run through the flowers, blue larkspur, white daisies, lying down on them, smelling them, deciding they were proof there was a God.

All those people, telling stories about Anne, people who have known her for six months or a year at most, acting as if they knew her more intimately than he did. It is like being at the funeral of a stranger. People whispering, "Massive stroke. On the tennis court. Poor thing. So unexpected." Strangers regard him with an unsavory combination of sympathy and curiosity. His own children, Jeff and Carrie, standing beside him, glance at him from time to time with the same furtive expression: *How is he making out? Is he falling apart? And if not, why the hell not?*

People from home come, droves of them. People he barely remembers from their ten years in Huntington and from scattered months of home leave there. People Anne has known since childhood. People from all over Ambler County, Quarryville, Green Hope, Springfield. All his paperwork, all his plans for his own orderly death, have not prepared him. He stands there, stunned, listening to people tell each other how sorry they are, watching people cry for the loss of beautiful Anne, watching them embrace her sister Celia, her new best friend Reese, then finally approach him with hesitant eyes, reach out for his hand, muttering, "I'm so sorry for your loss."

He hadn't known his wife's friends. He hadn't known his wife. Not very well at all lately. It eats the liver out of him.

On Saturday, all Rand has to do is dress for the funeral. Someone brings him a plate of scrambled eggs, too wet, he likes his dry, and buttered toast. He sets the plate uneaten on the dresser. His collar is giving him trouble—neck gets thicker in old age—and Carrie helps with the closure.

Jeff's face seems different this morning, shiny and pink, and it takes Rand a minute to figure out that his son has shaved off his mustache and his fashionable stubble. His suit is borrowed, too short in the sleeves. The boy looks young, vulnerable as a rookie recruit.

At the funeral, Rand listens to the words but spends most of his energy trying to stand up straight. His body seems to keep wanting to sag to one side, as if it is looking for a tree to lean against. Carrie stands beside him, gripping his arm. Then it is over.

When they get home from the funeral, there is a moment when Carrie and Jeff have gone off somewhere and Rand is standing alone on the kitchen stoop, trying to see the world clearly, trying to see the world as Anne saw it. And failing miserably. At that moment he hears a crack, and an enormous tree limb falls out of the sky, bounces off the gutter and lands at his feet. Birds explode from the feeder, escaping in all directions, bursts of red, gray, yellow, and blue, Cardinals, juncos, goldfinches, jays. Years ago, in Long Island, Anne taught him their names and colors. The common birds, she called them.

God, he misses her. But it is more than that. Something twists in his heart, thinking of her voice, calling to birds. Her strong hand, filling the feeder. Her blue eyes, searing, accusing. Rand retreats inside, pours himself a bourbon over a single cube of ice. Gulps it down. Pours another.

He sees it now. Anne made a net of safety and friendship around them—and even love—that kept them alive and kept her happy. She flirted with plumbers, pleaded with grown kids to finish college, found jobs for friends' children, tutored illiterates, cajoled caterers, inspired artists, and cooked his favorite chicken curry, all in the same life, probably all in the same day, and he has known only the plushness of the sauce in his mouth, the whiff of her lemony perfume as she served him, the perfect mouthful of green peas, celery, chicken and almonds, like a sacrifice worthy of a lesser god—and the mess she left in the kitchen. He has known only the dust-free valences of a clean house, the immaculate mini-blinds filtering light, the fresh salt smell of a seasoned woman next to him in bed.

He begins to remember that he has not held back on his complaints about their new life. He hears his own voice needling, dismissing, complaining. He thought he was preparing her to live without him. Instead, he sees now that she was already living without him.

Every room is a reminder. The new house and everything in it were her idea. The Williamsburg prints, the Audubon watercolors, the deep soft sofa and the high-backed wing chairs. "No pink" was his sole contribution to the building of their last nest together. "No Chinese red." This last a snide reference to her one decorating disaster back on Long Island—a varnished and textured Chinese red accent wall that softened and dripped in the heat of summer and gave off fumes in the dead of winter, and which he had been certain would one day ignite and burn the house down.

So, there was no pink, no Chinese red, but instead a kind of warm mauve undertone to the whole scheme that fueled—like arterial blood under the surface of the skin—a lively glow along wainscoting, cushion piping, tassels and various complicated arrangements of fabric around windows. For forty years, Anne had kept a kind of elaborate hope chest of her mother's furniture in the old Long Island house while they were posted overseas—the dining room table that sat sixteen with all its leaves in, matching Chippendale chairs, a pair of wingbacks, a sideboard, a mahogany cupboard he could use for his gun collection, sixteen settings of family silver with ornate crests on the handles. After months of reupholstering, repairs, and polish, it was all very elegant— what she must have thought he expected—but it was also welcoming, clean, and bright. It was what she had wanted their life to be when they moved here. Welcoming. Clean. Bright.

"Rand," she'd said, across the dinner table one night back in Long Island, just after they decided to move to Stonehaven. "I want our life there to be different. I want a house big enough and nice enough for dinner parties. I need a social life. So do you."

"Anne, whatever you want," he said. But he had lied.

Once the house was built and the furniture brought out of storage and placed with care, he balked. The autumn after they moved, there was a series of newcomers' parties at various homes and posh locations around the Downs. There were a lot of them. It was almost like being rushed for a sorority, she bubbled. So many clubs to choose from, so many breakfasts and luncheons and cocktail parties. For a season, Anne barely had to cook dinner. They ate party leftovers, pressed upon them by new friends, complete with plastic forks and colored toothpicks. Thanksgiving and Christmas and New Year's went by in a whirl, all requiring new social rituals.

All that first year, Anne would head out exploring then come home and bubble about her latest conquest—a funny little health food market in Quarryville, a book club that read her favorite mysteries, a working artist's studio behind the shops, a tennis tournament, a tour of historic homes. He listened with half an ear, alert for news of party dates or obligations that might require his presence, letting the rest slide past in a partly irritating, partly comforting patter that was the familiar sound of Anne's life intersecting with his.

It had been late May before he heard her say it: "It's time. We have some social obligations. I want to get to know some people better. Let's have a dinner." Her eyes shone with anticipation. It surprised him how long it had taken, and he realized he had hoped she'd decided dinner parties weren't the thing here.

It was easy to deflect. There had been no malice in it, it was simply that he loathed dinner parties or any hubbub in his own house. He had put up with such as an obligation of Army service overseas. He was retired from obligations, dammit. All it took was a burst of temper, a flushed face. The threat of stress. His heart.

"Anne, my god, we're just settling in here. Let us for Christ's sake have some time alone after all those infernal parties."

Her face darkened. "If we don't do it now, we'll never do it," she said.

"Fine by me," he countered. "If I had my way . . ."

"You DO have your way!" she shrieked at him. "It's like you're already dead! Do you know what that makes me? ALONE. Lonely. No family. No home to enjoy. I might as well be a bag lady, living on the streets of Bangkok!" She slammed the kitchen door and went out for a ride in the car.

He was shocked. He had always counted on Anne's consideration. She was nothing if not a considerate person. But something changed between them after that night. Through that first summer, and into the fall, and the rest of the past year Anne had seemed resolved to go her own way, and to treat him with kindness, even gratitude at times, that he was around, and useful to her, and remembered to leave the New Yorker and the Times folded to stories of interest.

She went to church more. Got out of Stonehaven every day, into Quarryville, Green Hope, and Springfield. Made a wider circle of friends. Worked four days a week at one thing or another—shelter, food bank, school—was simply not home those days except to make the morning coffee, send him off on his walk, then rush out for tennis or work, not returning till afternoon, and then sometimes just long enough to make a plate for him, place it in the oven to warm, and go off to some party without him. He never saw her on Fridays.

After a time there was no longer any expectation of a new social life together. No expectation of more than the occasional courtly escort to one of the larger benefits held in what was known as The Livery, a reference to a horse barn that had once been here, now replaced by a new post-and-beam ballroom with heartwood pine floors and tongue and groove walls and ceilings—so much tightly fitted wood, it reminded him of a yacht. She had given up on him. But with quiet and steely resolve, she let him know he would not stop her. He could have the house, as his preserve, old growly bear. She, the bird, would fly through the open window.

Anne began to go to parties with girlfriends and other couples. There was a crew of old gals who ironically, and unofficially, called themselves the Stonehaven Widows—some of them really were widows, but the rest of them were golf widows or wives who were simply practicing cheerful, independent lives from their grumpy retired husbands. Only a month ago, at one of the couples' events organized by these ladies, Reese's husband George joked to Anne over his martini, "That man is giving you the eye. He thinks you're one of the Stonehaven widows." Anne had gone into the hosts' bathroom and wept. When she came out, disheveled, makeup smeared, eyes bright, Reese asked her where in the world she had been. "Kissing a strange man in a back room," she said. She came home and told Rand the story.

He knew what she was saying. "Doesn't sound like my kind of party," he said.

"No," Anne had said, evenly. Randolph Lee liked his quiet.

Well, he has it now, doesn't he?

3

Rand gazes at the long, six-leaved mahogany table, now covered in piles of food brought by neighbors, remembers how it lay shining and empty all these months, with a dried flower arrangement like a memorial in the center. Anne's dinner party, the one he had finally agreed to, tastes like dust on his tongue. She had been so happy that morning, effusive in the old way, and now he realizes she must have been hatching her plan—gathering recipes, guest lists, visions of table settings fizzing in her brain until that moment on the tennis court when it all exploded. She'd been cheated out of doing something she would have loved, and it was all his doing. Now the dried flowers are gone, and the mahogany carefully covered with a pad and a linen cloth, on top of which lies such a litter of casseroles, pies, brownies, baked chickens, deli chickens, green beans, baked beans, pound cake, even a baked ham.

There had been plenty to eat at Reese's house after the funeral. Strangers had crammed her kitchen and parlor, spilling over to her deck and the tiny courtyard behind. Reese hadn't had any leftovers except a box of chicken wings that came late, which she gave to Jeff, who sat outside in the dark on the deck steps after everyone left and ate them all. Rand had stepped out for air, saw him tearing the flesh off the tiny bones, flinging the bones into the yard. The fury in the boy had frightened him. He'd quietly stepped back into the house.

All the food on Anne's table now is a fresh load, delivered with efficient promptness over the last twenty-four hours, and it is just for him. Unopened. Wrapped in plastic. Some of it still warm, like the whole wheat cinnamon rolls Reese somehow found time to throw together.

Cakes and casseroles have clearly been pulled from freezers where Anne told him ladies kept half a dozen such recipes at the ready for the inevitable demand, the ghoulish obligation of those who live among the old. These are all marked "thaw for two hours" or "ready to cook" with instructions taped on the plastic wrap on oven temp, minutes, and covering with foil to keep from over-browning.

There are plates of fresh-made sandwiches and entire meals tucked into blue plastic boxes, one with a cluster of matching plastic forks and napkins, as if the giver expected him to set out on a picnic.

There are baskets of fruit. There is a case of grapefruit. They must have been thinking of Anne when they sent that. Rand's medications all react with grapefruit.

All this food just for him.

It is an enormous picnic—a mountain of food, really—for so few ants. He has run off just about everybody but Jeff and Carrie.

Carrie is camped out upstairs in the guest room with her camcorder, her mother's letters and journals and photo albums, and her iPhone to keep her connected to her paralegal job in L.A., from which she has taken a two-week leave. Jeff is staying on Reese's couch rather than his father's. "It'll be less mess for you, Dad," Jeff said, cautiously, testing the waters. His father agreed. Jeff had clearly been relieved. Rand and Jeff have not gotten along well in recent years.

Let's face it, Jeff is kind of a bum. Never happy with his job. Always looking for a way out. Never bothering to marry any of his short-term girlfriends. Calling Anne late at night, getting her up at all hours. Rand would find her sitting in her bathrobe in the kitchen with reheated coffee, talking out his latest failure, bad breakup, lost job. Who is he going to complain to now?

Maybe Reese. Not him.

Rand has no idea who to call to deal with all this food. Surely someone will come and take it. He has no room for it in the refrigerator. If he calls Reese, she will be offended, she arranged it all. She doesn't know that Carrie, thin as a rail, eats only desserts and Diet Coke and wheatgrass shakes. Jeff eats only meat and spaghetti, as far as Rand can tell, and though his son can really pack it in, there is no way in hell he can eat a whole ham before he leaves Monday, which is tomorrow. Nobody else will come over. To the few who asked when they could visit, Rand has said, "Maybe in a couple of weeks." He can see Reese is exhausted. She will definitely take a day off before she comes over to check on him.

George is zonked. Turns out his heart is broken. He confided this after the wake, over his fourth martini. "I hate this," he said simply. "She had so much life in her. It's going to kill Reese. Everybody. We were all in love with her." Rand looked at him, incredulous. *What about me?* he wanted to shout. George saw his look. "You'll be fine, old man," he said. "The Stonehaven widows will keep you fat, just don't fall into their trap."

Rand almost hit him. George edged away, raised his martini glass in salute, and fled. George would not be coming around to nibble on chicken wings anytime soon. Thinking about it, Rand's heart pounds with rage, then twinges with guilt, then sags with sorrow.

Rand rummages in a drawer for the Stonehaven Downs Community Resource Directory and starts flipping through. Food Bank. That's one of Anne's things, isn't it? They take food, don't they? "Hello," he says, surprised someone is there to answer the phone. "I have some food . . . well, some of it's frozen. I don't really know what it is. It's from . . . a party. Casseroles and things. You can't? Oh. Oh, I see." He hangs up the phone. Those damn people think he's out to poison them. Nothing homemade. No pies or casseroles. No chicken curry. It is amazing that he can not get rid of all this food.

It reminds him of what the pastor said in his eulogy—young man that he hadn't ever met, but who somehow had known Anne well. He'd said, "What if Jesus made a meal and nobody came? What if he had created the miracle of the loaves and fishes, and there was nobody there to share it?

"The miracle of Anne's life—" the boy had gotten a little choked up here, his collar constricting his bobbing Adam's apple—"was that everybody shared it. We all sat at the table with Anne. She was a gift for us from God, and some of us have feasted with her long years, others invited late to the table. But, oh, the comfort of that meal together. It shall not leave us."

Rand picks up two pies, a pound cake, and the baked ham and finds places for them in the refrigerator. Then he unrolls a yard waste bag from the box, snaps it open, and begins to scrape the food from Anne's feast into the garbage. The dishes must be washed and returned. He will lie and tell people he enjoyed their contribution. No, no, he can't face that. He will look up their addresses in the Stonehaven directory and return their casserole dishes, shining and clean, on their doorstoops when they are not at home. He will enclose a note: *Thanks so much. Rand and Anne.*

"Dad, what are you doing?" Carrie rubs her eyes and stares at the open bag of garbage.

He starts guiltily. Then holds his ground. "Just cleaning up," he says.

"But Dad—" Carrie looks at him quizzically. "It's perfectly good food. It's for us to eat. You know, so we won't have to cook for a while."

"I saved some of it. All this will go bad. It may already have gone bad, I have no idea how long it's been sitting here."

"Dad," Carrie said, getting an expression just like her mother's when Anne was about to decide to take over something. "I was just going to freeze it for you. Why don't you let me do it? There's plenty of room in the box freezer." She peered into the trash bag. "Don't like curried chicken any more?" she said.

"I like your mother's curried chicken," Rand said. "The rest can go to the dogs."

"Oh, Dad." Carrie has tears in her eyes. "I miss her too."

She didn't even give him the chance to say it. He misses Anne. God, he misses her like an arm or a leg—no you could lose one of those and get by. He misses her like a set of lungs. He misses her like fresh air. He has been drowning in this cheesy Southern thickened air, this false camaraderie, and she has been his only source of oxygen for months.

The phone rings. He hands Carrie the trash bag and picks up the phone. "Yes?" he answers. "Okay. Yes it was. Yes, thank you. Good-bye." He looks at Carrie. Carrie is sorting casseroles by size and shape.

"I don't even know who that was," he says. "It's going to be like that for weeks." Rand holds the receiver in his hand, bumfuzzled. "She was *crying*."

Carrie stops sorting. "Dad?" she says. "Will you make a deal?" This is their old signal for serious talk. When she wanted to go to Berkeley and he wanted her closer at Swarthmore, she came to make a deal. When she wanted a strapless outfit for the prom and Anne wanted her shoulders covered, Carrie made a deal. When Jeff was winning at Monopoly, but she had Boardwalk, she could always make a deal. Carrie the dealmaker. She usually made a *good* deal, where everybody felt like they got something of what they wanted. She would make a terrible lawyer. She thought about others too much.

"What's the deal," he says.

"The deal is, I'll answer the phone while I'm here. I'll be here two weeks. You don't even have to think about it. And if I'm not here, you agree to screen calls with the answering machine and only talk to people you want to talk to."

"Okay," he says. "You win." Carrie knows he does not suffer fools or undue sentiment gladly. Thank god for Carrie.

Two hours later, once the casseroles are sorted into What We Will Eat This Week and What We Will Eat Next Week and What We Will

Never Eat in a Million Years But Jeff Might, Carrie sits at the kitchen table sneaking a coffee loaded with cream and sugar toxins, not on her vegan diet. Rand is napping in the study. Jeff is at Reese's. She answers the phone to what seems like a crank call.

"Hello, Lee residence, Carrie speaking," she says.

"Tahk tah Miss Ahn?" a childish voice says.

"Who is speaking, please?" Could this be a friend's grandchild, some special protégé?

"Miss Ahn, Miss Ahn!" the voice rises to a squeak.

"I'm sorry, I need to know your name," Carrie says. She's heard of burglars calling houses of the dead on the day after the funeral, hoping the family is away.

"I am Bobo," the voice says. "Sorry you ah dead."

Carrie hangs up.

4

Monday morning Rand wakes with plans to go for a run but ends up standing there in the clothes closet, touching Anne's camel's hair coat, her silk dresses, her suit jackets, clutching them to his breast and choking on the scent of her new cologne, which he'd never known the name of till now. He'd found the spritzer on her dresser and choked up at the smell, then at the label.

It was called "Happy."

Her clothes are faintly lemony with it; the scent clings, telltale as smoke in the clothes of a secret smoker.

Now his body slumps to one side and he slides to the floor, dragging a pile of clothes with him. When Carrie pokes her head in the bedroom door, she finds him huddled on the floor of the closet, his face buried in the tumble of cloth. "Dad? Dad! What's wrong!"

Rand pushes the clothes away. "Looking for some shoes," he mumbles. "Where the hell are my Nikes? Got to clean out this damn closet."

"Dad," Carrie informs him, "nobody cleans out a closet this soon. Anyway, I'll take care of it. I might want some of her things."

He looks doubtfully at his daughter, who has never seemed to know conventional wisdom about anything, much less closet cleaning and death. And she has never shared her mother's taste for tennis togs and double-knits. Carrie's always been strictly a thrift store fashionista—her taste running to plastic purses, zigzag patterns, and micro mini dresses. For a moment he imagines Carrie in one of Anne's outfits. There's . . . a resemblance. Delicate nostrils, tilted eyes, and faint brocade of freckles. He can't breathe, looking at her.

He needs to get out, exhale a little bit of the soupy Southern spring air, inhale the hot incense of the Gooley pine grove. It reminds him, just a little, of the sea breeze at Montauk.

Rand scoops his Nikes out of the closet, tells Carrie, "Time to get back to the routine. Doctor's orders, you know." Carrie looks at him suspiciously, opens her mouth as if to protest, but then closes it and lets him go his way.

Rand heads down the road, not even stopping for stretches, for fear that a passing car will stop, a neighbor look out at him, someone he's never seen before, and express sympathy, tell a story about Anne that he's never heard, some intimate moment of her life, make him feel even more a stranger in his own marriage. He ducks across the railroad overpass, having escaped public scrutiny.

By the time he gets to the base of the Gooley ridge, he has a cramp. He walks it out, leans against a tree, does the requisite stretches, finally sits down and massages the knot in his calf. A mockingbird flits by, lands on the pine needles at his feet. Turns and looks at him, squawks, and flies off.

"That's right," Rand says. "I'm sorry too."

Mockingbirds were Anne's favorite. She liked the way they open their wings in a one-two count, throwing shadows on the ground, flushing the bugs from their hiding places. She liked their two-tone wings that flash white when they fly. She liked to quote Whitman's mockingbird poem, written when he lived on Long Island, "down from the shower'd halo, up from the mystic shadows—." But what she really loved is the call.

Back at her mother's house, summer after summer, confused by the lights of the suburbs or drunk with love, a male called all night long, from the top of the low hill on which they lived. When they moved here, another mockingbird sang "praises," as Anne called it, from the top of the telephone pole at the end of the drive. Anne hatched an experiment last spring around this time. She planned to play *The Barber of Seville* over and over on the stereo whenever she saw the bird in the yard.

"Will he pick it up?" she said. "Bet fifty cents."

"It sounds to me like he already knows it," Rand answered. It irritated her so much, because for once he had listened, and he was right. The bird had a call that sounded just like "Figaro, Figaro, Figaro."

"Maybe," Rand said, "he was training *you*."

Rand shakes his head and looks up. The Gooley pines have caught a breeze and their needles shimmer down at him, greenly. He hears a sound like laughter. Is it behind him? Above? He gets up. Leg okay. Enough reminiscing. He finds his trail, and begins to run steadily, slowly, straight up the hill. If someone catches him here, it will be sweating, working out, too busy to talk, not mooning about the past with his hands over his eyes. If someone finds him here, he will somehow still be moving.

THE OUTSIDE WORLD

O the mother's joys!
The watching, the endurance, the precious love, the anguish, the
patiently yielded life.
O the joy of increase, growth, recuperation,
The joy of soothing and pacifying, the joy of concord and harmony.
O to go back to the place where I was born,
To hear the birds sing once more,
To ramble about the house and barn and over the fields once more,
And through the orchard and along the old lanes once more.
—Walt Whitman, "A Song of Joys," *Leaves of Grass*

1

JOLENE WAS BORN IN 1966, IN HOLLY, NEBRASKA, to two farm people of a splinter Mennonite group. They sprang from a race of German immigrants whose roots dug as fiercely into the black prairie soil as those of the giant holly tree which a century before had given the town its name.

Although they never would have said it this way, the land, to Jolene's parents, was twined with their idea of religion. Sin and faith were, quite simply, equated with earth and sky, and the separation between man and God was bridged mostly by great storms hurling thunderbolts and whirlwinds.

Jakob and Merlee were hard-working people whose sect allowed cars, but no chrome; colorful skirts, but only hooks to fasten them; reading and education, but no swearing; electricity, but no dance or drink. Men wore hats, but women were not required to wear caps, and sometimes they wore coveralls instead of long skirts if work required it. Their Holly Chapel had split from the Old Order Mennonites over an argument about whether it was suitable to add organ music to the spare four-part a cappella voicing of hymns. The Old Order was against it, they said because it was vain, but perhaps it is truer to say that it was because an organ would have drowned out the excellent voices of some of the leading families' sons and daughters. So now, on warm Sunday mornings, when the windows were open, the strains of organ music from the upstart Holly Chapel could be heard across town in the silences between speaking at the mother church.

As parents, Jakob and Merlee were rigid and careful with Jolene, an only child. Girls were not such a blessing as boys, but if they worked hard they could be a good help in the house. They loved her dearly, but Jolene was a careless girl, who liked to run in the fields and did not like to do her chores, wear shoes, or braid her hair. She liked squishy mud between her toes and hot summer days with meadowlarks. She carried the barn cat's spring litter into her secret place in the hay loft and played "family." She cried when her father found them where she'd hid them.

"Papa, save this one, this runty one," she would plead. "I'll take care of it. It won't be any trouble."

He would look exasperated, then kindly say, "I will, Joey," then go about his chores and forget his promise and drown them all in a bucket.

She would come home from school and they would all be gone and she would storm to her room and cry. Finally, her eyes stinging and sore, she would stand at her bedroom window and look across the field. Jolene remembers Nebraska as flat and gray and stubbly, with a sky that looked also like stubble, slightly blurred. When she thought about floating up and away, that sky always dampened the thought. Even in summer, when the sky was hot and blue, it seemed to press down like a steely dome, holding her in place, as she lifted her arms, reaching, longing to fly away.

Jolene's parents weren't poor, but they didn't spend money on frivolous things. They washed dishes by hand, kept the windows open in summer for cross ventilation, cooked out with charcoal piled in an old trash can lid, a square of wire mesh for a grill. They read books from the library. They insulated their house, and bought new tires for their tractors before they bought them for their car. "We live simply," her mother would instruct. "Not like the others. Scripture says, 'Be not conformed to this world.'"

This saying confused Jolene. *We're not different from anyone,* Jolene thought. *We are just like everyone else at Holly Chapel.* But she soon learned. She noticed that of all the families who went to her church, hers was the only one with one child. Of all the families, hers had no one to play with. Her parents were older, more solemn than the young mothers and fathers. They held themselves apart, even from their own relations. Jolene noted these things and saw that they were indeed different, and so was she.

Sometimes her parents watched Walter Cronkite on the news, on a small black and white set that got poor reception. Scenes of war, protests, black people marching, yelling, fires, hippies, and more wars played out on the fuzzy TV screen all through the seventies, their daughter's tender years. Jolene watched these scenes with interest and fear, and when she was small, she hid behind her father's straight-back chair so she could feel the protection of the sturdy wood bars, and her father's sturdy boots and ankles, between her and all those strangers. Her parents believed the news to be instructive, however, and explained to her that the world was full of violence and shame, but that living apart would protect her. They knew their daughter was smart, and if she would only learn to do her chores, she would someday be an asset to the community.

Jolene went to the Holly Mennonite Chapel, sitting in silence next to her mother, hands folded in her lap, feeling the scratchy fabric of her homemade dress poke the backs of her knees. Sometimes she listened to the service, but most Sundays she let the words roll over her like water. She would watch a fly circle above their heads, imagine it was the embodiment of the Holy Spirit, wonder how it chose where to land. She liked how some of the scriptures sounded, especially the words of Isaiah, but he always sounded mad, all those *Woe be unto you's.*

Jesus was incomprehensible. The Sunday school teacher always talked about how kind he was, but Jolene read the stories and he did not seem kind to her. In the stories, he was not gentle. He was strange and fierce and wandering. He left his mother and father and went walking in the fields, not really doing any work there, but seeing through everyone he met. He seemed like one of the hippies she'd seen on TV, someone who might wander aimlessly and show up anywhere. She sometimes looked for his head and shoulders rising above the wheat, his mouth chewing the sweet end of a seed stalk, when she scanned the fields for birds and creatures to make into friends.

Every evening before supper, her father would say the same prayer.

Let me be grateful, Lord, for these thy gifts.
Let me be mindful, Lord, of where I may serve.
Let me be waiting, Lord, for signs of thy presence.
Let me welcome the stranger, Lord, for thereby do we serve angels unawares.

Jolene loved the part about angels unawares. But she'd never seen one. Angels were men, she understood from Bible study, and they were usually tall and handsome, like her uncles, but wore no hats. They had halos, like Jesus. But, unlike Jesus, they were always showing up at your house. She began to expect a visit, even though there were no strangers in the town of Holly, and all the people who came to the farm were relations, aunts or uncles who'd come to work for a day.

One day when she was six, she saw a tall man walking towards her through the wheat with deliberation, and her mouth went agape. He wore no hat, and his hair glowed like a halo around his head. His arms swept the air like slow bird wings, and he seemed to be singing. She ran back to the barn.

"Papa! Papa!" she called out. "I see him!"

"Who?" her father said, puzzled.

"I see him in the field!"

"Which field?"

"The ANGEL," she said. "The Angel Unawares. He's coming like you said."

Her father gave her a strange look. Then he set down his tools and went outside.

It was her uncle. His truck had broken down on the two-lane. He was taking a shortcut to come bale hay, and he'd been using his hat to knock away the persistent attack of a horse fly, and had been singing a hymn as was his practice while walking.

Her father had a good laugh about it at the dinner table with her mother. But later, after Jolene went to bed, she heard them talking in the kitchen. She crept to the door and opened it a crack. "I thought it was him," her father was saying. "When she said that. Just for a moment I thought it might be him. He would be a man now."

"Oh, Jakob," her mother said. A strange sound then. A ragged sound. Her mother was crying.

"We should tell her," her father was saying. "It's time she knew. Maybe she makes things up because we've never told her."

Told me what? Jolene leaned closer to hear.

"He was the sweetest boy," her mother was saying. "He was an angel unawares, if ever was. And now we have her. A girl with wayward ways. Maybe you're right. Maybe we should tell her. Settle her down a bit to know the real grief in the world."

There was further murmuring from her father. Calming sounds she knew so well.

Jolene went back to her bed and pulled up her covers. She lay in thought for a time. It was in this way that she came to the realization that she had had a brother, and that he had died, and that her mother didn't love her the way she loved him. The loneliness she'd felt for years began to make sense. A missing brother, a spirit hovering around the house and fields like a small lost bird. A mother who glanced away from her and looked out the window, searching for her other child, the one she loved most.

Jolene's loneliness cleaved to this hurt and found a strange comfort there, in this knowledge of the boy she never knew, and this explanation for the feeling that her mother did not want her close by, had let her run in the yard and fields instead of making her come inside like other girls. She waited for days for them to speak to her of this, but they never did, so she took the knowledge and folded it away, like a secret message, deep inside her heart, and went on about her business. In her play, she sometimes included this mysterious boy, whom she named Peter. Sometimes she played Jealous Sister and sold him to the Pharaoh. Sometimes she wove him a coat of many colors out of grass and wildflowers and left it for him in the yard to pick up and wear, marveling in the morning if it was in a different place, or gone. She gave him useful things to do and charged him with watching over her small creations: neat caches of seeds and flowers, supplies for seven years of famine, which she'd heard from the Bible could come at any time.

A few months later, a truck driver, a black man, stopped in downtown Holly, distraught after running over a dog. Jolene listened to the kids talking about it at school. "Brother Gruber took him in," a girl said, "and fed him dinner and they stayed up tending the dog. The man told him stories about New Jersey, driving on the big highway they have, and a big wreck he saw. He told Brother Gruber there was nothing left of a man in that wreck but his wallet worn through to the dollar bills, soaked red with *blood*." The girl was enjoying telling the tale, especially the part about the blood.

"Did the dog get better?" Jolene asked.

"No," the girl said. "It died."

"What was the man like?" Jolene asked.

"Judy Gruber asked him if she could lick his arm. She thought he was made of chocolate! Do you believe that? She's so dumb."

Jolene was struck with envy—why hadn't her parents had the truck driver to dinner? Why hadn't they taken care of him and his dog? She could have heard stories about all kinds of things. She could have taken care of the dog. She could have seen a real black person up close, something that she had never seen except on TV.

"We never have new people here!" she complained that night after her father's prayer. "Nobody ever comes here unless we already know them!"

"Why, Jolene," he said mildly, "You're still wanting an angel visit, is it? It doesn't have to be somebody from out of town. It can be anybody. You can be kind to anybody." He paused. "Like me or your mother, for example."

"Or my brother," Jolene said. "But he's not here."

Her parents both went silent. Her mother made a sound in her throat like a small bird caught in the chimney pipe.

"What do you mean, Jolene?" her father asked. "Who told you that you had a brother?"

"Nobody told me! *You* didn't even tell me! You liked him better than me!"

Her mother reached across the table and slapped her.

Her father stood up, knocked his chair back to the floor. His face red and swollen with anger. "Who said that to you?" he said.

"Lord forgive me," her mother said, staring at her own hand. She looked up. "Jolene, child, I'm sorry."

Jolene ran to her room and slammed the door.

What happened after that changed everything. Her mother came, not her father, and sat next to her on the bed. Her mother stroked her hair and kept saying, "My sweet precious girl, my sweet girl." Finally Jolene had cried enough angry tears and she opened her eyes and stared at her mother.

"Will you forgive me?" her mother said, her flyaway hair escaped from her bun, her face careworn with worry.

"I forgive you," Jolene said. She opened her arms and let her mother hold her, the soft folds of her mother's breasts and belly warming her. But she held a thorn-prick in her heart: the knowledge that her mother could reach out a palm and hit her, any time she spoke the truth.

In this way, Jolene learned to fold her knowledge inward, to fold her hands with passive obedience, and to conform to the outward ways of her world.

Jolene's mother began to keep her closer, teaching her to take tiny stitches in their homemade dresses, teaching her the family recipes for apfel dumplings, beef pot pie, sausage, scrapple, spice cake, and stewed tomatoes; teaching her the secrets of women's work. Jolene's spice cake always came out funny, with broken eggshells in it or large air pockets that made it collapse, and her stitches were clumsy, crooked things. But her mother was patient, and at least her stitches got better.

Once a week, on Saturdays, her mother dropped her at the library, where instead of instructive books about history or social issues, Jolene read books about children transported to strange places—she wanted to be Lucy in Narnia, Anne of Green Gables. She yearned to follow them, pretended she was them, in her hay barn games—the rare times she was now able to escape her mother's guiding hand.

When the time came, she learned her catechism and was baptized, a ritual that was surprisingly uneventful. There was no dove dropping down from heaven. Her long skirt still scratched the backs of her knees, and she found herself more worried about whether it was riding up in back, showing her undergarments, than about the power of the holy spirit.

She did well in high school, watched her teachers for signs of any new or surprising knowledge, got A's in both English and Math, the teacher's pet in all her classes. In 1984 a teacher helped her get a scholarship to the University of North Carolina at Chapel Hill, which she chose because the sky was powder blue all the time there, according to college literature, and the average daytime temperature in winter was fifty degrees. They had never heard of minus fifty. Never seen the ground so hard that it shattered a dropped tin pail, never froze their fingers together inside their mittens, the moisture from the skin like Superglue if you forgot to dry your hands after washing dishes.

Her parents were called in to speak with the teacher. They came home chastened and bewildered. To her great surprise, they let her go.

"If it's what you want, Joey," her father said. "The teacher says you're very smart."

"Be careful," her mother said, her eyes filled with visions of Jolene swept up in hordes of raging outsiders, young people, hippies, college students.

Jolene couldn't believe her luck.

When they left her at the Greyhound station, bags packed with new underwear and three new outfits, her mother gripped her in an uncharacteristic embrace. "Be good," she whispered in her ear. "Work hard." The fear in her mother's voice was like a horsefly buzzing. It was all Jolene could do to keep from swatting her away.

"Yes, Mama," she said.

She stepped into the bus, showed the man her ticket, found a seat, and looked out the window, expecting her parents to be there waving. But they were gone.

She was a little sad, but soon the world flying by outside her window took her full attention.

2

When she got to Carolina, some of the kids there were as wide-eyed as she was—their parents farmed tobacco and went to church three times a week. But she was a hick compared to them. They watched TV sitcoms in color. They knew about going to the beach, laying out to get a full-back tan with your straps undone, streaking your brown hair with lemon juice highlights, getting your nails done for special occasions, designer jeans that hugged the hindquarters and thighs. (Jolene had carefully not brought *any* jeans to college. She'd brought skirts. What a dunce.)

They'd all grown up watching *Happy Days* and *The Rockford Files* and *Saturday Night Live*. They knew about how to drink wine and what a hand job was (was it what she thought it was?) and how to get a guy to light your cigarette and lean in to touch his hands around the flame, then stare up into his eyes over the smoke, just like in the movies. Unlike the people of Holly, Nebraska, and contrary to her own expectations of the South, the students here had gone to school with black people. They didn't say mean things about them. In fact, plenty of students here actually *were* black people, roaming the quad in packs as loud and confident as any other student cliques on campus. Her dorm mates knew about sexually transmitted diseases, though in the eighties they still whispered what they knew. They knew about sex.

One of her roommates had sex all the time with her boyfriend back home, and talked about it late at night, after lights were out, her voice floating disembodied in the room, saying things like, "He says he really loves my belly button. He calls it his *little* booty. Sometimes he comes there if we don't have a rubber. Hey, Jolene, you ever try that?" Jolene's face would go hot, and she'd mutter, "Not really," and be grateful for the darkness covering her flush. The other girls would laugh softly, but not without affection for their backward Nebraska roommate.

What Jolene knew about sex was from watching cows and rabbits mate, dogs getting stuck together. In seventh grade she'd read *Gone with the Wind* in a beat up paperback a girlfriend kept hidden in a paper sack. *Gone with the Wind* was pretty much all Jolene knew about sex. It captured her imagination for days. The scene where Rhett carried Scarlett upstairs, with its rush of words and flush of feeling and utter lack of detail made her swoon a little. That, and the warm moist feeling she got for an older boy in eighth grade one fall, a boy who completely snubbed her.

At college the boys stayed away from her. She wasn't like the other girls. She didn't know how to flirt. She raised her hand and got called on. She aced the tests. And sometimes she watched the people in the quad and the dining hall and hid the wonderment she felt that such a world existed, and that nobody seemed to know she didn't belong here.

The only place she fit in was in the classroom—especially in the classroom of a certain graduate student who taught the literature of Transcendentalism. Professor John, he told them to call him. He was in the habit of stopping his lecture and going very quiet, closing his eyes, stroking his long moustache, and speaking in rhyme:

> All things are current found
> On earthly ground,
> Spirits and elements
> Have their descents.
>
> Night and day, year on year,
> High and low, far and near,
> These are our own aspects,
> These are our own regrets.

As he spoke, she watched his tender eyelids, his lips pursed forward with pronunciation of special words as if he were kissing them. He wasn't handsome exactly, but he had a strong nose and chin, the skin on his cheekbones was taut and tan like a cowboy who'd lived outside, and his droopy mustache looked like it had been part of his face for a long time. It took a while for her to figure out he was reciting poetry, and that some of it had been written by Thoreau—who knew he wrote poems? The only poetry she remembered from high school was *Spoon River Anthology*, which they'd had to read aloud in class and was all about death and murder and bitterness between married people. But these lines, sounded out in Professor John's low voice, made strange sense to her, as though, if she were just a little smarter, a door would open to profound meaning.

He sounded so sad when he said those words, "our own regrets." Then he opened his eyes and said, " 'All things are current found'— now, what does that mean to you?" She raised her hand. "It means—I think it means—everything is here right in front of us. Like there's a mystery to solve, but open your eyes and you can solve it."

One of her classmates rolled his eyes, and a girl giggled in the back, but the teacher dropped his chin, closed his eyes, and almost smiled. "Good," he said. "Good." Then he opened his eyes and the blue of them pierced her and she had to drop her head and pretend to take notes because she knew she was blushing.

He called on her a lot after that, and once she was sure she caught him staring at her hair.

Walking out of class one day she heard girls talking about Professor John. "He was in Vietnam," one of them said. "It's so cute the way he closes his eyes like that," a second one said. "Yeah, girls, but his pants are so baggy on his butt. Who *dresses* him?" They fell into each other's arms, collapsed with giggles.

Jolene walked away, humiliated for him, scornful of the girls. Didn't they get how smart he was? Here was a man who actually quoted poems from memory. She hadn't known you could do that. She went to the library and took out a stack of books, carefully selecting poets she'd heard him mention—Emily Dickinson, Thoreau, Walt Whitman, Robert Frost. She also picked a Sylvia Plath off the shelf, just to have another girl.

The Thoreau volume was slender, and some if it she didn't get— some of it didn't seem all that smart, to tell the truth. But she felt disloyal thinking that, so she moved on to Emily Dickinson, who seemed like someone who could have lived in Nebraska, wandering around her parents' farm, writing about books taking you on far travels, and ordinary things like bird song and bees, but then throwing in zingers about how the human heart works and how death is like a friend who shows up and surprises you and takes you for a tour on the way to your little house under the ground.

She liked a lot of the Whitman, though she wondered how in the world he kept writing so many strung-together sentences without his hand falling off. Frost made her see people in New England, self-contained, sad, and pure, but Plath was a disappointment, she seemed so mad at everything. She read and re-read the poems she liked, tried to memorize a few lines. It would be hard to fit poetry into conversation here on campus, but she would be ready if the opportunity ever arose.

Jolene went home for the summer after her first year of college and looked around and realized her parents were anachronisms—and not very interesting ones at that. They weren't eccentrics like New England country people in Frost poems. They weren't passionate about their religion, like the Baptist student group that stood out in the Pit, calling out Bible verses. At school she'd seen James Agee's book with those photographs of Dust Bowl people. Her parents were more like that. It was embarrassing. They wore flannel shirts over long underwear in winter. They had a wood stove. They had an old dented Edsel, not even a station wagon, with the chrome bumper blacked to keep them from being too vain when driving. Her mother made biscuits from a bowl of flour she kept under the counter, a towel draped over to keep the flies out. Her mother still wore an apron all day long and a long skirt underneath. Her mother's hands were old and freckled and she used Jergen's lotion that smelled like candy apples. Her mother never heard of Charlie cologne or Chanel No. 5.

Jolene spent the summer of her freshman year moping around the farm, reciting lines of poetry to the fields, falling into her old habits of forgetting to latch the gate leading out of the dairy barn, forgetting to feed the biddies, missing the secret caches of eggs in the hen shed, forgetting everything but the clear hot sky and the buzz of cicadas and the feeling of cold green pond water against her skin.

She was good at two things on the farm: hand milking—dreaming and squeezing the teats with her cheek resting against the fragrant flank of a placid cow—and taking care of motherless calves. Nursing them with bottles. Cuddling them and brushing them, imagining it comforted them the way a mama cow would with her wide tongue.

One day her mother came and stood in the barn doorway, watching her, without making a sound. Then she sighed. Jolene looked up, startled. Her mother rarely strayed to the milking barn. Her mother's eyes were on her, lingering, shadowed. "Joey, you'll make a good mother one day," she said, the familiar voice cracked with unfamiliar emotion. Her mother seemed to want to say more, but then her brow creased with some inner worry, or an unspoken prayer, and she departed for the kitchen.

Jolene knew she would make a terrible mother. She was sure she would leave a door unlatched or let a kid get run over in traffic. She was always losing things. She liked to be left alone. She didn't even like to be inside, where all the women's work was, cooking and sewing and cleaning. As she turned back to her task, she began to think about how many ways her mother—both her parents—had concealed the real ways of the world from her. In the real world, people watched fun shows on TV, and went to the beach. In the real world, people read poetry and recited it out loud, put nail polish on their toes and actually knew some black people. In the real world, people fell in love and had sex without being married and talked about it to their girlfriends. They swore oaths constantly, as if it didn't matter. Jolene's hands knotted on the teats and her cow lifted a hind leg as if to kick. "Oh, Sal, you just don't know," Jolene said, leaning her forehead against the smooth flank.

Every day that summer she saw how backward her people were, herself included. At school all the girls on her floor were drawling sophisticates, wearing fabulously skinny jeans and knit shirts with stretchy bras that were barely there and showed nipple. They didn't have baggy Levi's and shirts you had to iron and bras from Sears that made cones with points under their shirts. Her roommates had short flashy streaked-blonde hair or shoulder length bobs with spritzed bangs, and they had curling irons, blow dryers, and hot rollers to shape their looks. Jolene had bone-straight black hair down to her waist, shiny and ragged at the ends. She hadn't let any of her roommates cut it during the year, even when they begged, even when they made fun of her: "You're just an old hippie! Look at all those split ends! Go to Woodstock, please!"

They told her boys didn't like that look any more. But Jolene was attached to a ritual of soaking her hair with Johnson's Baby Oil, then washing it in Johnson's Baby Shampoo, rolling it in a towel, and letting it air dry in the sun. She brushed it and brushed it, leaning forward and letting it fall, brushing all the way to the ends. She picked out her split ends and snipped them with a nail scissors.

She dreamed about Professor John, his pursed lips reciting poetry, calling on her, staring at her hair, stroking it with his big rawboned hands. That moustache, long hair, passionate voice. Thin, but with ropey muscles in his forearms when he pushed up his sleeves. When he talked, he seemed so serious, but now and then his hair would go askew and his hands would float up in wild gesticulations and his voice would crack, describing his vision of the world of Emerson and Thoreau. His jeans didn't fit worth a hoot, and part of her loved him for it.

Jolene wrote poems all that summer and packed them in her bags when it was time to leave.

"One thing they haven't changed about you, Joey, is that hair," her mother said. "I do love that hair. Like a horse's tail, shining in the sun. You get your hair from me."

Jolene looked at her mother's hair, iron gray and curled in a thin braided bun at the nape.

Now she got the feeling her mother wanted to touch her, run her rough hands down the back of her head. Other parents hugged their kids all the time, patted their hair. But her family were all frozen in place, herself included. The moment passed. They said their good-byes.

She almost remembered then, the thorn so carefully concealed years ago, but she felt only a dull ache. Something about her parents broke her heart.

When she got back to school that August, she asked her roommate to cut her hair short, changed her mind, then compromised by taking half off. She would never wear her hair in a bun. She would never be gray. She oiled it, washed it, laid it out on a towel in a patch of sun on her bed. The sky outside her dorm window was warm pale blue. The sun glinted on her skin and it was oozing hot outside, hot and thick and humid, and there would be a thunderstorm, and unlike Nebraska you could see all the tiniest movements of the air in the leaves of green trees above your head. The trees were like magnificent women with long hair, waving their arms and dancing. She could write poetry about this.

It was just like Emily Dickinson said:

> The leaves unhooked themselves from trees
> And started all abroad

She did not find Professor John in her class syllabus that fall and she was devastated. She thought he would be teaching Transcendentalism II. She got up her nerve and asked the department secretary why that course wasn't listed. And where was the teacher who taught it last spring? "He dropped out," the Carolina girl drawled. She scratched her head with her pencil. "Couldn't take the pressure, I guess."

Jolene walked away, a blast of air-conditioning making a chill on her back where her hair used to hang in a protective drape. If somebody like a graduate student brilliant teacher could drop out, what else could happen? She was sad about it all week, started wearing her hair in a ponytail as a kind of penance, she couldn't have said for what, but maybe for cutting it. Finally that Friday her roomies got tired of her mooning around, said, "Honey, there are lots more boys out there." They took her out and handed her plastic cups of beer and purple punch at a frat party. "Drink this," they said. "Damn, it's not going to kill you to have a little fun." She drank.

She got drunk pretty fast, didn't like the way she felt—slow and dull-witted. A boy came up behind her, tugged on her ponytail, slurred, "You got the blackest hair I ever seen," then wrapped his arms around her from behind, ran his palms over her breasts and started kneading them like a kitten kneads its mother's teat to suck. Something in her body responded, and she sagged into him for a moment, then something in her belly revolted and she elbowed him, but he would not let go. He staggered backwards and pulled her with him to the floor. She landed on his soft chest and belly, heard his head crack on the plank flooring.

People around them looked down and laughed, and she took the opportunity to break his hold and roll away. Her shirt was pulled out of her jeans. She looked down at the boy in disgust. He gazed up at her, eyes glazed, rubbing his head, said, "Baby, don't be so mean!"

Jolene found a bathroom and tucked her shirt back in. Looked in the mirror. Clear skin. Black hair. Green eyes. Unfocused green eyes. She had to get out of there. Was there something in the beer? She'd also had punch, which had tasted really weird. She felt like throwing up. But she hated throwing up, so she decided it was time to go home.

When she got out into the soft air of the night, she saw the boy who'd grabbed her was puking in the bushes. So much for frat boys. She felt her head whirl, her feet stumble. She made an effort to place her feet with care. This must be what it was to be drunk. She didn't like it.

As she walked, she became more and more aware of the revolt in her own stomach. It would take another ten minutes to get to the dorm. She was going to have to find a bathroom. Greenlaw Hall? No, that was long since locked. Lenoir Dining Hall? Ditto. The undergrad library? She knew all the work study kids at the desk. She didn't want to walk past them looking desperate and drunk. Besides, the bathrooms in there were . . . ick. Davis Library was open. Lights on. A couple of grad student types reading away. Somebody was coming out. She couldn't make it. It was too late, she turned her body toward the meager shrubbery alongside the library's brick entry and let it fly.

"Jo? Jolene? You okay?"

She knew that voice. Professor John. Her dreamboat. "Go away!" she said and let fly another volley, stumbling and falling to her knees. She felt his hand on her back, the precise place where her long hair used to be. "Hey," he said. "That's all right. You just go ahead. Best thing for you. Get it all out."

Humiliated, coughing and vomiting, she whispered, "Go away," again, but didn't mean it. That hand on her back would keep her safe from dying, if she was dying. The man's shadow was a welcome protection from the glaring streetlight that made her feel exposed. "It's okay," he said again. "You're okay."

"I'm *sick*," she said, starting to cry. This was worse than anything that had ever happened to her. This was no ordinary throwing up. Something was really wrong. "I can't breathe," she husked, and threw up again, almost falling into the bushes. Oh horrors. Oh she should just die right here. "Go away," she moaned.

"Alright, okay, you are sick, you are right about that, you are dead right about that. I'll take you to the hospital if you want. You might need that. But there's always a wait in line there. And I've got my car right here. My apartment is three blocks away. And I'm an Army medic, I've got something that could help."

She could smell her own breath, sour, stinking. She moaned and turned away. But he was still talking.

"You drank a lot of beer, right? And maybe some purple punch? Don't worry about me, kid, I've seen a lot worse. If it's still bad in a little while, I'll take you to the emergency room. But I think you might be over the worst of it before long."

There was a lull in the vomiting. Just the horrible acid taste in her mouth and a whole-body weakness. She caught her breath and began to cry in earnest. He tucked his arms under her arms and pulled her to her feet, put his strong, ropey arm around her and pulled her along to his car, an old Buick with stuffing coming out of the bench seat. She saw that it would be all right to sit there, even with her clothes and hair flecked with vomit. She moaned and threw up down the side of the car.

Now she had chills. He pulled an old blanket out of the backseat and wrapped it around her shoulders. How did he know? She huddled in the bench seat and moaned and cried, just a little, mostly out of humiliation now, she was no longer afraid. This man she knew was a good man was going to take care of her. This was no groping boy. This was a man who knew what he was doing. Too bad he would never look at her shiny hair again without thinking about this—"Stop the car!" she said. He pulled over. She opened the door and stuck her head out. When she'd finished, he reached over, closed the door, and pulled quietly back into traffic. As she wrapped his rough blanket around her, she felt a new discomfort. Her bowels were loosening in a strange way. She clamped her legs together and prayed to hold it in a little longer.

They made it to his apartment and he unlocked the door and pulled her in, turned on a light, put his arm around her and shepherded her directly to the bathroom. She groped for the commode and knelt before it and he pulled her hair back, his fingers firm and strong on her head. The toilet and floor around it were sparkling clean and she felt horrible, splatting her innards all over them. "Go away," she said, immediately knowing he would do it, even though it was his own bathroom and she had no right to tell him what to do.

"Okay," he said. "I will. But I'm right here if you need me."

When he left, she pulled down her pants and sat on the john as hot liquid shot out of her. She had not been entirely successful it holding it in. Her jeans and panties were soaked. It was hard to believe she contained so much foulness. When she felt the urge again, she grabbed his trash can—with a clean white plastic liner in it—and threw up into that. She felt like smears of body fluids were all over her hair and legs and the floor and tub. She stayed there, freezing with the air-conditioning, the blanket pulled around her, shaking and puking for what seemed like hours. Finally she found herself leaning against the back of the commode, exhausted, wanting more than anything to sleep.

It was cold. She had to get warm. She pulled the blanket around her shoulders more tightly. She had to clean up the mess before he saw it this way. She sat there, dazed, for a few minutes, then reached over and turned on the tub water. Pulled off her jeans. Found a tube of Crest on the counter, took a dab and swished it in her raw mouth, spit and rinsed. Found a roll of toilet paper under the sink. Began dabbing at streaks of vomit on her arms and legs and throwing the toilet paper into the commode. She flushed it clean and then dropped her nasty pants onto the floor. No way she could wear those again until they were washed. Then she wadded up a handful of toilet paper and started wiping the floor. See, Mama? she said to herself. I can clean a bathroom if I have to. She was shivering, but she threw the blanket into the tub and started running hot water. She could wash that, at least, before he came back and saw how she had ruined it.

There was a tap on the door. "You okay in there?"

"Yes," she lied.

"I'm coming in to make sure."

"No!" she said. "Don't come in!"

"You can take a shower," the voice said.

"Oh," she said. "Okay." She saw now that the tub had a shower head and a shower curtain pushed over to the side.

"I'm not looking," he said. The door creaked open and he laid a pile on the floor: clean towel, clean shorts, and tee shirt. "They'll be too big," he said. "But it's something."

"Okay," she said. "Thanks." She suddenly felt so warmly toward this new creature, this John the medic who had seen her sick and disgusting. She said faintly, "You can come in." As soon as it was out of her mouth she hoped he hadn't heard. She was practically naked! She was gross! But he had. John the medic, John the prof, stood in the doorway looking at her.

"You're blue," he said. "Damnation, this air-conditioning is way too high. Let's get you in the shower." She stood aside, arms crossed over her chest, shivering and exposed, in her shirt and bra. He turned on the shower, adjusted the heat. "Good thinking," he said, pointing to the blanket in the tub. "Just leave your other clothes. There's a washer and dryer down the hall. I'll do them in the morning."

He was being very careful to look at the shower, or the floor. Then the mirror. She caught his eyes there. Steam rose from the shower and fogged the view, and he turned and looked at her.

"You're so cold," he said. "We have to get you warm."

He rubbed her arms with his hands and lifted her shirt over her head. Reached around, unclasped her bra. "Come here," he said.

She slipped into his arms and felt those ropey forearms against her back, his warm tee-shirt cotton against her breasts. He rubbed her back in big circles, over and over and clasped her to him. "Oh my sweet girl," he said. "Oh my sweet."

She was getting warmer. He didn't touch her hair at all.

He helped her into the shower, said, "Too hot?"

She shook her head. It was wonderful. Clean warm water streaming off her head, washing all the crud away.

"Just a minute," he said. He stripped down to his boxers and stepped into the tub. He stood in the stream of water next to her, rubbing her arms, her back, soaping her there, not touching the private parts at all. She blinked water out of her eyes, but everything remained a blur. She could feel his rubbery thing sticking out toward her, bumping against her leg.

"Here," he handed her the bar of soap. "You wash the rest."

She rubbed the bar of soap against her crotch and belly and breasts and felt the soap stream off her, the blanket beneath their feet like the muddy soft bottom of the pond.

Then he was smoothing her hair away from her face, moving under the stream of hot water, and opening his mouth to her neck and ear and mouth. His hands moved to grip her buttocks and he groaned. She felt something spinning inside her.

"Go away," she said faintly, but now she could feel his hair, lips, nose, cheeks, head brushing against her breasts in the stream of water and she felt him pull her to her knees, and he joined her there, and just held her and held her until his body and hers shook with the fever of him, his heat and his strength.

He shut off the water and toweled her off. Then pulled her to his bed, which he had fitted with clean sheets. It was a double bed, like her parents had, and she wondered if only virgins had small narrow beds like hers.

He helped her slip under the covers, put a cup of steaming tea to her lips, said "Drink this," and watched her drink it.

She could not look at him. After all that kissing and touching in the shower, he had not tried to do it to her, the thing her roommates had talked of so many nights. She had grossed him out, or maybe he didn't really like her that much. Maybe she'd liked it too much. She remembered moaning and shivering with pleasure. She looked at her tea, some kind of strange-smelling herb, sipped, and when she was done, lifted the empty cup and looked up, afraid and shy and feeling the power and exhaustion in her body.

He took the cup and said, "Now sleep."

She closed her eyes. His clean sheets felt strangely intimate against her skin. She had never slept without pajamas before. She felt him kiss her on the forehead. Then she slept for what seemed like years.

When she woke, she knew exactly where she was. Her legs had gone diagonal on the big bed and she had twisted all the covers into a tangle. She had the bed to herself.

I have spent the night in a man's apartment. Professor John's apartment. His bed.

He must have slept somewhere else. She sat up in bed and looked around. Light seeped through the basement windows and picked out the spartan furnishings—one chair, a brown sofa covered with a rumpled blanket and a pillow. A coffee table, a lamp. A card table with two chairs. A desk made out of a door and file drawers, one of those enormous IBM typewriters on top, piles of papers neatly squared as if in some kind of intentional order.

A poster of something familiar hung over the desk—that bridge in California, the beautiful one that looked like an angel's harp, red against a bright blue sky. He was standing there, back to her, fully clothed, at the kitchen counter, cooking bacon, and it actually smelled good to her. She stretched and yawned. Drat! Where were her clothes?

He turned and looked at her. "Ready for some breakfast?" The way he said it seemed the most natural thing in the world. Yes, she nodded. She dimly remembered an offer of clothes. "Can I have . . . a shirt or something?"

"Right there." He pointed. The folded tee shirt and runner's shorts lay at the foot of the bed. "Your clothes are almost dry. They're in the dryer down the hall. I didn't want to leave you here alone, but you looked like someone who likes to have clean clothes. See if those fit. I'll go check the dryer."

She waited till he'd left the room, reached out and pulled the shirt and shorts under the covers, wriggled into them. They smelled like soap. He was such a tidy man.

She felt suddenly that she had to get up and make the bed. It was a tangle. She began smoothing the sheets and tugging the covers back into some kind of order. She fluffed the pillow, centered it at top. She folded the couch blanket into a neat rectangle, laid the pillow on top. What about the bathroom? It must be a terrible mess. She went to check.

It was spotless. It even smelled good. Her bra and panties were draped on a hanger over the air-conditioner vent, almost dry. He had washed them. Boys do things like that? This one did. She almost cried. At what awful hour had he got up to do all this? Or was it later than she thought?

There was a clock in the kitchen. It was almost noon.

What were those piles of papers on his desk? There were five of them. Each top sheet had a different title, something about Henry David Thoreau, squarely in the middle: "Henry David Thoreau and the Cycle of Life." "Henry David Thoreau and A Way of Being." "Henry David Thoreau and the Ecotrope." "Henry David Thoreau: A Life Worth Living in the Woods." "Henry David Thoreau Comes Home in Our Time."

Had Professor John really dropped out of graduate school? Did he love Thoreau so much that he would write papers on him without having to?

She lifted one of the title pages and peeked at the first page, scanned the first paragraph.

"Henry David Thoreau," a voice came from behind her, "never had a washer and dryer." She jumped, and dropped the page, turning to face him. He lifted one finger in the air and intoned, "He hung his drawers on alder bushes and washed his bare bodkin in a clear pond with the tadpoles, or sometimes dipped a cloth in a pan of hot water heated on wood coals. Do men—or I should say, women—really benefit from the modern conveniences of today? Think of the pleasures of washing in the woods."

It was exactly the paragraph she had read.

"Well, in this one case," she said, "I guess they do."

He laid her clothes on the bed with a flourish and gave her a wry grin.

"You were always the smart one in class," he said. "Are you hungry?"

She nodded.

"Come on then, let's eat."

He laid before her a warmed plate with bacon, eggs, and grits. "Army rations," he said. "Get you ready for the march."

"The march?"

"You have anything to do today?"

"Um," she thought quickly. Her English paper could wait till Sunday. None of her classes was very challenging this semester. She hadn't had a challenging class since Professor John's. "Not really," she said.

"Let's go for a walk. I want to show you something."

It was as if last night had never happened. She felt suddenly shy again, spooning his Army food into her mouth. He had seen her throwing up. He had kissed her in all kinds of places. She blushed thinking about it. He had washed her *underwear*. Then he had slept chaste on the couch. She looked up to find him staring at her.

"Look," he said. "I shouldn't have done that last night. Shouldn't have got in the shower with you and all that. It was completely unfair. I just like you. You were my favorite student. And since I'm not teaching anymore, maybe we can be friends."

"Friends," she said. "Sure." She wanted to feel happy about this, but found that she did not. "Just friends" is how all the dorm girls dumped their boyfriends. He didn't like her after all. After last night. After being . . . *naked*. But now he was talking again.

"Let's try this," he said, his fingers resting lightly on the table, the way they did before he would give an assignment in class. "Let's spend this one day together—*not* sick and *not* in school—and see if we enjoy it. Anyway, there's something I want to show you."

"Okay," she said. He liked her after all. She was already half in love with him. He was so good at so many things. Maybe he would know how to take care of her strange little dreaming heart.

She changed into her own shirt and his jeans—her pants weren't dry—and she stuffed her bra into her purse because it wasn't quite dry either, but also because she found she liked the feeling of cloth loose against her breasts, her breasts swaying a bit as she walked. She liked the possibility that he wanted to touch them. Kiss them. Open his mouth to her.

He packed some apples and cheese and bread in a rucksack, and they got into the car, which she noticed he had also cleaned up. He wouldn't tell her where they were going. But she knew that to make it through this day she had to be more than the girl who got sick all over him and then let him kiss her in the shower. She had to be more than his favorite student. She had to be his companion of the mind. She had to stop thinking about wanting him to touch her, and think about Thoreau.

"What are those papers on your desk?" she said. "They told me you dropped out."

"I did. I decided I don't need them telling me what to do every minute. I miss the teaching. The students. But I don't miss my thesis advisor." He shook his head.

"Why?" she said. She meant, *Why did you miss the students, the teaching, was it because of me?* But he was thinking about his advisor, Dr. Grunwold, and for a moment his face twisted in anger. "Let's not talk about him," he said. "You want to know what all those papers are. Well, I'm writing a book about Thoreau. And I don't have to have a Ph.D. to write a book. I can just write it."

"Sure," she said, as if she knew what she were talking about. "You've written a lot of it already."

"About half," he said. "The thing is, I'm not really sure I want to keep going." He sounded wistful. "The thing is, I think I want to *be* Thoreau, not write about him."

"What do you mean? Like, go live on a pond?"

"Exactly," he said. "You'll see. We're almost there."

They drove down a winding country road, then came to a little town, a stoplight and a block of brick storefronts, their awnings sagging, a few people on the street, looking in shop windows. "Quarryville," he said. "There's an ice cream shop here."

Jolene peered out the window at the old-fashioned parlor, with its lacy iron chairs and striped awning, just like the one back in Holly. "Oh, let's stop!" she cried.

He pulled the Buick to the curb and they picked out cones of old-fashioned ice cream flavors at the counter as if Baskin-Robbins had never been invented. The most exciting flavor they had was Butter Pecan, so she went for that. John had strawberry. They traded licks. The girl behind the counter said hello to John as if she'd known him a long time, then turned and stared at her. "And who might this be?" she said.

John introduced them. "Jolene, Saralyn."

"Jolene," Saralyn repeated. "What a pretty name. How'd this fool end up with somebody like you?" Jolene didn't know what to say. What did she mean, fool? And it wasn't as if they'd "ended up" together exactly. Not yet anyway.

"Just lucky," John said. He put his arm around her. Jolene blushed.

"Guess so," the girl said, shaking her head. "Watch out for this dude," she advised. "He got his head in the clouds. Big dreamer. In high school we called him Big Chief Wannabe."

Jolene stared at her. This girl knew all about John, and Jolene knew nothing. She hadn't even known he grew up here. When they got back in the car, she was quiet. Then she said, "How do you know her?"

"Saralyn?"

"Yes."

"I've known her since I was little. We went to school together." He could see that she was worried about something. "What is it?" he said.

"Why did she call you that name? Chief Wanna—?"

"When I was in school, I got interested in the Indians who lived here long ago. Studied my family tree. Figured out I have some Tuscarora in me. I guess I drove everybody crazy with that for a while." He looked at her. "Anyway, don't pay too much attention to people in Quarryville. They live in their own little world."

She was sure Saralyn had been a girlfriend. She tried to remember what she'd said: *How'd this fool end up with somebody like you?* As if she, Jolene, were somebody special, someone from an exotic place superior to this world.

They passed through the town in less than five minutes, and now the curving two-lane road was opening up to rolling fields and patches of deep pine forest. "Ambler County," he said, as if that explained something important. They crossed a narrow bridge and she looked down to see the rushing water, the old mill, the dam above the falls. "Sissipahaw River," he said. "On this side, the old cotton mill, on that side, cliffs." A ridge rose on the far side of the river, covered with pines of a darker hue, enormous trees rising to shade out the midday sun, so that it flickered through in patches, making a shadow dance on the road as they passed.

"The Gooley pines," he said, and again Jolene was sure the words had some kind of sacramental meaning, as if they'd crossed a boundary into a deeper place. The next words confirmed her thoughts. "My people were Gooleys, way back. Roll down your window. Smell those pines."

She opened the window and inhaled. A faint hot whiff of sweetness, like incense, in her nostrils.

There was a gap in the ridge and a dirt road cut off to the right at a sharp angle. John eased the car onto the road as if he'd been doing it his whole life, braking just enough to make the turn, not enough to skid on gravel, slowing to keep the dust from rising, and something about it felt so familiar in her body that she looked around sharply to see if she'd been here before. Nothing but a farm road, a creek crossing, the far side of the ridge opening up to an old barn, a house, a pond.

Who lives here? she wanted to ask. But she kept her silence. Something was about to be revealed. She knew enough to wait.

Three deer burst from the field and flew across the road just in front of them, and John flung out an arm as if to keep her from going through the windshield. Her mother used to do the same thing when she was little.

"I'm fine," she said, turning to look at him.

"Good," he said. "I should have remembered."

"Remembered what?" she said.

"They like to cross this time of day." He nodded toward the deer, now bounding through the pasture. Sun in her eyes, she watched them bisect the glimmering field, insects and dust motes and birds spinning in the thick warm air above the grasses. He slowed, and she could hear meadowlarks warbling in the hedge. How long since she had heard that sound? It pulled at her heart.

"*Split the lark and you'll find music / Bulb after bulb in silver rolled,*" he said. "Emily Dickinson." He glanced at her.

Oh, that was one of her favorites! How did the next line go? She couldn't remember. "I love that one," she said, "It always reminds me of spring onions, how you peel them open and they're all silvery and slick inside."

"Ah," he said.

Spring onions! Why had she said that?

He turned again, onto the dirt driveway to the house, and again she knew some familiar thing. To get to her parents' farm you braked on the main road, turned onto gravel, and that sensation, from floating on asphalt to hugging the washboard ridges, was in her body's memory like breathing. It was different here, though. In Nebraska, you could see everything. The sky changed to storm and you could watch it coming for miles. Here, the land unfolded like a mystery, shadows and ridges and bowls of orange clay, trees and grasses and birds skimming the shape of the land. Here, the land held secrets in blue shadows around every curve.

He reached for her hand, led her from the car, gave her a tour of the broken-down farmhouse, with its low ceilings, iron bedsteads, and flat-board kitchen walls. "Heart pine under the paint," he said, running his hand over the rough boards. "Hand sawed. My great-great grandfather cut the wood and built this place, piece by piece."

"That's a lot of work," she said, staring at the floor, walls, ceiling, all rough wood, whitewashed. The boards were two feet wide or more in places.

"He knew how to work, that's for sure. They had a sawmill down by the river, water powered. One of the first things his people did, back in 1851, when they got here, put in a sawmill."

"That far back?" she said. "Wow." She didn't know how far back her parents' farm went, only that there had been a grandmother there once, her father's mother.

He pointed out a leak in the ceiling where rain had run down the wall to rot a floorboard. "Got to fix that today," he said. He pulled some tools and a piece of tin out of the rucksack, placed them carefully on the counter, and led her into the yard.

There was a hand pump in the back, and without thinking Jolene picked up a tin pail full of rainwater and primed the pump.

"You've done that before," John said.

"I grew up on a farm," she said. Water gushed out, cold and clean, and splashed at her sneakers. "Looks like the water's good."

"Taste it," he said.

She cupped one hand and took a slurp. "*Cold*," she said. "You try it."

He cupped both hands while she pumped, scooped it up to his mouth to drink, and splashed his face with the rest. "I had it tested last year," he said. "They used DDT here in the fifties. But the water's fine. Hand dug, back in the thirties, over 25 feet. There's a spring too. Come see."

His face was lit with pride and interest and a different expression, one she had not ever seen when he was in class. Something sensual around his lips, as if he found the entire prospect of the farm—its land, water, outbuildings, dwelling—delicious.

She followed him to the spring at the edge of the woods, a deep pool lined with rocks. "It runs all year," he said. "It's not like some springs in the summer. It gets plenty of water. I dug it out for watering livestock, but it's big enough to lie down in."

"Big enough for you?" she said, gauging his tall lanky frame against the pool.

"Big enough for two people," he said.

She felt her cheeks go red, but he didn't seem to notice.

Now he laid his palm on an enormous round stone with a curious smooth dip in the center. "Indian stone," he said. "For grinding corn. There are a lot of them around here. Used to be a big village by the river."

"When?" she asked. It sounded like he'd seen it.

"Long time ago." His eyes were far-off, seeing something long gone. She'd been wrong about his cowboy face. What had he said? *Tuscarora*.

She followed him to a pond nestled at the edge of the pasture and they squatted by the water. Wood ducks paddled at the far edge, and a blue-flashing kingfisher buzzed their heads, chattering. She remembered a line, but was too shy to speak it: *God bless his suddenness / A fellow in the skies.*

"He's got a nest here," John said. "Every year. There's a phoebe too. And almost every night a blue heron comes by and fishes."

"I love blue herons," she said. She remembered watching one back home pick out all the fingerling bass her father had just stocked in his fishing pond.

"Follow me," John said. He grabbed her hand and pulled her to standing, then turned up a steep pine-straw path into the woods. Almost instantly they were in cool shade. The trunks of the pines beside them rose from the gloom like pillars of some ancient temple.

She looked up. Far, far up, the green-gold crowns of the trees sparkled and shifted against blue sky. "Wow. They're so big. What *are* they?" she asked.

"Good question," he said, as if he'd been waiting, like a professor, for the bright student to notice something new. He stopped in the path and spread his arms wide. "The Gooley pines," he said, "are a relict stand of white pines left from the last Ice Age. Never been cut in seven generations, and longer. In fact, most of these are 500 years old. The story goes that the farmhouse was built from a single pine—one they felled just next to the sawmill, they never could have dragged it there."

"Wow," she said again. She was going to have to find something more intelligent to say.

He turned to her, focusing with laser-blue eyes. "My sentiments exactly. Wow."

"You like it here," she said. "A lot."

He turned and looked up, as if some kind of blessing were falling on his shoulders. "It's my Walden," he said. "It's where I want to spend the rest of my life."

He hunched his Army pack and tightened the straps. "Come on. Race you!"

He charged the hill, and she scrambled after, yelling, "No fair! You didn't count to three!" and slipping on pine needles, laughing and tripping and dodging the enormous tree trunks until she caught him at the top of the ridge and leaned into his pack, catching her breath.

"I win," he said. He stood solemnly looking down. She moved beside him to see.

Below and beyond them lay a broad field strewn with boulders and blazing with wild asters tinged gold and purple in the late afternoon light. The rocks caught the light and cast broad swaths of blue shadows. In the distance shone a glimmering curve of water, the Sissipahaw River, glimpsed through a tangle of sycamores, grapevines, and river birch. She looked up at his face, his hair tinged gold and eyes shadowed blue deep in their sockets.

As if he were answering a question hanging in the air, he named it: "Indigo Field."

Something in the name brushed against her soul, moth wings moving to light.

They picnicked in the field, backs leaning against a sun-warmed boulder. He sliced cheese and apples and bread with his knife and fed her pieces, one by one.

"Good," she said, chewing. "These are good apples." There was something wild and spicy in the taste.

"Bushy Mountain Limbertwig," he said, and she thought he was beginning to recite another poem until he explained that was the name of the apple. "There's a couple of trees here, planted way back. If you wrap them in paper, they'll last till June. The old varieties are the best." While they ate, John told her about Indigo Field, the Tuscarora who lived here once, his parents long since dead, his father and aunt who grew up on the farm, his dream of living here and making a life and family of his own. He was so sure of himself, Jolene thought. Imagine being someone who talked about the past, dreams for the future, things that went so much deeper than daily chores and distractions. She could see spending her life with this serious, strange man. His dream was part Walden, part homestead, part poetry.

She could see how she could help him. She knew how to live on a farm. She knew how to work. She could see cows in the barn. She could see herself milking them, dreamily, and bringing frothy pails of milk to him like prizes won at the state fair. She could see swimming naked in his pond, lying beside him in his "two man" spring, picnicking in the Gooley pines. She could see raising chickens and patching up the old house. She could see being her mother, only young, and happy, and so in love.

They lay on their backs and watched the late afternoon clouds, muscular and passing in rows, like a kind of parade, across the azure sky. She felt a prickling heat where his arm barely touched hers, and the sweet dry smell of the rocks and asters spiced the air. Some kind of energy rose from her core and warmed the insides of her legs, where the rough jeans he'd loaned her rubbed.

"There's a mule head," he said, pointing to a lumpy cumulus.

"And a unicorn," she said, pointing to the one below with a strange long finger swelling out of its head.

They named the clouds—horses, cherubs, Indian chiefs. Then he turned to her and said, "You would make beautiful children." He watched her.

She blushed to the roots of her hair. She didn't even know how to "do it." She couldn't imagine making children. That was some distant, faintly medical thing that involved grownups and aunts and parties with pink or blue iced cookies shaped like ducks and knitted booties and things called layettes, and who knew what they were? It involved secrets behind closed doors, and lots of mess to clean up. But his eyes seemed to be seeking an answer. Children or no children? Me or not me? She reached up and pulled his mouth down to hers. *Here's my answer. Yes, you. Yes for now and yes to whatever comes, my Lord you are so beautiful, yes.*

He kissed her and pressed his face against hers, then kissed her hair and collarbone and cheeks and eyelids.

She opened her eyes. "All I know," she said, "is the kissing part."

He sat back and looked at her. "Shall we fix that?" he said. He was not teasing. He was really asking.

She nodded.

"Say it," he said.

"Yes," she breathed it into his ear and buried her face in his neck. She watched his face, his lips, memorized his ears, the wheat-color hairs on his chest and arms, the golden brown of his mustache and hair. *Remember this,* she said to herself, *and this and this.*

He pulled off his shirt and shoes and pants, and there were his legs, furry and strong, and at the center his penis, a soft pink fruit in a nest of gold. She touched it and it rose to her and pushed against her hand.

He groaned. "My sweet," he said. "My very sweet." Then he slowly, patiently kissed and sucked every part of her as he undressed her. Where he kissed, her skin warmed and then tingled, as the open air cooled the spot. She wanted to wrap her arms around him but he gently held her down.

"I want to see you," he said.

So she lay back and watched him, and when he finally began pushing himself inside her, she saw the change in his face, his eyes closing in a convulsion of happiness. It stung a little and she gasped. He opened his eyes and looked at her with the sweetest expression she had ever seen on a man. It was as if he were looking at her soul. She wondered what he saw in her face. Then he started moving, pushing, and she had to squeeze her eyes shut and just feel what was happening to her, to him, and then to both of them together.

They lay on a bed of dry grasses, sprawled open, and she wanted to crawl into his arms, she felt so soft and exposed. The clouds were still marching across the sky in formation, but now they were lit differently, from the side, and their edges shone pink and gold. He rolled to her, wrapped his arms around her. "Cold?" he said. "Yes," she said, "cold." But she was not cold exactly. She was tingling from head to foot as if she had been dipped in hot water and lost a layer of skin.

This is the great secret, she thought, *the answer to the vast loneliness of skies.* Sex that joined two people and filled them, left them pleasured and whole and full of life.

He helped her into her tee shirt and pants and laid his jacket over her shoulders, then said, "Come here, I'll keep you warm." She snuggled against him.

He looked down at her. "All better?"

She looked him in the eye and said, "You fixed me good," and it made him laugh and laugh and it was the bravest thing she had ever done. She was proud and happy and stayed that way for days.

When she got back to the dorm it was almost eight. John had repaired the roof, bought her a burger in town, and made love to her again in the broad bed in his apartment. She'd wanted to stay the night, but he said, "Remember, you've got that paper. English paper." She was a little hurt that he thought he had to remind her, but then he said, "Look, I want to be with you too. You'll want a change of clothes and your roommates will be wondering where you are. Go home, shower, sleep. Let me take you to breakfast in the morning. We have lots to talk about. I have some things to do. Meet me at Breadman's? 10 a.m.?"

"Okay," she said. "I'll be there."

When she got to her room, she learned that twenty girls from her dorm had gone to that same party on Friday, gotten horribly sick, and had spent the night at the clinic. It seemed like a year since then, but she listened to the stories and the evening began to come back to her like a distant illness. Someone had spiked the punch with a chemical so foul, it could have killed them in higher concentrations. It was a scandal. The frat would be shut down and investigated. Her mother had called, worried that Jolene hadn't phoned at her usual Saturday morning time. Drat, Jolene thought, well it's too late now. They would both be at Saturday night Bible study. They didn't have an answering machine. She would call them Sunday, even though it was against some kind of rule her parents had about work and using machinery on the Sabbath.

With all the hubbub, no one asked Jolene where she had been. Nobody commented on the strange clothes she was wearing, or John's oversize jacket. No one noticed the new glow in her face.

Jolene showered and slipped into her narrow bed. It was a little strange to be back on campus, she felt so changed. *This is what it feels like not to be a virgin. I wonder if anyone can tell.*

And now, I'm different from before
As if I breathed superior air,
Or brushed a royal gown.

She let her nightgown ride up to her hips, felt her skin slide against the smooth sheets, and almost groaned in pleasure. John was coming to take her to breakfast tomorrow. They'd spend the day together again. She fell into deep sleep, clutching her pillow to her chest.

3

The next three weeks passed in a rush of days, gorgeous days spent with John, lonely afternoons attempting to catch up on her studies, feeling peeled and tingling and completely unable to focus. The only thing she could read and pay attention to any more was poetry, and none of that J. Alfred Prufrock stuff, either, it had to be sonnets or Robert Burns or Emily Dickinson and her bees and eternity. She was reading with opened eyes, as if the world had been a secret to her and now was suddenly revealed in words. She aced a poetry paper on "Emily Dickinson: Repressed Sexuality on the Page." Then she flunked her Sociology exam.

She was shocked. She'd never flunked anything in her life. She hardly ever studied. It had always been enough to read, take notes, and go to class. But she'd been skipping classes. *Wild nights,* she thought, *wild nights. What did you think would happen?* she scolded herself. But the scolding was half-hearted. She found that she really did not care very much. That shocked her too. She'd lied to John about her class schedule so she could spend whole days with him at the farm. She had been coming home late, going straight to bed, exhausted. She hadn't stayed up to read her chapters. She forgot to call her parents on Saturday again, heard the thin voices at the end of the wire as she lied about her Saturday morning schedule. "Jolene," her father said, worried, "I hope everything is good. Are you keeping up with your studies?"

"Sure, Papa," she said, shocked at how easily she was lying these days. "I'm doing fine."

"Do you have some nice girlfriends?" her mother said. "Are they nice girls?"

That stopped Jolene. She didn't really have girlfriends. She had roommates. "They're okay," she said, thinking of the girl who swore like a sailor and was keeping two boyfriends going at once.

"We want the best for you," her mother said, and she could hear the question hanging in the air: What has become of you?

"I'm fine," Jolene said, and that at least was true. "I'm happy. This is a great place." She smiled. "Don't worry, Mama, I am fine. How's the farm? How's Holly Chapel?"

She listened with half an ear to the recitation of daily chores, animal lives, church news, barns raised. They finally said their good-byes.

"You could come here," her mother said, "for your mid-term break."

They missed her. She was surprised. But she was so behind on her studies. And then of course there was John.

"Got lots of studying to do," she said. "Better stay here."

"Good then," her mother said. "God's blessing to you."

"And also to you," Jolene said. All the other kids said "I love you" when their parents called. There was a moment when she could have said it. *You can be kind to anybody, your mother or me, for instance.* This was a gift she could give them. Something she had learned in the Outside World. She opened her mouth to try it, but there was already a dial tone. She placed the phone gently back on the cradle, that thorn twisting a bit, but the ache was dull by now, and the rush of excitement at seeing John again soon soothed her heart.

In early November she blew a midterm in Biology. Staring at the grade on her test, she began to feel a terrible dread. This shouldn't be happening. What was wrong with her? She was afraid to talk to anyone about it, especially John, who seemed to care a lot about how smart she was, and what a good student. When the call came from the Dean's office, she knew she was in for it.

She stood holding the scrawled message from her roommate, her body warm and moistly oozing from an afternoon in John's bed. Now she felt the dread in her arms and legs. Her parents would be so angry.

She hadn't called them in two weeks. She had not been able to tell them about how badly school was going, and she certainly could not tell them why. Her mother would get very quiet, and put her father on the line, and he would say, in his mild voice, "We are so disappointed in you, Joey. This is such a big opportunity for you. We thought this was what you wanted." Now she'd have to face the music.

She *would* do better, she would convince them and the Dean that she could still do the work. She would finish college. She would. First in her family. She would make them all proud.

The secretary didn't make her wait at all. She gave her a look of pity, and ushered her right in. The Dean rose from behind her desk. "My dear," she said, her face lined with sorrow. "Please come and sit down. I have some bad news."

"I can do better," Jolene squeaked. "I know I can. I've been skipping classes, but now I'm ready to buckle down."

"No, no," the Dean said, shaking her head. "That's not it. Don't worry about that right now."

They didn't care about her grades? It was a strange relief, but then she realized they must have found out about her trysts with John. There must be some kind of rule they were breaking. She hadn't told much to her roommates. But it wasn't a secret exactly, with all their Breadman's dates, their walks down Franklin Street hand in hand in broad daylight. She wouldn't give him up. No matter what. She couldn't. Her body had a loyalty that could not be broken. John was her family now. She could feel juices seeping into her underpants. She hadn't stopped to shower. Horrors, she wondered if the Dean could smell the evidence.

The Dean was speaking in a low voice. Something about a freak accident. Drunk driver, narrow bridge, heavy car going off the edge. Jolene didn't understand. Why was she talking about an accident? She looked at the Dean, confused. The Dean had seen this look before. This incomprehension of death, the young face shutting out knowledge. She cut to the chase. "Your parents, dear. They died. Late last night. We've been trying to find you for hours."

The breath went out of her. She finally saw it. A narrow bridge. A stranger coming across, not knowing the protocol to stop and let the other pass, or being too drunk to care. Her father swerving to avoid it, the car falling like dead weight into the water. The dark water entering the car, rising and swallowing them, her parents' last thoughts being of Jolene, how she had once again forgotten to call, had fallen away from them, gone to the Outside.

This was her punishment, to live to see the slaughter of those innocents, her parents, to know she could have been there, protected them somehow.

She wrapped her arms around herself and moaned.

"Oh my dear," the Dean said, completely misunderstanding. "I am so sorry."

Late that night in John's bed she woke with a start, having dreamed of them, driving slowly and deliberately to their fate, encountering at last the stranger, the "angel unawares," and accommodating him. She sat up in the dark room. She could see all too clearly the blackened chrome on their old Edsel, their lives constricted to those old narrow lanes, their clothes threadbare by choice, their lives safely barricaded from what they called the Outside World, and she wrapped her arms around her knees and cried with pity for them, for having lost their first child, and now another, and for how she would miss terribly those Saturday calls, protecting them from the knowledge of her ruined purity, having the chance to say a few words of comfort and connection, stupidly believing she would have more chances.

She was in the Outside World now. She was on her own. There was no going back to the safe world.

She turned to John and clutched his back and held on.

The next morning she flew out to their funeral. The college paid her ticket. She stared out the window of the incomprehensible silver machine and saw the whole world spread below, beneath a scattering of clouds, beautiful—roads, farms, houses, hills, forests articulated by early light and shadow—until it all disappeared under high cloud cover and all she could see was the world of upper sky, strangely illuminated and empty of life.

An aunt and uncle picked her up at the airport, took her to their house, where people already gathered around the plain wood double caskets laid out on a table not far from a table of filled pies. Jolene laid her hand on the raw wood, smelled pine and baked custard, felt her stomach revolt. Which one was which? The caskets were closed. Emily's old poem came to her:

> I never lost as much but twice
> And that was in the sod.
> Twice I have stood a beggar
> Before the door of God!

An aunt hugged her to her breast. The possibility of living with the aunt came up. Jolene remained vague about future plans. Truly, she had no idea what to do. She'd felt a little sick on the plane, and then again at the funeral, and now she walked through all the ceremonies and gatherings in a daze, slept where she was told to sleep, signed forms she was told to sign. One morning, her aunt and uncle spoke of the farm. The farm would go to her uncle, if she agreed.

She hesitated for an instant, wondering if she should bring John here just to see the place of her youth. The tiny town of Holly, created in 1866 with its bold main street slanting across the carefully squared blocks, held no charms for her. She had no intention of living with her aunt and uncle. Her aunt's face was creased and worn with duty. There was no affection in it. At the funeral, church people had greeted her, asked about her studies, then walked away to murmur with the neighbors and family they knew better. Her parents had never invited the stranger, and rarely the neighbor.

She had been on the outside too long. They knew she'd never stay.

The aunt and uncle glanced at each other. We can pay more, the uncle said. Whatever you need. You should finish your college.

Without even trying, she negotiated a good price for the farm and funds were consolidated into a piece of paper, a cashier's check. Just like that she had no place to go.

Her aunt drove her out to the farm the next morning to claim whatever personal things she wanted. Summer's dizzying fields of green corn now lay gray and shriveled, stalks bitten with frost. Tenants would live here now, or no one. The uncle had already gathered up her father's tools, just some old horse halters remained, hanging on pegs and covered in cobwebs. Her favorite barn cat was nowhere to be found. Her milk cow had stopped producing and been sold. Her aunt had butchered the Rhode Island Reds she'd tended as chicks. It took just a season or two for the animal life on a farm to birth, produce, die. But the land and the sky stayed the way she'd remembered them, as if caught in perpetual winter, gray clouds lined up in rows like some smeared mirror image of the fields.

She found herself yearning for the capes of green and gold grass covering soft hills in the pastures of John's farm. It was so different there. The blue shadows stretching from the boulders on Indigo Field. The towering Gooley pines like cathedral pillars. The soft drama of an evening sky. The shouting of so many birds, who gathered, John had told her, at the cusp of ecosystems—hill pasture, mature pine forest, river bottom, and old field.

She took the single family photo, a posed picture of a church reunion before she was born. Her parents stood in the back and children lined up in front, their restless faces blurred. Her mother and father so young, her mother's hair glossy and dark, escaping her modest bun and curling around her face, a face careless with joy, arms holding a child that must have been her brother.

She took some cracked china plates and teacups. Her mother's sewing kit, a quilt. And a lovely handmade cradle. She remembered the story her mother told, some grandfather had made it back in Germany. She stroked its carved end pieces, made of some golden wood she did not recognize.

She thought about John's love of his grandfather's place, his dream of raising a family there, his capable hands trimming tin for the roof, the way he let her help him by just giving her things to do, assuming she knew how to do them. She was raised on a farm. That was apparently enough for him. And now that farm was gone. She'd never really had a dream of her own. She felt, imperceptibly, her life seeping into the shape of the deep pool that was John's world.

She flew home and took a cab straight to his apartment. The door was locked, her key was at the dorm, so she sat on the stoop and waited. And waited. The afternoon dimmed. It started to get dark. She hadn't called him in two days—her aunt had no phone. She dozed, head leaning against the door frame, her winter coat wrapped tight around her though the November night was mild.

She woke up to a car door slamming, footsteps, John's startled "Jolene? When did you get home? My god." She rose to meet him, plowed her head into his chest, and almost knocked him over. She wrapped her arms around him and would not let go. "Jolene?" he kept saying, "why didn't you call me? "

She moaned into his chest. He held her arms and pushed her back, looked into her face. "I sold the farm," she said. "I can't ever go back."

"You have a new farm," he said, "our farm." She knew by the look on his face that he loved her for being an orphan like him, and he pitied her. She did not care. She claimed him then, and his land too. "Our farm," she said.

She would pump water, saw logs, build a barn, whatever it took.

She would move with him to the farm and they would make a life together, free of family constraint, like Thoreau and Emily Dickinson. Their bodies would sing the dawn chorus, like the birds, and they would live like children in the woods.

Jolene dropped out of school. They married in December. It was a sunny day, with that Carolina blue sky and a brisk cold breeze. They stood in the farmhouse parlor, which she had painted and fixed up with a hooked rug, sofa, and two overstuffed chairs from the used furniture store in Carrboro. John said she should set aside her farm money as a nest egg, but she spent a few hundred dollars of it on new pots and pans, plates and cups, a china cupboard, lumber for a new floor in the kitchen. This was how people did things in the Outside World. You spent money, you fixed up, you had new things sometimes that had some shine to them. Still, her lifelong training in frugality limited her to used furniture and just four place settings. Four should be enough for now.

The only wedding guests were John's Aunt Tawley and Uncle Rupert, the ones who owned the farm and were selling it to John. The local magistrate presided, and Jolene served tea and carrot cake afterward on her new plates. The carrot cake was a little lopsided, she never could get it right with cakes. Jolene felt a moment of panic when she saw there were five people for her allotment of four plates, but the judge begged off, having another appointment. The elderly aunt and uncle stayed. They sat in straightback chairs, quiet, and stared at her and the new furniture.

"It looks different in here," the uncle said.

"She fixed it up right nice," the aunt said back to him, as if Jolene were not even in the room.

The uncle turned to John. "How you doing with that hay crop? Any of it spoil after that rain we got?"

With that, the conversation turned entirely to farming and weather.

Jolene sat serenely in her new dress, hands in her lap, watching the three of them talk, enjoying the feel of the heavy red velour bodice embroidered with pink and purple flowers and the skirt that flowed all the way to the ground. She was sure no one could tell what she'd finally figured out—she was pregnant. Hadn't had a period since mid-

September. Her skinny belly was strangely rounded at the base. She would give John his precious children. They would make up a family from scratch, fill the gap in both their lives, and John would be so happy.

She sat there, pondering these things, while the aunt rocked in her chair and the uncle talked hay. They left a present of a speckled clay pitcher, something of John's mother's. "This has been passed down for a long time," the aunt said, and Jolene knew she must never crack or break it, though it was already chipped down to the red clay along the spout.

When Jolene told John later that week, his face lit up with joy. Though it scarcely seemed possible, now John was more loving than before. He brought her coffee in bed, and when she had some morning sickness, brought her raspberry leaf tea he concocted himself from a recipe in a book of midwifery he'd found in the house. She regained her appetite quickly, and through the winter he cooked and fed her hearty stews and brought delicacies from the little shops in Chapel Hill—baklava and kiwi fruit and organic apricots. She tried out recipes from his mother's cookbook, a *Fannie Farmer* with an ancient broken binding. Its pages were stuffed with scraps of paper and recipe cards and newspaper clippings spattered with grease in places and crusty with dried sauces she picked at with her fingernail, and it was all held together with a fat rubber band. In spidery handwriting, the cards held recipes for things she'd never eaten before—spiced peaches, chocolate pound cake, stewed turnip greens, fried okra, and lemon chess pie. "What's chess pie?" she asked John.

"Let's try it out and see," he said. He rolled out dough from scratch and they sat and ate two pieces each, the soft sweet filling melting on their tongues. "We have something like this at home," she said. "Lemon custard pie. But this is different."

In the spring, John traded his old Buick for an even more ancient pickup truck, which had been spray-painted orange and used for target practice, but still ran. One hilarious afternoon he taught her how to drive a stick shift, rumbling across the pasture in first gear, stalling out, trying again, till she got the feel of it.

He found an old tractor to restore, and planted an enormous

vegetable garden, one he tended every day. He brought her the first sugar pod peas and radishes, strawberries he'd tended from plants since last fall, greens and broccoli, and wild mushrooms he found in the woods, a patch he'd harvested since he was a little boy, so he knew they were good. She ate it all except the mushrooms, which she'd always loved but for some reason could no longer stomach. When her belly became too big, they made love in different ways, and each time she felt like his rich juice was helping that melon in her belly grow.

She murmured to herself a line from her beloved Emily, and wondered now if the scholars were right, that Emily had never married.

I'm wife; I've finished that
that other state . . .
How odd the girl's life looks
behind this soft eclipse.

It was John's idea to use a midwife, and Jolene agreed easily. Midwives, not hospitals, is how her people gave birth. And didn't John have medical training? She felt completely safe in his hands. Her mother had taken her to visit at a birthing just once, and Jolene remembered waiting and listening from the kitchen as a stout woman with a kind, wide face bustled in and out of the birthing room, finally carrying a red squinting infant howling with life. "An easy birth," the midwife said. "Hush now, child, Mother is resting." Jolene had seen the deft way the midwife carried the child, the kindly authority she held over child and mother, the mother's beaming face when they were finally allowed to enter. It had been a happy birth. Jolene could see hers just like that.

But—how to find a midwife here, where she knew no one?

John said, "I know someone. Maybe she'll come out of retirement for us."

"I want to meet her," Jolene said. She envisioned a rosy wide face and a stout body, dressed in a long plain dress and apron, exuding warmth and competence.

John said he would work on it, and Jolene waited with anticipation. Finally, when Jolene's melon belly had become the size of a prize watermelon at the State Fair, John said, "Let's go. She's home. I think she'll do it."

"You haven't asked her?" Jolene said, alarmed.

"Some things are better done in person," John said. "Don't worry, sweet girl. She's amazing. You'll love her."

But will she help us? Jolene wanted to say, but she kept her face and hands composed, waiting, her long training in feigning patience once again put to use.

John helped her into the truck, and she settled her weight on the seat. He turned down a farm road that crossed their hay pasture, and followed a faint track that led into the woods. "She lives in the woods?" Jolene asked, unable to contain her curiosity. The Gooley pines loomed overhead, cooling and shading their path. Images of Hansel and Gretel, breadcrumbs and candy cane houses, all those Brothers Grimm stories, flitted through her mind. Jolene wondered, fleetingly, if this midwife were a witch of some kind, John had been so reluctant to reveal her identity.

"It's a shortcut. She's our closest neighbor. Her family has had a farm here forever. Since before I was born. I can't wait for you to meet her," John said. The eagerness in his face like flickering sunlight.

"Tell me her name, at least. Please just tell me her name."

"Didn't I tell you?" John said, a little surprised. "Sorry. It's Reba Jones. I call her Miss Reba." The truck rattled across a plank bridge, the trees parted, and sun shone on a large yard and a small brick house. As they pulled around to the front of the house, Jolene saw them: three enormous figurines of winged women, their bodies roughly carved from blocks of hickory, their faces and hands painted black, with large staring blue eyes.

"What are *those*?" Jolene asked. They scared her half to death.

"The black angels," John said. "The story goes that her father carved them, after Reba's sister died. Apparently, her sister had blue eyes."

"And she was *tall*," Jolene said, trying to joke, but she immediately felt ashamed under the stare of the angel looming above her.

The screen door creaked. A face emerged, a body. "Well, Mr. John, I see you found you someone. Finally."

Miss Reba Jones was a stern-faced black lady who could be eighty, could be sixty, her face was so slender and clear of wrinkles. But her eyes gave her away—old eyes magnified behind thick lenses and a body blocky and awkward, rocking side to side as she walked with her cane.

John introduced them and Miss Reba took Jolene's arm, brought her to a large chair in the parlor, and bid her sit, then settled in her own chair.

Miss Reba studied the two of them. "You forget to shave?" she said to John.

John rubbed his jaw. "I'm growing a beard," he said, grinning. "Once it stops itching, it'll be less bother. You like it?"

"It sparse," Miss Reba said. She nodded toward Jolene. "What you say?"

"It's . . . fine," Jolene said. He hadn't said anything about a beard. Why hadn't he told her?

"You sit and rest awhile," Miss Reba commanded. She turned to John. "You come help in the kitchen."

Left alone, Jolene stared around the room. Every spare surface seemed to be covered with crocheted doilies in rainbow colors.

Miss Reba and John returned with plates of chocolate cake, a tray of iced tea and glasses. Miss Reba served her a china plate of cake and a fork, poured the tea, handed her a glass, and settled in her own chair opposite. Jolene did her best to balance the cake plate on her knee, barely able to see it over the expanse of her belly. She set her tea down on the doily covering the chair arm, carefully lifted the plate, cut a bite of cake, put it in her mouth, and ate. She tried her best to sit up straight, but with the sweet crumbs, thick icing, and cool sweet tea melting together on her tongue, she gave up and sagged into the comfort of the chair. "So good," she murmured. Why didn't they have chairs like this at their house? Why didn't they have chocolate cake? She needed to learn how to make it.

Miss Reba and John were chatting about the farm, the hay, the chickens, and Jolene watched them. Miss Reba nodded at things John said, but she noticed that even when he tried to be funny, she barely cracked a smile. Finally Miss Reba set down her cake plate and her tea and peered at Jolene over her black-rimmed glasses.

"You mighty quiet," she said.

"The cake was good," Jolene said. "Thank you." Was now the time to ask? She glanced at John.

"You about to pop a child," Miss Reba said, "Less than a week."

"I—I guess so. It's been nine months," Jolene said. "Or about that, anyway." She realized that she did not know exactly how long it had been. Wasn't she supposed to know? She looked at John again, as if he might have a way of calculating such a thing.

Miss Reba held out her broad palm, said, "Come here. I can check it."

Jolene stood awkwardly, obedient as a child, but also terrified. She stepped to Miss Reba's chair and waited.

"Go sideways," Miss Reba said. Jolene turned to the side, aware of the enormous swell of her body, the sway in her back, the weight pressing on her spine and her hipbones, down to knees and ankles.

Miss Reba laid one hand on her belly, another at her back, and she began to move her palms, in circles, slowly, over the thin material of Jolene's dress. The heat of her smooth hands eased the ache in Jolene's belly and back. Jolene closed her eyes and began to relax.

Miss Reba stilled her hands and hummed. *How odd,* Jolene thought. *Like she's warming up to sing.* But the humming felt good too. Suddenly the baby gave a terrific kick, right on Miss Reba's palm. Miss Reba's face opened in a smile, her large white teeth revealed, crooked and friendly. "Oh, he ready to fight. He ready to come into this world."

John was beaming. Jolene knew he wanted a boy.

"It's a he?" Jolene said. "How do you know?"

Miss Reba's face all serious again. "You carrying low. And he's large, bigger than a girl. Might be a hard birth," she said, "but he's turned right, so it could be smooth. Either way, you strong enough to carry it."

"Miss Reba," John said, "will you come for the birthing?" His face so earnest and sweet, Jolene thought, how could she refuse? Jolene wanted Miss Reba to be there. She wanted it now.

"I got to ask," Miss Reba said. She turned away, looked up at the mantel. Jolene followed her gaze to a photo of a lovely young woman with chocolate skin and light eyes. It was as if Miss Reba were asking the photo what to do.

Jolene felt a tingling on her spine. Now Miss Reba closed her eyes, swayed a bit, muttering under her breath, jerking her elbows out to the side. It was as if Miss Reba were warding off some danger in the room.

Miss Reba's eyes flew open. She turned and eyed her. "You not from around here. You got people here?"

Jolene shook her head. Was this some kind of test?

"She's from Nebraska," John said. "Don't worry, we won't say a word."

"Say a word about what?" Jolene said.

"Mmmm-hmmm," Miss Reba said.

"About using a midwife," John said. "Some people around here think you have to have a doctor."

Miss Reba turned back to face John. "I come. But you got work to do before the day."

"Whatever you say," John said, grinning. He turned to Jolene. "Miss Reba attended at my birthing," he said.

"She did?" Jolene said.

"That's right," Miss Reba said. "And he turned out all right, I guess."

John laughed, his head thrown back, a real belly laugh. "Glad you think so, Miss Reba. Not many agree with you."

"The Bible say, 'Be not conform to this world,'" Miss Reba said.

Jolene sat with her mouth open. Miss Reba, quoting Bible sayings like her mother? She considered. Miss Reba was a different kind of person, and it wasn't just that she was black. She was *odd*. Maybe Miss Reba knew something her mother knew. Being different was okay. If only her face were a little more jolly, like the midwife back home. It seemed Miss Reba's solemn face was allotted fewer smiles than was the common measure.

Miss Reba taught them how to breathe together, showed them some herbs they could gather from Indigo Field and dry in the sun. "Drink this, four times a day, from here out," she said. She scrawled the recipe on a scrap of paper.

"Meadow mint tea," Jolene murmured. Just like back home.

"Then, make this one for when you start to feeling the labor pain," Miss Reba wrote down another recipe, told John the herbs. "This one hard to get," she said. "Take a pinch every day till the pain start." She handed John a small jar labeled Birth Root.

"That won't hurt the baby?" John said.

"No, just make him ready, make mama pain softer."

Miss Reba confirmed that John still had a copy of the *Midwife's Companion* she had given to his mother forty years ago. She told them both to read it, cover to cover.

"When you done," she said, "baby come."

How in the world did Miss Reba know that? Jolene looked at her like she might be a witch after all.

"Might need to read fast," Miss Reba said. Her mouth curved in what might be part of a smile.

Jolene laughed. Miss Reba might not wear a long gray dress, nor an apron, nor have a wide kind face, or rosy cheeks, but she had some laughter tucked into a corner of her heart and some healing in her hands. Those would be good things at a birthing.

Finally, on a hot day in June, the child was born, a son, and it was a surprisingly easy birth. John drove to get Miss Reba at the first sign of labor, and she came with her black satchel and kit of herbs and potions. She spent the morning singeing juniper branches in a fry pan on the stove, then massaging sweet smelling lotions onto Jolene's belly and back, legs and feet, arms and hands. "Got to keep the circulation," Miss Reba said. Miss Reba washed her hair with sweet almond oil, spread it out on a pillow in the sun to dry. How did she know this was Jolene's great luxury, her great vanity? Jolene lay on the double bed, feeling massaged and glowing and aching and lovely in her halo of hair. She had forgotten her fears of Miss Reba. She was certainly capable, so far, if not exactly warm.

John would have had her birth down in the cool spring pool he'd made, but Miss Reba said it was too cold. Calm, almost eerily placid, the long serious black face of Reba Jones broached no discussion. "That old clawfoot tub be just right. Fill it with warm water," she instructed John. "Test on your inside elbow." So Jolene birthed her first child into warm water, her legs spread in a squat, which Miss Reba said made a child come faster.

There was a moment when everyone in the room seemed to be covered in warm water, tears, and blood, and the sun shone through the window and Jolene saw the baby's scowling face, shiny and red, his mouth open and tongue sticking out, his head small and elongated, his eyes squinting at her like a Chinaman's and his arms and legs, fat and flailing. She laughed in pure exhaustion and delight until she hiccupped and John had to make her drink tea out the wrong side of the cup to make it stop.

Miss Reba pulled the placenta, inspected the child, wiped him clean, looked at his face thoughtfully, and said, "This baby born on a Friday at midday. This boy be the delight of your soul. I put my special blessing on him." She closed her eyes and held a hand to his forehead and sang mumbled words Jolene could not hear. Then she spit on her thumbs and wiped the baby's closed lids, gently. She reached into her bag and found some oil, poured a bit into her hand, then began to rub it on his head, molding it round and smooth.

John said later he'd heard of the head molding, but if he'd known Miss Reba was going to spit in the kid's eye, he'd have drawn the line.

They called him Beauregard Simpson Blake—Beauregard for John's great-grandfather, who'd been named after the Civil War general; Simpson for Jolene's mother's maiden name. He was Bobo for short, and he quite simply became the pleasure of her days.

At first everything seemed as magical as it had been before. There was that hot, sweet weight against her chest as she carried Bobo in his sling. There was sleeping in the sun, the three of them on a blanket, baby tucked between. She would look at John, kiss his neck, and murmur, "Here we are, the Blake family." He would look at her with a glow in his dark eyes like he knew the secret of happiness, and it lay before him.

There were late strawberries and asparagus from the garden, there was nursing, a strange pulling at her nipples making heat in her body almost the way John did. There was the way John looked at her while she nursed, and the gentle, luscious lovemaking that made her lush new rounded body feel golden, and worthy of worship.

There was that funny face, those wriggling arms and legs. There was tucking the baby in that lovely cradle made by some German ancestor, and then rocking and singing him to sleep. The baby was docile and quiet, and they took it as a sign that they were specially blessed in their world apart from the world.

As the months went by, Jolene watched him, changed him, and nursed him. The baby stayed docile and sweet, and his eyes a bit unfocused, never seeming to hear her say his name, as if he hadn't quite made the transition from womb to world, and was still swimming in a dim red pool, underwater. He had the habit of flipping his hands up on his chest and resting them there. Jolene got the image one day of a child sitting in church, passive, hands folded, pretending to pay attention to the sermon, much as she used to do. It was as if he were daydreaming, lost in his own world, where conversations took place that she was not privy to. He was such a good boy. She could not believe her good fortune.

On the farm, their daily life centered on the baby. John left only to get supplies—diesel for the old tractor he was fixing up, corn for planting, laundry soap for Bobo's diapers. Jolene was just as happy to stay home and play out Bobo's routine—up at four, feeding, diapering, playing outside on a quilt when the weather was fine, napping on the screen porch when it rained, reading to Bobo, talking to him, and finally, letting him lie there, quiet, while she read her poetry. She had not given up Emily Dickinson, but now her poems seemed more like playtime rhymes than incantations before love.

"Has it feet like Water Lilies?" she said, tickling his toes.

"Has it feathers like a Bird?" She fluttered her fingers.

He wiggled, smiled, and gazed unfocused at some world over her shoulder.

Sated on poetry, and the sweet unfocused smiles of Bobo, Jolene would nap with the baby and wake to John's return from the fields, his kiss on her cheek, mustache and new beard tickling her awake. "Hello, beautiful," he would say. "Hello, beautiful yourself," she would say. John would take the baby and she would make dinner from whatever he brought in from the garden: broccoli, sugar peas, carrots, beets. Sometimes Miss Reba came by with a dressed chicken or two, or some blackberries to trade for whatever John was growing, and John would make an old-fashioned Southern fried chicken dinner with blackberry cobbler. Sometimes they made do with a few eggs from the layers, some dried apples stewed with sugar and cinnamon, and dandelion greens steamed with butter.

John bought her a small flock of laying hens and once they were settled in, he traded chicks and farm work for a bred Devon cow. After she bore her calf, Jolene milked her twice a day, resting her head against the flank, humming, the baby tucked into a basket at her feet. It was a sweet paradise world, smelling of honeysuckle, pine, and mowed pastures, and humming with bees. Emily Dickinson would have loved this world, she sometimes thought, dreaming lazily in a hammock and gazing up at the shifting patterns of pine needles above her, then down at the fine dark swirl of hair on her baby's head. That hot burst of milk at her breast, the flesh of a tiny hot being attached to her own flesh. Emily might have been a maiden lady, she thought, but she understood the delicious pleasure of the world.

One day when Bobo was about ten months old, she caught his eyes staring at her while she milked the cow. She picked him up and smiled and said, "Bobo is a good baby!" and all manner of silly things. A few days later, on a picnic in Indigo Field, she watched him staring at a swallowtail butterfly that flittered above his head, and suddenly his hand went up, as if to grab it.

When he couldn't reach it, he burst into tears of rage.

All through his next eight months, Bobo was alternately ecstatic and howling. Jolene and John were taken by surprise at the change, then decided that after all, this was how babies were supposed to act—they cried and then they smiled and laughed. Bobo's crying never lasted more than a day. But sometimes he rolled his body back and forth, back and forth, over and over, like a boat rocked on high seas. Sometimes his rage was so great it seemed he would simply burst out of his skin, like some malevolent creature, and fly in to the air screeching, arms and legs pummeling the air. Then sometimes he looked at them with so much love and delight, they were sure he was blessing their happiness.

By the time the boy was two, his hair had come in thick and curly and black, but his chubby legs had gone a bit flaccid and thin. That tongue pushed out when she tried to nurse him, he would howl in frustration as he failed to attach, as if he, never the strongest baby, had forgotten how as he grew older.

What she did not say to John was *Why isn't he walking? Why isn't he talking?*

When she put Bobo on the grass to crawl these days, he just lay there, grunting, and if a butterfly lit on the grass, he watched it carefully, but did not reach for it, or repeat the word as she said it over and over and over: *Butterfly, Bobo! Say Butterfly!* Sometimes he would say "buh

buh buh buh." But that could mean anything. He said it when he saw John, or when she held a cookie before him, or when he was in the bath. For the last two months, it had been his only word.

She had vague ideas about talking at two years—or was it walking?— and an image of lively three-year-olds taking over their mothers' lives with incessant demands at barn raisings and church gatherings back in Holly. She had nobody to ask. She caught herself thinking of calling her mother, then felt the familiar dragging at her heart, *you don't have a mother any more.* A woman should have a mother to ask such questions of.

She briefly considered trying to track down an aunt back in Nebraska, but she had never liked her aunts, so what would be the point? She had not invited them to the wedding. She had not even told them about the child. And she'd had the distinct impression during her last visit that all her relations were glad to have the farmland without the complication of a young woman attached to it. She remembered that unkindness and turned away from the connection.

John's elderly aunt and uncle had showed little interest in the young married couple since the wedding, and Jolene couldn't imagine calling up Aunt Tawley and asking her advice. Who else did she know here? There was Saralyn from the ice cream shop. Jolene had no intention of confiding her worry to someone who was probably a former girlfriend of John's. There was her odd neighbor Miss Reba. But the old lady had no children of her own. What did she know besides birthing? Besides, she remembered what John had said after Bobo was born, when she asked him about the strange blessing Miss Reba sang for him. "She's probably put a spell on you," he said. "People say she has the power." He was kidding, but there was something dark and unfathomable in Miss Reba's eyes.

As the summer passed, she thought about going to the library to get a book, but didn't want John to see it, and didn't want the librarian knowing her business, so she waited and hoped and noticed that, month by month, things didn't seem to be changing much. Bobo wasn't eating enough to grow, and he wasn't changing enough to grow up.

In August, on a broiling hot day, she finally broached the subject with John. "There's something funny," she said. "He's not lively like he used to be."

"Nobody's lively on a day like today," he said. He wiped his forehead and neck with his bandanna.

"I mean it, John. Something's not right. Not just today." Why couldn't he see it?

John looked at her thoughtfully. Looked at Bobo. Picked him up. The boy dangled arms and legs passively, rolled his head side to side, cheeks flushed with the heat.

"Maybe it's time to switch him to cow's milk. Maybe some molasses in it. That's a spring tonic, it says in the midwife book. I think he'll be all right when the weather changes."

She tried those things. Bobo liked the new milk. He gained a little weight. But not much changed. She pored over the midwife book, which had a section on child health and diet, herbal tinctures to make a thrifty child. Thrifty. She remembered that word from home. It meant thriving. She began to brew teas and seek out herbs in the pastures and forests, mix them into his warm milk bottle. She began to mix a raw egg into his milk, and blackstrap molasses. She massaged his arms and legs to increase blood flow. She gave him warm baths followed by cool washcloth rubs, then wrapped him in a hot towel, which he seemed to enjoy, kicking with more energy than she'd seen. She determined to set aside her dreamy ways, her poetry reading, and make this baby thrifty.

One day she paged to a section with pictures of babies who were terribly deformed. Oh how it tore her heart, the perfect sweet face ravaged by the misshapen cleft palette, the Siamese twins joined at the belly, the chubby baby leg with a swollen club foot. In those days, it was clear, such children did not often survive. At least her baby wasn't like that. *What could be wrong, really?* she asked herself, gazing into Bobo's wide gnome face. When her Bobo laughed, his eyes crinkled up like one of those little trolls she'd read about in the fairytales of childhood— his face wide, joyous—and her heart eased. *Good things come to those who wait,* she told herself, remembering her mother's aphorism against worry, against impatience, and in her heart the stirring ache was stilled, for a time.

The fall passed, then winter, then spring, and her hope faded as Bobo remained much the same—alternately happy and raging, confined to a world he could reach by rolling, although he was able to roll sideways a little further than before. The fear that he might be damaged became a knowledge that he surely was damaged, or "slow," but she tucked that knowledge into a dark corner of her heart, where John could not see it, and went on.

With March came a new worry. John was having trouble with Uncle Rupert's accounting on the hay. Hay was part of the trade John was making for mortgage payments. John paid partly in hay bales, partly in cash from his sales of produce and other things. In the summer, John made cash from a roadside stand. People from Quarryville and the university would pull over and buy corn and beans, squash and tomatoes, leaving quarters and dollar bills in a cigar box that John checked every day. In fall John cut and sold firewood, then Christmas cedars, to tide them over. But by spring there was always a rough patch when there wasn't much to sell or trade until May cutting. John always had it figured that last fall's hay would cover March and April payments, but this year Rupert had a different idea.

"He says the hay last fall didn't cover the payments this spring," John told her. "He never said anything like that before."

"We could trade milk," Jolene said. "There's plenty of that."

"Bobo needs that," John said darkly. "Besides, they don't drink milk. Upsets her stomach."

"Or cheese. I know how to make cheese," Jolene kept on.

"Milk, cheese, same thing," John said. "Can't you understand? We need some cash. He's talking about breaking the deal. He's talking about—." His voice broke.

"About what?" Jolene asked, worried now too.

"About raising the price. Selling to someone else for cash. He needs the money, I guess. Aunt Tawley's heart medicine costs way more than they can afford. They're pretty broke."

It shimmered in the air between them, the question of getting a job. Working off the farm. Neither one of them would say it. Neither one of them wanted it.

That night she couldn't sleep. The farm held them all together. It shook her to the core, the thought of losing it. What would they do? Where would they go? She could not fathom it. Then she had an idea.

She told John about it at breakfast the next morning, while he drank his coffee.

"I can pay it," Jolene said. "I have money. It's just sitting there, in the bank."

"I don't want your money," John said.

"It's not for you, it's for us," Jolene said. "I need this farm too. Bobo needs it. It makes all the sense in the world, John."

"I don't like it," he said. "What if there's an emergency? What if you need it for something?"

"Don't be silly," Jolene said. "We don't need a thing. Let me do this, John. Let me do something for you, for a change. Besides, if Uncle Rupert can change the deal any time he wants, we need to get this settled."

It was this last argument that finally won John over. They needed the freedom from worrying about farm payments. He wanted the farm securely his. Theirs. He nodded.

Jolene's heart flooded with joy. It was his life's dream, and she was going to give it to him.

On Monday, she dressed in one of her old college outfits, a plain white blouse with no collar, and long cotton skirt, fastened with one of Bobo's diaper pins. She had gained some pounds around the middle. She stuffed her bank book and old college ID into a cloth bag, along with some fresh diapers, gathered up Bobo, and got in the truck with John.

Rumbling into downtown in their battered orange truck, Jolene saw heads turn at the sight of them. Other drivers eased through Main Street in shiny new Chevys, tapping horns and shouting out to neighbors, stopping mid-street to say hello on the sparkling spring day. But John wasn't doing any of that. He was just looking for a parking space.

A woman stared at them from the sidewalk, then pulled her children away, as if they shouldn't see such a sight. Jolene pulled Bobo closer, smoothed back the tendrils of her dark hair that had escaped from her loose braid and made a cloud around her head. Now she remembered Saturdays in Holly with her mother, walking to the sewing shop or library in their plain long dresses, while town girls and mothers regarded them with cool stares. "Just like Holly," she murmured. "What's that?" John said. "Never mind," she said. She turned and looked at his long whiskers. How had she not seen? He had been growing out his beard, and now he almost resembled a boy from home.

He pulled over in front of the bank. "I'll drop you here," he said. "I've got to go to the feed store."

"But I thought you would come with me," she said. Truth to tell, she was a little afraid of banks. Her people had never used them.

John shook his head. "People talk in this town. I don't want people saying I took your money."

"But, what if they—?" She stopped. She didn't want to sound stupid. But she was worried. She'd never taken money out of a bank before, just put it in.

"What?"

"What if they won't give me the money?"

"Don't worry," John said. "This is what you do." And he instructed her in exactly what to say.

Jolene kissed him, picked up Bobo, and stepped down from the cab. The plan was to meet in half an hour at the ice cream shop, then off to Uncle Tawley's to surprise him with a check. She felt a strange thrill. She was going to buy the farm for them today. She was going to make John happy, happier than she'd seen him in a while. She was going to save the day. As long as she and Bobo could get through this and walk out with a check. For the first time in a long time, she knew exactly what to do.

She remembered to ask for Mr. Ridley, the banker who had so kindly taken her uncle's cashier's check and placed it in an interest-bearing savings account.

"Miss Jolene," he said, beaming, holding out his hand. He seemed genuinely glad to see her. She wondered if he would be so happy when she told him her mission.

"Mr. Ridley," she said. Bobo wriggled in her arms. "And who is this?" Mr. Ridley said, in a sing-song voice, as he pulled out a chair for her. "Is this a new addition to the Blake household?"

"This is Bobo," Jolene said.

"Hello, Bobo," Mr. Ridley said. Bobo was staring at the ceiling fan and slowly waving his hands. "What does he see up there?" Mr. Ridley said, and laughed.

Jolene resisted the impulse to poke Bobo and make him respond. Mr. Ridley was regarding the child with interest. "What a great lot of hair," he said. "How old is he?"

"He's two and a half," Jolene said. "He's a good boy, aren't you Bobo?" Bobo wriggled in her arms, then flung his head back and continued to stare at the ceiling fan.

"A good boy," Mr. Ridley agreed. "Very well behaved."

Bobo jerked his arms out and knocked Jolene in the head. "Ow," Jolene said. "Bobo, settle down." The boy's eyes went back to the ceiling fan.

She drew out her bank book and statements, which showed $112,300. It had earned twelve thousand dollars in interest in three years! Pretty good, she thought. Buying the farm would take most of that. But she would still have a couple of thousand left.

"I would like to withdraw one hundred and nine thousand dollars," she said. "Cashier's check, please." She said it just as John had instructed.

Mr. Ridley's smile faded, but immediately was replaced with a fresh one. "Some other bank luring you away?" he said genially. "Because I have to tell you we can give you a better interest rate now than almost anyone." He leaned forward. "We're in the money," he said, seriously. "You can't really do better than First. Your money could make five thousand dollars next year in interest alone."

John had said he might do this. Jolene was ready. "No other bank," she said. "Just some bills to pay."

Mr. Ridley leaned closer. "Is everything all right at the farm? Is John okay?" He seemed genuinely concerned.

"We're fine," she said. "Everyone's fine." She wasn't going to tell him what it was for. She wasn't going to be the subject of Quarryville gossip. John would hate that. "Just a cashier's check please," she said. "I don't like to carry cash." That last part she'd ad libbed. It sounded good. Like she had done this before.

Mr. Ridley moved some papers around on his desk. Picked up the phone, said, "Just one moment, Miss Jolene, we'll get you taken care of." Then he dialed his assistant, asked her to come in.

At this moment, Bobo kicked both his legs into her belly, and Jolene felt the diaper pin spring open, her skirt fall agape at the side. While Mr. Ridley was whispering on the phone, she set Bobo on the desk, held him steady with one hand, and fiddled with the pin under the table with the other. The pin popped open, stuck her in the thumb, sprang out of her fingers, and clattered onto the floor under her chair. Mr. Ridley was still busy on the phone, so she bent down to pick it up, and as she bent over, her cloth bag fell to the floor on the other side of her. "Drat," she said under her breath. She scooped up the diaper pin and the bag, and banged her head on desk on the way up, jerking Bobo so that he tumbled onto his back in the middle of the desk. The boy started to cry. Jolene grabbed him and bounced him on one knee, quieting the boy, then saw that her thumb was leaking drops of blood on the child's shirt. She was dabbing at it with a cloth when Mrs. Trent walked in.

Mrs. Trent was long and cool and had perfect short hair. She glanced at Jolene as if she didn't think much of her. "Yes?" she said. "How may I be of assistance?"

Mr. Ridley was looking at Jolene. "Are you okay?" he said.

"Fine," she said. "I'm fine." *I'm bleeding all over the place, the baby's crying, and my skirt is falling off. Just get me the dratted check.*

"Mrs. Trent, Miss Jolene here is one of our most valued customers. I wonder if you could tell her about the investment opportunity we have for some of our special customers?"

Mrs. Trent looked a little startled. But then she collected herself and began to speak. From what Jolene could gather, there was the opportunity to borrow against cash, at a favorable rate, in order to invest in a money market fund, which then earned a higher rate, so that you came out ahead in the long run, thus getting the use of your cash and saving it too.

She'd never heard of such a thing, and it didn't really make sense to her. "Are you sure?" she said, holding her skirt to her side with one hand, still bouncing Bobo on her knee, so that her voice came out in jerks.

"Very sure," Mrs. Trent said primly.

She stopped bouncing Bobo. "Well, it sounds like a good deal," she said. "I'll have to ask my husband."

Mr. Ridley said, "That's fine. When can he come in? I'd be glad to fill him in."

Jolene knew that if John came in, he would start to think about it, and if he started to think about it, he would back away from their plan, and if he backed out now, there was a good chance she wouldn't be able to talk him into it again.

"Well, I—" Jolene stopped. "I appreciate the offer. But I just want the check."

Mr. Ridley looked at her thoughtfully. "So be it," he said. "Perhaps another time."

He arranged for the check to be printed, and he gave her a new balance for her book. He shook her hand. "Mrs. Blake," he said. "Bobo." He reached out to grasp the boy's fingers and gave a slight shake.

She noticed that he had stopped calling her Miss Jolene. She stood, holding her skirt closed with one hand, holding the check with the other, bag dangling from her elbow, Bobo clutched to her shoulder. She walked out the door with as much dignity as she could muster. Mr. Ridley opened the door for them and closed it softly behind them. "Thank you," she whispered. She nuzzled Bobo's neck. "Thank you," she said again.

She had the money!

When she found John outside in the truck, it was all she could do to keep from waving the check in the air. But Bobo was fussing. She stuffed the check into her bag and lifted the child into her lap. "Let's go," John said. "Ice cream another time. Let's get this done."

They drove in silence down the long dirt road to Uncle Rupert's house. Aunt Tawley came to the screen door. They had never visited John's relations together. John always went by himself. Now he swung down from the cab, said, "I'll be just a minute," and held out his hand for the check. She pulled it slowly out of the bag. She had imagined a triumphant moment, the both of them standing there, holding hands, while Uncle Rupert bent over the deed, finally signing it over to them. But now Bobo was fussing again, clinging. She didn't want to take him into that house, make a scene. She held the boy in her lap. Watched John go inside alone.

He came out pretty quickly.

"He's not home. Do you believe it? Never been anywhere but his house or my barn in years, decides to go play checkers."

"Did you leave the check?" Jolene asked.

"Are you kidding? I want that deed signed. I'll wait." He patted his breast pocket. "It will be safe, don't worry."

For the next three days in a row, John stopped by his aunt and uncle's house. Then a fourth day. A fifth. Each time he told them when he was coming. Each time Uncle Rupert was gone. John grew more and more exasperated. He gave it three days, and missed him again. Three weeks passed in this way. It was clear that once Uncle Rupert knew they had the cash, he didn't want to sell. John wondered, suddenly, if the land was really his to sell after all. He went down to the register of deeds and checked. It was listed in Rupert's name. It was valued at $134,000, five thousand more than the price they'd agreed on ten years ago.

"I've paid him two thousand a year for ten years," John said. "Now he's holding back because of five thousand dollars. What a cheapskate. Some of this land should have come to me in the first place." John was pacing back and forth in the kitchen, furious.

"You should just go talk to him," Jolene said. "Work it out."

"He's the one who wanted a big cash payment. He's the one who had his eyes on your money, greedy old bastard."

Jolene was shocked. She'd never heard John talk like that. Saying words like that. "He's your family," she said. "And what do you mean he had his eyes on the money? Did you tell him?"

"I—he—he said he couldn't wait for me to pay it off. He said he had another buyer. We have an agreement! He thought I was some pathetic kid he could screw around with. I told him we could pay him tomorrow, if it came to that. He asked me where I got the money, like I'd robbed a bank or something. You should have heard what he said when I told him, he said— " John stopped, miserable.

"What did he say?" Jolene asked. "What did he say about me?"

John's face twisted in anger. "He said your people hold on to money. You *Amish*. He didn't even get it right. What an ass. I almost hit him." He looked up. Saw the expression on Jolene's face. "Oh, my sweet girl, I'm so sorry." He pulled her to him, murmured into her hair, "So sorry. Never meant for you to know any of this. You shouldn't have to—"

He was holding her so tight, her cheekbone pressed painfully into the button on his cotton work shirt, and she thought, *He thinks I am a child, a weak silly fool. He thinks I can't stand up to a bully.* There was a schoolyard bully back in Holly, used to hit the Holly Chapel Mennonite kids when he figured out they weren't allowed to hit back. "Peace be with you," the kid would yell, each word accompanied by a blow. "Amish Amish Amish." Until one day the Mennonite kids ganged up on him and six of them sat on him until he took it back. "I'm not Amish," one boy said. "Amish would kill you with a rake." Everyone knew he lied, but it was effective. They all thrilled with the gruesome possibility, none of them quite sure how you did that.

Rupert was being a bully. She pulled away and looked John in the eye. "Give me the check. I'm going over there." She would charge into their yard, barge inside, and say, *It's time you took this money. Sign the deed. I'm not Amish.*

"No," John said. "I messed things up. I'll fix it." He had that stubborn look.

"You're wrong," Jolene said. "This is my problem too. If they won't take the money from you, maybe they will take it from me." *I can be stubborn too. You have no idea how stubborn a Mennonite can be.*

John finally agreed that they could go together. Going together might change things. You never knew. He arranged for Reba to come stay with Bobo. They drove together in silence. Walked to the screen door. Aunt Tawley let them in. They sat in the parlor. Strangely, Uncle Rupert was home this time. "See you brought reinforcements," Uncle Rupert said.

"What in the Sam Hill have you been up to—" John began.

Jolene put her hand on his arm. "Let me," she said.

John was so surprised, he stopped.

"We have the money," she said. "If you don't need it, we can continue as before. Two thousand a year. You are our family. We want to honor our agreement. If you want to change the agreement, now is the time to say." *And an Amish would kill you with a rake.*

Uncle Rupert and John both looked at her in astonishment.

"Girl's got spark," Uncle Rupert said.

"She is not a girl," John said. "She's my wife."

"It's worth more now," Uncle Rupert said.

"So is the money," Jolene said. "It will earn you thirty thousand in six years. Mr. Ridley has good rates now at the bank." She nudged John. He pulled the check from his shirt pocket, unfolded it, held it up for them to see.

"We'll take it," Aunt Tawley said. "Rupert, get the paper."

There was a moment when the two men regarded the two women with amazement, as if they'd never seen them before. Then Uncle Rupert surprised them all by laughing out loud. "These women," he said, "must have put something in our tea. I'm blown if I don't think I agree with them." He shuffled off, came back with a yellowed deed, and a typed agreement. "Tear it up?" he said, holding up the agreement.

"Better to write on it, paid up," Aunt Tawley said. "And the date."

Jolene reached for John's hand. They watched Uncle Rupert scrawl his quavering name and date on the deed, and though it was not by candlelight, as she'd imagined, with a quill pen and a wax seal, she felt the sense of triumph she'd waited for. Did John feel it too? He was staring at Uncle Rupert with a funny look on his face. He looked a little like a child who did not believe the gift before him was really his. She squeezed his hand. He turned and nodded, gave her half a grin. *He is afraid,* she thought. *So afraid of losing this. More afraid of that than anything.*

Uncle Rupert blew on the ink, held it over a lamp to make it dry. "All yours now, boy," he said. "No hard feelings?" He held the deed like a question mark in the air.

"No," John said. He took the deed, scanned it, folded it, and placed it in his shirt pocket. "You still want hay? I'll charge halves like before."

"You'll take cash?" Uncle Rupert said. "I guess I've got some now."

"This week would be good. Before it gets too dry."

"All right."

Aunt Tawley did not offer them tea. They left, hand in hand, and John drove the truck a little ways down the road before he pulled over and said, "We did it. You did it. I can't believe it. You were amazing. The farm is ours now."

"Ours," she said. She wrapped her arms around the broad chest of the most stubborn man she knew.

For the rest of April and May, and into June, Jolene and John celebrated their ownership of land by walking its acres and boundaries, Bobo trundled along in John's arms. Bobo's third birthday came and went. The farm birds shouted louder, the fields seemed more lush than ever, the baled hay more golden and sweet smelling. One day they watched the aerial dance of a pair of hawks mating, tumbling in the sky over their heads.

"Oh look!" she said, '*A living, fierce, gyrating wheel.*'"

"Whitman, right?" John said. "Dalliance of the Eagles." He paused, remembered:

"*In tumbling turning clustering loops, straight downward falling.*"

"Yes!" Jolene said. "Then something about separate diverse flight, and—"

They both said it together: "'*She hers, he his, pursuing.*'"

The next morning, Bobo woke up hot and feverish. Jolene felt his forehead in horror. He'd never so much as had a cold before. He had to go to the doctor! Even John got worried. He gave Bobo a sponge bath to cool his fever, but the baby began to jerk and convulse in his arms, and then finally lay hot and quiet.

John breathed into his mouth, pressed the tiny chest, over and over, but the pulse stayed weak and the fever burned. He threw Jolene a look of controlled panic and said, "Start the truck."

The emergency room in Quarryville quelled the fever with tubes and fluids, explained that this happens with young children sometimes, cause unknown. He would need to stay very quiet for a few days and take lots of naps. After the doctor left them, the nurse turned to Jolene and said, "How's he progressing? Is he talking? Does he have consonant sounds?"

"Well, he says one thing," Jolene said. "He's a little slow I guess." She suddenly felt herself flush under the stare of the nurse.

"What about the Down Syndrome?" the nurse said. "When was your last checkup?"

"What?" Jolene said. "What syndrome?" Bobo had a syndrome? Jolene looked at John with horror. John looked back steadily.

"He's fine," he said. "It takes time."

Jolene felt the heat of dismay, fear, then rage rise in her head while voices swirled around her. There was something terribly wrong with Bobo. She had known something was wrong. John had known too, and had said nothing.

"You'll need to go to a specialist," the nurse said. "Let me give you a referral." She bent her head to write down a number, which apparently she knew by heart. When she offered Jolene the paper, she rested her other hand on Bobo's curly head. Bobo laughed and wriggled his arms, almost as if he wanted to touch the nurse. "They are beautiful at this age," she said. "And it just gets better. My son is eight. He's a bucket of love." She gave the two of them a fierce look. "Don't neglect this. You'll need to check his heart on a regular basis. There's a correlation with heart damage. Plus you'll need special training for him—language, speaking, managing emotions."

Jolene sat stunned, listening to the list of symptoms she should have noticed, things she should have done, holding on to Bobo's frail knees with one hand. Bobo's heart was damaged? John would not look at her. She snatched the paper out of the nurse's hand so fast, it tore in half. Gathering up both halves and stuffing them in her pocket, she said, "I didn't know."

"I know," said the nurse. "That's why I told you."

On the way home the baby slept in Jolene's lap, and she sat there silently staring at him. Those funny hands. The slanted eyes. That was Down Syndrome. Why had she never seen it? Back in the schoolyards of Holly, they called kids like this *retarded*. She hadn't known there was another name for it. She had a dim recollection of a schoolyard giant back in elementary school, a large pale girl with freckled skin who towered over the rest and whose uneven gait and beaming smile were strangely frightening as she chased the first graders. In a fierce whisper, so as not to wake the child, she hissed at John, "You knew!"

"I suspected. I didn't know for sure. I didn't want you to be unhappy." He drove carefully, as if speeding might unleash more feeling.

"Unhappy!" Jolene moaned. "I can't believe this. What did she mean about his heart? Is he going to die?" Her voice had risen to a wail. Bobo woke, blinked his eyes and fixed on her face. He began to cry with Mama.

John set his jaw and drove.

The doctor was good with Bobo, conducted his exam gently and with good humor, tickling his feet and making him laugh. But when it was time to talk with Jolene and John, he lost his patience. "Surely you knew something was wrong?" he said. "He's three. What about the natal doctor? Didn't he tell you?"

John's lips closed in a tight straight line. Jolene thought guiltily of Miss Reba Jones and her strange ways. The doctor drew his own conclusions. "Natural childbirth, huh?" he said. "You do know this is the twentieth century. A baby needs a doctor—has he even had his shots? Don't you know there's a measles epidemic?" The doctor was angry. "People like you—"

"Listen," John said, cutting the doctor off, "we're here now. Just tell us what to do."

The doctor seemed about to say something, then changed his mind. "First of all, we'll give him his shots today. Then there's his heart. You'll have to bring him back every three months. He's got all the classic signs of a murmur. I don't think we need to operate, but . . . we'll have to see if his heart can keep up with his development."

"What else?" John said.

Jolene felt the panic rising in her throat. Shouldn't she be taking notes? Where was a pencil, a piece of paper? She had done everything wrong, wrong, wrong, and she had doomed her own child to some awful fate. While she rummaged for a pencil, Bobo looked at her anxiously.

"There's the issue of strengthening his legs for walking. You say he doesn't crawl. You see how his feet are turned out? We'll need some kind of bracing to help that. And you'll have to take him to PT for exercise. Walking can happen within the year if you keep it up."

"What else?" John said. Jolene could tell he was on a slow burn. They didn't have any money. They were living off the land. And here this man was giving orders for what sounded like very expensive treatment.

"Language. He'll need tutoring. Special classes as he gets older. You'll have to watch for any gifts or talents. He'll need to develop them for later. He's got a good chance of living into adulthood. The heart's not as bad as it could be."

The man seemed to think he was delivering good news. John took it badly.

"We don't have insurance," he said.

"I know," said the doctor. "You'll have to apply for Medicaid. Some of this is covered."

The doctor eyed Jolene with a strange mixture of pity, anger, and disgust. "Don't you read, Mrs. Blake? This is covered in all the women's magazines."

"My wife doesn't read *women's* magazines," John said.

Jolene thought guiltily of all her hours spent reading poetry. Emily Dickinson, for goodness sake. When she should have been reading— well, something useful.

"Well, John," the doctor said, "I might have expected this of you. But your wife seems a sensible person." He turned to Jolene, who was rocking Bobo from side to side. "You can take any magazines you want," he said, "from the stack in the waiting room." The look on his face said: *but I don't think you'll actually read them.*

"You *know* him?" Jolene asked, as they walked to the truck.

"I grew up around here," John said. "I know a lot of people."

"Why did he—" Jolene stopped herself and buried her nose in Bobo's hair.

"What?" John said, his voice like glass. "Why did he have such a low opinion of me?"

"Like Saralyn," Jolene said to the baby's tender skull.

John glanced at her, frowned. "I don't fit in with these people," he said. "I never have." He paused. Unlocked her door. Got in the truck. "You've got to understand this about Ambler County," he said. "If you don't fit in, you're sunk. You might as well hang it up. You just learn to live with it. You create your own world and ignore the outside world."

"The Outside World," Jolene repeated. Her parents had used that phrase to describe the world outside the town of Holly, Nebraska, the world outside the Mennonite church—excluding even the Other Mennonite church, from which Holly Chapel had split before she was born. She had thought that by marrying John she had joined the vast throngs of Real People in the Outside World, the world and people she'd wondered about her whole life, thought she'd find at college.

"I guess," she said slowly, "everybody's outside of some world."

She looked down at Bobo's skull, the soft place where the bones had finally joined, and through the fine curls she could still feel the tender pulse of this creature who also did not fit in and never would. "Oh, Bobo," she said, "your parents are misfits." And she began to cry again, hot tears splashing on the baby's hair.

John drove on, his lips in a tight line. "Dammit, Jolene, you don't get it," he finally said. "Sometimes it's a *good thing* not to fit in. Sometimes it's a very good thing."

"'Be not conformed to this world,'" Jolene said.

"Exactly," John said.

It gave her no comfort to hear him agree.

4

Jolene insisted on paying for treatments, and the bills quickly emptied her bank account. They did not qualify for help because they owned their farm outright. So, against John's wishes, she called Mr. Ridley at the bank, who agreed to a loan against the land and sent papers for them to sign. The papers sat on the kitchen counter for three days. One morning she saw that John had finally signed them. The dark look in his eyes told her she'd been wrong to buy the farm, then risk it by borrowing, but soon the treatments began to work, and as they both watched Bobo's eager crablike progress across the floor, their worried hearts eased.

They had been too exhausted, distracted by Bobo's crying, to make love very much that year, but one night he reached for her again and began to make love to her. Then he paused, said, "Almost forgot." He pulled a condom from the bedside table and began to unwrap it.

"You don't need that," Jolene laughed. "We're married, remember?"

"Let's just be careful," he said. "We don't need another baby right now."

"Why not?" she said, and suddenly it seemed like such a good idea. They'd been careful for three years. She missed the intimacy of him inside her, his warm juice spreading in ejaculation. She was ready for another baby.

But he was adamant. He would use condoms.

When she learned about diaphragms from her stack of women's

magazines, she asked him to take her to the clinic. "Okay," he said. "Good." Apparently he didn't like the condoms very much either.

Now Jolene's time was spent on Bobo, to the exclusion of her farm chores. John hired Miss Reba to help a few days a week with the boy, drove Bobo to her house, or brought Miss Reba home, and the boy grew attached to the stolid old woman. In a year's time he learned to say Mama and Dada, Weba and Bobo, could speak at least one complete sentence—"Want cookie"—and was finally learning his A B C's song. He liked the letter 'A' the best, and when things made him happy, he tended to say "Aaaaaaaaaayz." He was able to stand up straight, as long as he held on to a chair. Before she knew it, it was June again, and Bobo was turning four.

At Jolene's insistence, they were having a party. She invited Miss Reba and instructed John to invite his aunt and uncle. "You really want them?" John said. "They're not my favorite relations."

"They're your *only* relations," Jolene said. She was adamant. Bobo needed family. He needed friends. Once Aunt Tawley and Uncle Rupert saw him, they would be charmed, she was sure. How could they resist him? She tickled the tender place under Bobo's chin and he laughed, as if in total agreement.

Jolene decorated the screen porch with wildflowers in jars and festoons of sweet-smelling honeysuckle and put a nice tablecloth and her new plates on the porch table. Aunt Tawley and Uncle Rupert arrived bearing a small gift-wrapped box.

"Where's John?" Uncle Rupert said, looking around the porch, his eyes passing over Miss Reba and Bobo and back to Jolene.

"He's gone off to the shed to get some kind of surprise. I don't have any idea what it is," Jolene said. "Anyway, please sit down." The two of them plopped into wicker chairs.

Bobo was busy scootching on his hands and knees across the porch floor toward Miss Reba, who was in the rocker with her hands reaching toward him.

"Don't he walk?" Aunt Tawley said.

"He's slow," Jolene said. "But learning."

"His daddy's brother was like that," Uncle Rupert said.

"Like what?" Jolene asked, her curiosity outflanking her anger.

"Slow," Rupert said, turning to stare at her. "Didn't live past ten."

"Rupert!" Tawley said. "What a thing to say. Miss Jolene, don't you listen to him."

"I remember him," Miss Reba said. "Slow children can be the sweetest." She pulled Bobo to her lap and he gave her a hug, pressing his smiling face against her cheek and kissing a sloppy kiss.

"It's the heart that goes on 'em," Uncle Rupert said. "They got a weak heart."

Aunt Tawley glared at him, then said, as if in explanation, "Rupert thinks it was the Indian blood coming out. They say it's bad blood makes a bad heart. John's daddy had a bad heart too, but he lived to a good age."

"Fifty-five," said Rupert, shaking his head. "That ain't such a good age."

"And how old are you, Uncle Rupert?" Jolene asked, her face burning. "How's your heart working?"

"He's seventy-two, Miss Jolene," said Aunt Tawley. "And I'm not sure I like your tone."

She and Jolene stared at each other.

"Anyway," she continued, "Rupert and John's father ain't related by blood. That's the whole other side of the family."

"My daddy had Indian blood," Miss Reba said, setting Bobo's feet back on the floor. They all turned and looked at her. "He lived to a good age. Longer than he wanted to live. That's a fact. Tuscarora blood only make you stronger."

"You don't look like you got any Tuscarora," Uncle Rupert said. "You look like a regular nig—"

"Rupert!" Aunt Tawley snapped. "Shut up. I mean it, just shut up."

At the sharp tone in her voice, Bobo's face jerked around. He watched Aunt Tawley with concern. She turned to Miss Reba and said, "I'm sorry. He's old. He's no fit company unless you want to bale hay. Best man around for that. We got to go." She turned to Jolene. "I hope Bobo enjoys his present." Jolene nodded, her mouth grim. They hadn't even said hello to Bobo. They had hardly looked at him. They walked to their truck and drove away.

Reba's old eyes seemed to have receded in their sockets. Her lips were in a straight line, firmly shut.

"Oh, Miss Reba, I'm so sorry. Please, please." Jolene looked around for something to do to make it up to her. There was the cake, uncut, untouched. "Please, have some cake."

Miss Reba's mouth moved a bit, forming words with no sounds. She stared at something past the screen, out in the field. Jolene could barely hear the words she spoke: "Ain't no Tuscarora blood makin' bad hearts. It's the curse on the whites. *Death in equal proportion, eye for eye. Tooth, tooth. Arm. Leg. Finger bone.*" She seemed to be quoting some scripture or incantation.

Jolene shuddered. Bobo stood there, unsteady, watching Miss Reba and his mama. Miss Reba rose and strode to the door and opened it without a backward glance.

When the screen door slammed behind her, Bobo toddled to the door and called, in his high voice, "Weba!"

It took Jolene a moment to get it that Bobo was walking.

By the time John came back in, carrying a large cardboard box, Jolene had forgotten Miss Reba, and had scooped up Bobo and was hugging him and covering his face with kisses. "He walked!" she said. "He walked!" John set down the box, put his arms around the two of them and swung them all in a circle, singing "Happy birthday to you!" while Bobo laughed and tried to sing along, "Ha buh da! Ha buh da!" They sank to the floor and John reached arms for Bobo, trying to get him to walk again. Bobo reached his arms up to be held.

"Reba didn't stay for cake?" John asked.

"Nobody stayed for cake," she said. She eyed the lopsided blue birthday cake on the table, its colors too garish to be appetizing, she had put too much food coloring in the icing, a whole bottle, and the word "Bobo" looping in gooey yellow. She was terrible with cake.

"Cay!" Bobo said.

"More for us!" John said. "I told you they were peculiar. Oh, I almost forgot. Bobo, here's your present!" He placed the cardboard box before the boy.

Bobo looked at his father, then at the box on the floor. A curious sound emanated from the box. A mouse squeak? Bobo scootched over and lifted the lid. A white puppy leaped up and licked Bobo on the nose, then tumbled into his lap.

"Ay!" Bobo yelled, giggling. "Aaaaaaaaayz!"

They ate the cake sitting cross-legged on the floor, and the puppy licked icing off Bobo's cheek as fast as his fist could smear it on. "Cay!" Bobo exclaimed as he chewed, and pieces of blue and yellow icing fell out of his mouth. By the end of the party, there were cake crumbs all over the floor, a puddle of puppy pee, and Bobo had walked across the porch five times in pursuit of his wiggly birthday present.

"Good present," Jolene said.

"I'll train him," John said.

"Wonder what Aunt Tawley brought?" she said.

"A spoon, I bet. That's what she always gave me. A silver spoon from the great Blake collection."

"How strange," Jolene said, and laughed.

"And look here," John said. He picked up a cloth packet that lay on the table. It was about the size of an envelope, and seemed to be stuffed with something lumpy.

"What is it?"

"Must be from Miss Reba."

"Open it," Jolene said. The look of it gave her the shivers.

John unfolded the cloth gingerly. Something fell into his hand. "A gourd," he said. "A gourd rattle. Looks like she painted it and added feathers and things. Looks like a chicken bone tied to a thread. Wonder what that's all about?"

"Ugh," said Jolene. "Put it away. It's creepy." She shuddered, remembering Miss Reba's strange talk of curses.

"Must be some kind of good luck charm," he said.

"Put it away, John," Jolene said. "I mean it."

He put in on a bookshelf in the living room. The next day, walking across the kitchen, Jolene stumbled on scraps of feathers and gourd torn to pieces by puppy teeth, and something that looked like it could have been a finger bone gnawed to splinters, exposing the dark marrow within.

5

They named the dog "Ace," after Bobo's outburst, and it became the word Bobo used the most. John kept his promise and trained the puppy in the basics. The pup seemed to train himself in more specialized skills: standing between Bobo and danger, standing still while Bobo gripped the tufts of fur at his shoulder, then guiding the boy as he walked.

By the time Bobo was five, Ace was a bundle of white fur and fluff, as tall as the boy, with a pointed nose whose shiny black had worn off in places from relentless digging of holes. The dog could catch a fish in the shallows of the pond in his jaws, kill a snake, a rat, or a rabbit, and swim across the pond on command, all the while keeping an eye on Bobo's every move. Ace sat where Bobo sat. He slept where Bobo slept. He moved where Bobo moved, his tail wagging slow and low, so as not to whack Bobo in the head.

He left Bobo's side one time that they could remember, when he and Bobo ran up to Jolene just as she was picking up a bale of spoiled hay for mulch. Underneath was a hatch of copperheads, six or seven of them, the tiny reddish-brown snakes squirming and hissing in the direction of Jolene's bare leg. Ace moved to stand in front of them, attracting their venomous fangs to his flank. While they struck at his leg, ribs, and nose, over and over, he calmly turned and dispatched them, one by one, then took off for the swamp. Bobo cried and tried to run after, but Jolene snatched him up and ran to the house.

For three days and nights they mourned Ace's passing, believing that no dog, not even Ace, could survive so many serpents' teeth. But Ace lay in the mud until the mud pulled the poison from his body. When he came home one morning, ragged with swamp briars and fur black as dirt, it was like the resurrection of Christ in the Blake household.

Ace was back! Long live Ace.

As Bobo grew stronger, Ace became his companion in everything he did. They explored Indigo Field together. Did Bobo's daily chores together—put fresh hay out for Blackie the cow, collected eggs in a basket, swept the porch and helped Papa pick things for supper. Sometimes they rode on John's tractor, and sometimes he let them ride in the back of his truck, bouncing across the pastures on a hay ride. John taught Ace the limits of Bobo's world, and Ace checked Bobo's every move, like a shepherd guarding a flock of lambs.

At five, Bobo began to want to explore, but if he tried to open the pasture gate, Ace body-blocked him and pushed him back until Bobo beat him with his fists and finally gave up. Later, when Bobo was able to escape the block, Ace simply stood and barked at him until someone came.

John taught Bobo his numbers, and Jolene read to him. Ace listened attentively, head cocked, just another student in class. Bobo sometimes made him sit and look at a book while he pretended to read in his half-formed voice. Sometimes Bobo moved Ace's paw to help count rocks: wah, doo, ree.

In this way, Jolene and John began to feel their boy was safe, and the blessing of Reba fell full upon them like honey, and the weeks and seasons and years passed in a sweet muddle of days until the boy turned six and the doctor said he should start to go to school. At first Jolene resisted, remembering again that pale giantess back in Nebraska, how the older children also chased her, and sometimes threw rocks at her strange bulky back and made her cry. But it seemed there was a program in the school, and a nice lady in charge of the program, so they took their precious boy to meet her and began to talk to him about being a big boy now and that meant you could go to school.

"Ace too?" he asked.

"Ace will stay here and wait for you," John said.

"Not going, Papa," Bobo shook his head and set his chin.

"You can teach Ace things that you learn," Jolene said.

Bobo thought about that for a minute. "Teach Ace?" Ace barked and wagged his tail. And so it was decided. Bobo would go to school for the fall semester, afternoons only, in a special program.

In the fall, John drove Bobo to school for the first time, and Jolene stayed home, keeping desperately busy so that she couldn't think about all the things that could go wrong. Before they left, John chained Ace to a shade tree in the back yard, but when she went to check on him, he'd slipped his collar and his tracks in the soft dirt of the driveway showed he'd followed the truck. When John got home, Jolene was on the phone. Nobody had seen Ace. Not Reba. Not the school. He didn't come home that night. Bobo was inconsolable. He refused to go to school ever again, and John had to hold him tight to keep him from running into the woods to search for Ace.

The next day the principal called. Ace had been waiting at school for Bobo. He was disturbing the morning classes. Racing around the school, herding children into tight bunches, sniffing and poking them with his nose, and barking. The dog barked and barked and would not shut up.

John brought Ace home in the truck. Bobo's first two days of school were ruined, and Bobo blamed Ace, yelling at him, "Bad Ace. Bad Dog!" until Ace's head drooped and he slunk under the porch to hide. The next day Jolene sent Bobo to school and barricaded Ace in the house. He jumped out an open window. The day after that, they put him in the shed, but he dug his way out. Then Jolene locked him in the old root cellar, and he howled a ghostly howl all afternoon, and when they finally let him out, his paws and gums were bloody with clawing and chewing at the wood slats of the walls.

Jolene couldn't stand it anymore. Bobo would stay with Reba the next day while they baled hay. Maybe Reba could help them find a teacher. Bobo didn't have to go to school. Truth to tell, she would rather he stayed home where she could grab him and smell his head and watch over him. But when Reba came to pick him up, she squinted through her glasses and said, "Why this boy not in school?"

Jolene explained.

"Mm-hmmm. Mm-hmmmm. That don't seem a good reason. He got to go to school." She turned to Bobo. "You like school?" she said.

"Yes! Yes!" he shouted. "ABCDEFG. Nice teacher. Kids!"

"You know the dog can't go," she said.

"No Ace," Bobo agreed.

"You got to tell him that, boy. He don't understand."

Jolene looked at Reba. Did she really think Bobo could talk to Ace and Ace would listen?

Bobo stared at Miss Reba, then called Ace to his side and made him sit. Then he started to talk to the dog in his special dog language.

Miss Reba turned to Jolene and said, "Boys like to ride the bus. There's a bus they got for the specials. He can ride with the specials. Dog can't smell your tires and follow that way."

Reba had spoken and Jolene could think of no other solution. Bobo would ride the bus with the other special children. Ace could stand with him at the end of the road, Bobo would say "Stay," and Ace would stay.

When the bus dropped Bobo off at four, Ace would be there. Strangely, it worked. What Bobo said, Ace did.

John and Jolene felt oddly bereft going about their business without the company of Ace and Bobo. Some afternoons Jolene would wander from her chores, done quickly and efficiently without Bobo to watch, and go visit John out in his fields. One afternoon she brought him lemonade. One afternoon she reached out with her arms to be comforted and John held her tight. It was a steamy fall day, so when he said, "Pond swim?" she said, "Yes!" with delight and raced him, taking off her farm clothes and slipping into the warm, soupy water.

It had been so long since they'd been alone on the farm without Bobo to worry about. They laughed and splashed and kissed and played, then lay on the shady banks. Jolene turned to John and kissed him again, stroked his belly. "I could get used to this," Jolene said. She was wondering, a little, why he hadn't made love to her yet.

She kissed his cheek, moustache, neck, ear, and nose. She stroked his belly, let her hand rest on his penis.

John smiled, then looked at her seriously. "We should be careful," he said. "We shouldn't be doing this without planning ahead. Don't want to take a chance."

"I think it's time," she said, stroking the hair out of his eyes. *Time for another baby. Time to put the diaphragm away.*

"Time?" John said mildly.

"We should try again," Jolene said. "Bobo's in school now. We have a little time. We could make a little girl. A little sister for Bobo."

John made a strange hunching movement with his shoulders, then sat up in a crouch on the pine needles, his genitals hanging like heavy fruit, his backside pale, his back brown and wide. "I don't think so," he said.

"Why not?" Jolene said, sure she could jolly him out of whatever his objections might be.

"Bobo is why," he said.

"Bobo would love it," she said.

"Don't you get it?" John said. "Bobo is our responsibility for the rest of his life. He will never survive without us. I can't stand to think we would create another child like him. I can't stand it."

"You *love* Bobo," Jolene said. She was as sure of this as she was of anything. She'd seen him hold Bobo in his lap, cuddling him, and showing him plants and flowers and hay bales and bugs, joyful in the boy's attachment. She'd watched him lug Bobo across the yard as the boy stood on one of his large boots and clung to his leg. She'd seen him whirl the boy in the air while Ace barked and barked and the boy screamed in delight. She'd watched them sleeping together in the hayloft, in the hammock, on the pine needles by the pond. Bobo was the joy of his days.

"I love Bobo," he agreed. "But he's my fault. It's in my family, not yours. My sperm. My genes. I can't stand that he might die. I can't stand that it might happen again."

"Your *fault*," Jolene said. "Your *fault*. My god, John. He's not a mistake, he's our sweet boy. How can you say he's your *fault*? You should be ashamed."

"I am ashamed," he said. "And I can't do it. You'll have to keep using something, or I will. We'll have to be careful. If you want another baby, maybe we could get a donor or something."

"*You're* giving me another baby," Jolene said. She knocked him off balance and sat on him. Looked him in the eye as his penis stirred, then fell.

"See," he said. "I just can't do it."

She touched his penis and watched it rise in her hand. She gave an experimental lick. "Jolene," he groaned.

She kept licking. Maybe if he like this part, she could get him to do it for real.

6

John was serious about no babies. He insisted on watching her put in her diaphragm now before they made love, which made her nervous, so she started putting it in every night before she came to bed. "It's there," she would say when she slipped in beside him. He would check for the chemical-smelling goo with his hand. Then grunt, turn toward her, and wrap her in his arms. In this way their love life sparked, and Jolene hoped for a miracle.

When he stopped checking, Jolene found herself skipping the diaphragm part, just injecting the goo. Then, one night, exhausted, she used nothing at all. Surely he could tell. He knew her body so well. She considered his lovemaking that night to be a kind of assent, a softening of his stance.

When she found herself pregnant, she didn't tell him for weeks, then months, waiting for the right moment. She was sure it was a girl, a girl with curly light-brown hair like John's and wide blue eyes and a mouth that laughed out loud, arms and legs that would climb trees. This girl would be the darling of their days. Everyone would love her. She would name her Emily, for the poet.

Then one day there were cramps and there was blood and lots of it and after making lunch and finishing chores and sending Bobo off to school, she stuffed two sanitary pads in her panties, took herself upstairs to bed and let the baby flow out of her while listening to the hum of John's hay baler in the field, back and forth, back and forth, gathering up life into tight square blocks while she was letting go of everything. The sound seeping through the open window maddened her like flies at the windowpane, so she closed the window and lay in the heat, sweating, until the sound became dimmer and dimmer and she became more and more exhausted and finally slept.

John found her, leaking blood all over the spread, pale arms flung out in exhaustion. The medic in him took over and by the time Bobo got home from school, he had her cleaned up and drinking beef broth to replenish her iron.

When Jolene told him how long she'd been carrying, John was furious. "Why didn't you tell me?"

"I wanted to wait. Wait till I was sure it was okay," she said. She'd hoped he would accept the idea of a baby, once it was further along. But he blamed her.

"You made this happen," he said. "You did."

"Yes," she said. "I made it happen. And you. Oh, John, you would have loved her so much, she would have been your darling girl."

"You have lost your mind," John said coldly. "And this is what happens. Don't you know this is what happens?" He sat looking at her, then stood up and walked to the doorway. Rested his hand on the frame. Turned halfway toward her. "I can't trust you," he said.

"No," she said. The word seeped from her mouth like a breath.

And like that, the smell and heft of him was gone from her bed. He slept in the spare room, the one that would have been hers, the one that would have belonged to the darling girl with light-brown hair.

As John turned away from her, he turned to Bobo, with all the love and attention a doting father could muster. Where he'd been attentive before, now he was fanatic in his attention. Jolene, watching the two of them, sometimes wondered if John believed Bobo would be dying soon, and this was their last time together. The quality of his attention had become driven, almost strained, compared to the easy love of earlier days.

Bobo thrived under the attention, learned to swing a whiffle bat (though he hit the ball rarely), learned about fishing (but didn't like to kill the fish), got better at catch (still dropped the ball, but no longer cried when he did). The boy scrambled alongside his father, scooping hay up to fluff it, attempting to drag sacks of feed into the barn, an inch at a time. It was beautiful to watch them together. But she missed Bobo at her side, following her every move. And more than that, there was something tough and guarded in John when she was around. She was his Jolene, but not his love. She had become . . . Bobo's mother.

Now Bobo would leap out of bed in the mornings and race to John's room and jump on his father. "What's foh today, Papa?" he would say. "What's foh today?" John took him on walks through the woods, taught him to crawl across a log from one side of the creek to the other, taught him to jump over ditches and get up without crying when he fell—well, not crying much. John showed him what poison ivy was, where snakes lived, where turtles nested, and how to train Ace to do tricks. Soon Bobo was putting on shows for the two of them after supper.

"Roll, Ace," he said, and Ace rolled over.

"Beg, Ace." The dog sat up on hind legs and panted.

"Jump, Ace." The dog jumped over a stick and trotted back to sit in front of Bobo.

"Fetch, Ace." Bobo threw the stick and Ace fetched.

After each trick, Ace returned to Bobo, sat, and looked at his face, grinning.

"He's so well trained," Jolene said. She turned to John. "When did you do this?"

"I didn't," John said. "Bobo did. All by himself."

Jolene remembered what the doctor had said: *Watch for any special gifts or talents.* This was a gift. This was a talent. Bobo could train animals. She filed it away for later, when he might need it.

Months passed. John did not return to her bed. She refused to beg. She could be stubborn too. But, finally, one night she stood in the doorway of his room and watched him. He was not asleep. He sensed her there. He opened his eyes.

"Come to bed," she said. "Just come to bed. I promise I won't . . ."

"I don't believe you," he said.

She felt the color go out of her face. Not to lie next to her husband, her John, that beautiful chest, back, legs, those beautiful eyes. "I'll—I'll get an operation," she said. It just fell out of her mouth. The minute she said it she knew she never would.

"I should do it," he said. "It's easier when men do it."

"No!" she said. Then, "Maybe." Her body twinged with the thought of it, the thought of John hurt. "Come to bed now. I can't sleep."

But he held his ground. Jolene was devastated. They'd never really fought. But something about this felt very final. Her belly, though it should have healed by now, still felt sore and empty from the miscarriage. How could it be that John would not hold her? Jolene padded to her bed and lay on her stomach, feeling a dread she'd never felt before. Everything she wanted relied on John loving her. If he did not, she would live all alone, in her own house, for the rest of her life, as her family moved like underwater creatures around her. *I envy seas whereon he rides,* she mouthed. But Emily's words did not fit. John was not on any journey. He was in the room next door. But he was gone.

She wept, feeling as desolate as those cold Nebraska skies and gray fields she'd grown up knowing so well, and had long since tried to escape.

Jolene learned about John's stubbornness that year. He stuck to his guns. They did not speak again of operations. She watched him and Bobo, appalled, disbelieving, that her family no longer seemed to include her. John still spoke to her kindly. He still ate the food she put on the table, and she still cooked the food he brought in from the garden. She did her chores, her milking. She ironed Bobo's shirts for school, even though all the kids wore tee shirts with their jeans, even Bobo knew that, and complained, *Want Teeez, Mama!* So she let him wear tees, but ironed them too.

Jolene held on in a frenzy of chores. Cleaning out the cow barn, sewing patches on all their clothes, darning socks, canning and freezing everything in sight, including an attempt to pickle eggs from their small flock. She would prove that she was worthy.

Or die trying.

Jolene stayed up late on winter nights, sewing or waxing the kitchen floor, painting the kitchen cabinets. She fell to bed exhausted, sometimes sleeping on the couch, just to keep from thinking of what awaited her upstairs: an empty bed, a husband who no longer loved her body. When, she thought, hugging her arms around her chest, when in the world did he get like this? Why did I never see this before?

One warm day in February, a bluebird got in the house and flew around and around, banging into window panes and skittering along the tops of walls, then swooping up the stairs. She followed it into the spare room where John had been sleeping. She closed the door, opened the window, stood back. The bird bounced from wall to ceiling, knocking loose plaster onto the floor in sifts of white grit. It clung to the slat wood wall and eyed her, then moved its head from side to side, seeming to sniff the air. Finally it darted to the open window, slipped out into freedom. She watched it arc into the sky, headed to the Gooley pines. She pulled the sash shut.

She had not come into this room since John's decree. Something had changed. On the table next to the bed sat John's big IBM typewriter, the cover pulled off, and a blank page inserted, as if someone had considered typing, then walked away. She tapped on some keys, but they did not make that satisfying smack against the paper, making words. Nothing happened at all. It was turned off. She looked more closely. No one had touched this typewriter in ages. The onionskin in the platen was yellowed and crisp. Beside the typewriter were his chapters, laid out in a neat row, but the top pages were curled with sunscald from the window, and clots of loose plaster from the ceiling now scattered across them like sugar.

She remembered that set jaw from the day he explained about his book, and not needing a degree to finish it. The look in his eye when he mentioned his thesis advisor. Almost vengeful. Proud. John had always been this way. She had never thought his fierce powers of rejection would be turned toward her.

Now here was his book, abandoned.

She swept the room, brushed the plaster off the paper and the bed, and closed the door.

In March it rained for week, a cold rain that brought a chill to the house and made spring seem far away. One night a fox got to the young chicks and the few old biddies who survived refused to lay. Then Blackie's milk began to dry up. It was finally the prospect of no longer having the daily contact with Blackie's warm slick flank, her earth smell, her silky teats, that filled Jolene with grief. She sat there, weeping against the cow's rib bones, wiping tears with milky fingers, when Bobo walked in with Ace.

"Mama cry?" he said. "Don't Mama cry."

He came up to her and put his arms around her waist and she cried even harder, and then Bobo began to cry too and the two of them had a good cry together, Ace circling at their feet, anxious, bumping them with his worn-off pink-black nose, and Blackie turning to watch them with her great glistening eyes.

It was as if Bobo had caught her own grief and his small body magnified it. Now she was crying because his little frame was so shaken, his face so woebegone. Jolene finally wiped his squinted eyes with her shirt and said, "No, Bobo, Mama's not crying any more. Mama's happy. Stop crying, Bobo." She stretched her mouth into a smile for him. He looked at her face then buried his head in her belly.

"This has got to stop," Jolene said. Suddenly she was angry. This wasn't the way it was supposed to be. This wasn't what was promised her. This was wrong. She needed somebody to talk to. A woman. The only woman she knew was Reba. *If that's what you've got,* she said aloud, *then that's what you get.* It was something her mother used to say.

She grabbed Bobo's hand and pulled him to the truck. Ace jumped in beside. Keys in the ignition as always. Turn the key. Drive. It was that simple.

John was out in the field. He would never miss them.

7

Reba lived just a half mile down River Road, and Jolene took that route because the forest road would be muddy after all the rain. She realized, with a kind of shame, that she hadn't been to Reba's house since that first time. John always drove Bobo there, or Reba arrived at the farm to babysit in her big Chrysler sedan. Jolene had practically forgotten how to drive John's truck. He'd taken care of all their needs and errands off the farm. She ground the gears when she tried to shift into third.

Reba was in the yard feeding chickens when Jolene pulled up. Now she saw what she hadn't really seen on her first visit: small tidy brick house. Chimney leaking a smudge of smoke. Big old Chrysler parked in the yard. Red Ford truck sagging to one side in the back. And the strange thing she did remember: black angels, carved like totem poles from huge logs, placed around the front yard. Three of them.

Miss Reba looked up. A slow dawning expression on her face: suspicion, then caution, then pleasure. "Weba!" Bobo called out the truck window, waving frantically. He unlocked the door, scrambled down, and ran to her, wrapped his arms around her legs.

Miss Reba put hands on hips and said, "Miss Jolene." Then looked down at Bobo and said, "Well, boy, how'm I s'posed to get anything done around here with you stuck to me like that?"

"Chikin," Bobo said, looking up at Miss Reba.

"Yes, boy, chicken. Come help me feed." Miss Reba took his hands and filled them with corn from her apron pocket, then set him loose and watched the chickens crowd him, pecking his shoes where he had dropped a yellow clump of seed instead of scattering it. "Like this, boy," she said, showing him a hand closed, then flung open. Bobo grabbed another handful out of her pocket and flung it straight up, and it fell on them all, raining down corn on chickens and people and angels alike.

"Oh, Bobo!" Jolene said. "Don't waste it!"

"No waste," Miss Reba said, brushing corn from her hair, letting it fall to the dirt. "It all come down in time." She regarded Jolene with her black eyes, nodded, and said, "You best come inside. Dog stays out."

Bobo said, "Stay!" and Ace lay down on the porch stoop, eyeing the chickens carefully.

Jolene took Bobo's hand and entered the parlor, blocks of light from the windows illuminating the dark furniture: a sofa, a recliner, a small table, two chairs, everything covered in those crocheted throws in rainbow colors.

Miss Reba pulled a red plastic truck out of a drawer and handed it to Bobo. "Play here," she said, pointing to the rug. She explained to Jolene, "I like him to stay on the rug."

Jolene stared at the picture on the mantel: a beautiful black girl, about eight years old, grinning in her Sunday best, pigtails and buck teeth.

"You?" Jolene said.

"Danielle," Miss Reba said. "That's my Danielle. She grown now."

"Daughter?" Why had she been so sure Reba had no children?

"Niece."

Miss Reba did not seem inclined to say more.

"She's lovely," Jolene said. "She must be a beautiful young woman."

"Yes," Miss Reba said. "Inside and out."

Again, Jolene felt a chill in the air and did not ask further questions. It had been a mistake to come here, what had she been thinking? She'd been desperate. She would have to make up some reason for her visit. She couldn't possibly ask this formidable black woman about how to fix her love life. How to fix her marriage. Jolene stared at her hands. What could she say? She needed chicken feed! That was it.

"Miss Reba," she said. "I just came by to see —"

"You like sweet tea?" Miss Reba said. "I got some. And cake. You like cake, boy?" She turned her face to Bobo.

"Cay!" he crowed. "Cay, Mama!" He grasped his hand at the air surrounding Miss Reba, as if it were filled with sweetness.

Jolene swallowed. Still hanging in the air was the memory of Bobo's birthday party, years before, when Miss Reba had left, insulted. She couldn't insult her by leaving now.

"Thank you," Jolene said. "I would love some."

Now Bobo was making truck sounds and carefully moving the toy in a track, following the swirling pattern in the rug as if the swirls were roads, and the edges were the confines of a world contained and safe.

She sat watching Bobo play while Miss Reba got plates and cups and brought them on a tray.

Miss Reba placed a plastic saucer next to Bobo on the floor. "Cay!" Bobo cried. He grabbed the slice in his hand and it crumbled and fell in clumps in his lap.

Jolene reached to pick up the crumbs but Miss Reba laid a hand on her arm. "Let him be," she said. "It's ladies' time."

Jolene sat back, startled at this open invitation. "I—" she felt words bubbling, spilling into her mouth. "I don't know what to do," she whispered.

"Mmm hmmm." Miss Reba nodded, pushed her glasses up her nose.

"He—he—" she couldn't say it.

"Mister John," Miss Reba said.

"Yes. John."

"You afraid, afraid about his love." Miss Reba's eyes were closed.

"Yes, yes, that's it exactly. I mean, really, Miss Reba, how can anybody live with a husband who won't—who won't—" She could not say it. How could Miss Reba possibly understand. She had never been married or had children of her own. And yet the words kept spilling, "Who won't come to my bed," she whispered

"Mmm-hmmm." Miss Reba was rocking now, in her recliner. Rocking forward a little, then back, eyes still closed. Then she snapped them open. Jolene stared at her, abashed. Those black glittering eyes, enlarged by thick glasses. They seemed to magnify Jolene's little secrets in the open air.

"You strong enough to carry it," Miss Reba said. "But you got to have a charm."

"You mean, like magic?" Jolene remembered the gourd rattle Miss Reba had left for Bobo's birthday present. She wondered if Miss Reba knew through her powers how that silly puppy Ace had chewed it into splinters.

"Don't truck in magic. It's a spirit blessing. And a charm. Let me think here, mmmm hmmm."

A charm? Jolene watched her as she closed her eyes again and hummed a tuneless song. A love charm? It made her think of Shakespeare, and A *Midsummer Night's Dream*, all those fairies flitting about, getting it mixed up who should love whom, and turning people into donkeys. And what about those angels in the yard? What were they supposed to be? She didn't like them.

"Sometimes . . ." Miss Reba was talking with her eyes closed. "Sometimes the spirit of a man goes bad on him. He can't be with a woman, gets afraid. Some bad spirit inside. Afraid he'll hurt the woman." She sat up suddenly. "You know. You know exactly. But you don't believe me. Don't matter. Works anyway."

Miss Reba rose up, rustling, and walked to the windowsill, where a watery green glass gallon Mason jar was half-filled with arrowheads. She fished around with her fingers, deep in the jar. Pulled out a stone that was not pointed at all. It was shaped like a lozenge, rounded at each end, with a subtle flange in the middle, all around. "Grinding stone. For fine corn. This what you need."

Miss Reba stroked it with her fingers, rolled it between her palms, said some words Jolene did not understand.

"Put it in the pillowcase. Hold it, till it warm, before you sleep. Then let it go. It will help you."

Miss Reba handed her the stone tool. It felt warm and smooth in her hand. A worry stone, like her father used to carry. That's what it was. A worry stone. She felt calmer already. Miss Reba was a friend after all. She understood more than seemed possible.

"Thank you," Jolene said. She slipped the stone into her pocket.

"Have some cake," Miss Reba said.

"I will," Jolene said. She perched the cake plate on her knee. Cut a bite with her fork. Placed it in her mouth. Perfect. Lemon pound cake, just like her mother used to make. There were flecks of green in the cake, and there was a haunting aftertaste. Lemon and . . . what?

"I put the rosemary in," Miss Reba said. "It's for memory."

Miss Reba knew Shakespeare? Well, maybe so. She knew as much as that poet about herbs and their meaning. Jolene was completely charmed. "For memory," she said, nodding. "This cake reminds me of my mother."

They chatted about this and that, about cake recipes and the weather, about Bobo's haircut and the hay fields, for more than an hour before Jolene realized the time and begged her pardon. John would have come back from the pastures by now, and it would be hell to explain why she'd taken off like this. She fingered the charm in her pocket. "Have you got a bucket of chicken feed we could borrow?" she said. "We're out."

"Right out there on the porch." Miss Reba said, as if she understood completely the need for chicken feed.

Jolene placed her cake plate carefully on the tray, finally noticing that it was fine china, yellowed with age, laced with roses and edged with gold. "Thank you," she said. "Thank you for the ladies' time. Next time, come to my house?"

"We'll see," Miss Reba said. "You got to learn to make a proper cake."

Jolene turned, remembering Miss Reba had left before tasting Bobo's garish, lopsided birthday cake. Was she still insulted after that disastrous party? Then she saw Miss Reba's lip curve. Miss Reba was chuckling. Jolene laughed. "I'm terrible at cakes," she said, "but I'll try." She thought of her mother's lemon pound cake. "I'll learn."

"Try, try," Miss Reba said, "and then succeed." She lifted a carton of hen's eggs from a stack by the door, handed it to Jolene. "You got to have fresh eggs for cake. These pretty fresh."

John heard the truck from across the field and came running. "My god!" he swore at her, through the truck window. "My god, you didn't even leave a note! Where the hell were you? Where the hell did you go?"

"Weba!" Bobo called out. "Weba has cay!"

"I went to Miss Reba's," Jolene answered, strangely calm, fingering the stone in her pocket. "We needed chicken feed. And you know, it turns out it's really rude to visit without having cake."

"Cay, Papa!" Bobo held out a foil-wrapped paper plate. "Weba say it for you!"

John took the plate.

"It's lemon-rosemary," Jolene said. She slipped out of the driver's seat, clutching the egg carton to her chest, then hefted the pail of chicken feed from the truck bed.

John lifted Bobo from the truck. Ace leaped to the ground. "Papa!" Bobo said. He wrapped his legs around his father's waist. "Papa, I feed the chicks. Like this!" He threw both hands into the air, letting them open to the sky, and leaning back as if he were expecting corn to rain down on their heads.

"Good," John said. "That's good." The cake plate slipped from his hand. He held Bobo to his breast. "Good," he said, closing his eyes, then opening them, and looking at Jolene with something like fear. "Don't ever," he said, "scare me like that again."

Ace nosed the foil, flipped the cake into the dirt, and ate.

That night after Bobo was in bed, Jolene washed herself with water warmed on the wood stove. Then slipped into her bed, the stone charm in hand. It seemed to glow between her palms with its own heat. She slipped it into her pillowcase. She sighed and fell into a dreamless sleep, all the weight of the strange day falling away from her arms and legs and splaying them willy nilly, like split wood at a chopping block.

She woke with the moon glaring into her eyes.

She raised her head, expecting to hear something. John moving in the direction of her bed? No. The house was silent. Silly charm. She felt for it in the pillow. Still there. Cold now.

She rubbed the smooth surface with her thumb. It seemed to warm a bit with its own fire. She rose, holding it in her hand, and slipped out of her room, down the hallway, to the room where John slept, hair glinting silver, a trick of the moonlight.

He had been so angry.

He had not listened to her apology. He had turned his face away. *Filled with the bad spirit*, Reba said. Something terribly wrong, but this time she knew it was something wrong with him, something she could not fix.

She wished she knew a song or a murmur of words to say, a charm to pass over his head while he slept. Something to bring back the perfect union of their days and nights. She was tempted to lift the cover and slip in beside him. But he was so angry. It was as if there were a hard edge glimmering around him, something sharp that could cut the both of them. She had been wrong about everything. She had even been wrong about Miss Reba. How had she not known the goodness in that soul?

A bird called out the window. She raised her head. Outside, the fields shimmered with light. A full moon tonight. Clear sky. The weather had changed. It was a strangely mild night, as if March had invited May. Movement in the pastures. Deer? Somewhere out there, in deep thickets, does were heavy with young. Her belly filled with sadness. She wanted to live in the pastures, with the deer.

Jolene pulled on tee shirt and jeans and sneakers, wrapped a shawl around her shoulders, slipped into the hall, and headed out the kitchen door.

Moonlight and pollen and last year's seed and stalk, shimmering as she passed. Fresh sprouts of woodbine, blackberry cane, scrub oak branch, catching at her bare forearms and calves. The moon was higher now, smaller, poised like a ladle of molten silver, ready to pour. Scratches in her arms like sparks from the moon, instant heat, then lingering ache.

Here was the dark path through the ridge, the Gooley pines. Here were pine needles two feet thick like a moist mattress underfoot. Here was that muttering owl, wing breath swooping past her face. Here was the top of the ridge. Indigo Field below, rocks and grass, squeezed like a moonlit lake between the ridge and the river, the river behind a thicket of grapevine and sycamore, the two-lane road slithering like a black snake through it toward the water, loud fast-moving water speaking secrets to the soft air.

Here was the place she and John had lain together. A boulder gleaming with light, sheltering a soft dry grassy patch. *Deer sleep here,* John said, when they'd first come here. She had touched the flattened dry thatch and found it still gave off heat. John had pulled her down beside him, and they lay flat on the heat of the animals before them. John said the rock just below the thin soil here heated up during the day, kept its warmth at night, and deer knew it, so they came and added warmth of their own, especially on sunny winter days. Snakes knew it too, so there was always one asleep under the boulder, waiting its turn in the sun. It would be quiet now, he'd told her. Sleeping a snake sleep, dreaming snaky dreams.

They'd made love till darkness fell. Then they looked up.

"It's just a thin cloth between us and all that light." John said. They stared at the stars, holes of gleaming light in the dark fabric of the sky.

The light seemed to want to tear the cloth to pieces.

This is how things are put together, she'd thought then. *Not how I thought they were. Here is a secret world.*

Now she knelt down on the grassy patch, still damp from rain, tried to feel the heat with the palms of her hands. Now she flung her body flat on the grass, breasts and belly pressed against it, face buried in the thatch, smelling the new life in the earth.

Now she rolled onto her back, spread her arms and legs wide, shawl fringe clutched in each hand, eyes shut tight, listening. A *chuck-will's-widow, in the thicket near the bridge. The soughing pines. A sound like earth, sipping water. Sleepy bird chatter. Then silence, a rich silence, one that breathed and shifted in its sleep.*

Now she opened her eyes.

Gravity could not hold against the pull of all those stars. And that moon! Surely her bones would fly up like a bird's.

She opened her palms, let the light fill them, weight them. Now she felt it. Heat from the earth below. Ghost heat. Heat from a past time.

It occurred to her that she had never been so alone before. It occurred to her that she had not been Jolene before. Not since she was a little girl, daydreaming in a cornfield.

What had Emily Dickinson said about such things? *The soul selects its own society . . . then shuts the door.*

She felt the cool air sliding down from the pines to the river. The tips of her breasts, the tops of her thighs, cooled and tingled. She moved her hands to warm them.

She felt the cycling warmth of her season, the knowledge she always had of the movement of an egg within her body to the place of readiness, her body pulsing faster in anticipation of pollination. Then she felt the twisting thorn of fear in her chest. Fear of losing John, fear for Bobo's future. The ache in her heart was so heavy. A terrible question came to her: *Had she just made up the beauty in this world, and John's love for her, to fill the old ache of a lonely child, had she made up this life the way as a child she'd made up a missing brother and fields of angels, entire families made of flocks of chicks and litters of kittens?*

She let the tears leak from her eyes, slide to her temples and soak into her hair. Her hands clutched Reba's rock charm, the peeled-smooth pestle of river rock that was the exact shape to fit in her palm, oblong and rounded on each end, with the small decorative ridge circling the middle. She opened her legs, held it against the seam of her jeans, rubbing there for the comfort of it—the heat and hurt of it.

What had Reba told her? This was a pestle for grinding corn. Those Indian stones, worn into a smooth bowl shape from centuries of strong, bare-breasted Tuscarora women pushing stone against corn against stone.

Perfect, she thought. *I am a stone bowl.*

Now she held the pestle in the light, let moonlight catch and shimmer on the smooth polish from a century of hands and gripping. Now she unzipped her jeans, and began to rub, gently at first, exploring, then in a relentless rhythm, pushing, pushing, eyes squeezed shut, *remember it, remember John, remember this kind of love, pine smell of his hair, smoke smell of his shirt,* one hand free to squeeze the tip of the breast, mouth open, tongue, voiceless tongue, no one to hear the deep breath of the night sounds, the groan of the night collapsing on the heat of the animals who once lay here. The young animals. Her young self, opening to first love. Her first self, crossing the boundary into a broken world.

She lay there, spent, sorrowful, alive. After a time, she curled to her side and pulled the shawl tight around her shoulders. A chill mist seeped across the field and she slept, dreaming that rocks came alive in Indigo Field, gathered round, and watched over her.

A piercing note woke her.

It was still full dark, but above the ridge the setting moon hung, heavy and pink as flesh. From a branch above, a white-throated sparrow piped its downturned notes. She rose, feeling the chill in her arms and legs. The sparrow called again, just over her head, and she looked up, wonderingly. *Such sad sweetness in such a small thing. How had I forgotten such sweetness?*

She rubbed her arms and legs, felt the strength in them, the muscles of a country woman. She headed down the path back to the house, seeking warmth. There would be Bobo's smile, a warm wood stove, the prospect of fresh eggs for breakfast, enough left over for a cake. She pictured John taking a careful bite, his lips pursed as sweetness approached, and it came to her. John was scared. That was what was wrong with him.

The sparrow called again, from a branch above her head. Another answered, its song sweeter still, but quavering at the end.

What joys attend this life come quick and loud, unexpected as birdsong.

Had she read that somewhere? Had she made it up?

She would write it down when she got home, before the others woke.

ACKNOWLEDGMENTS

I met a writer once who told me that no one reads her work before it goes to her publisher. This writer is extremely famous and smart and can get away with things like that. My writing takes a village of kind and smart people to keep it going, make it better, and help me let it go.

Many thanks are due to teachers in the Warren Wilson Creative Writing MFA Program, all of whom inspired and cajoled and made me smarter (and sometimes made me want to speak like Donald Duck in order to better understand poetry), but especially to Susan Neville, Steven Schwartz, Antonya Nelson, David Haynes, Wilton Barnhardt, C.J. Hribal, Joan Silber, and Peter Turchi for their incredible kindness and seemingly easy brilliance. The writers there are no less teachers for me, especially Kathryn Schwille, Donna Gershten, Cindy Epps, Steven Mitchel, Tracy Wynn, Emily Pease, Linda Elkin, Greg Rappleye, and Kim Ponders.

Thanks to Gail Galloway Adams, Judi Hill, Ann Hood, Debra Monroe, and the writers of Wildacres Writing Workshop, for reading my first fiction drafts and providing encouragement.

Thanks to Georgann Eubanks and Marianne Gingher for their ongoing support and teaching, years ago, in my first fiction workshops at Duke Continuing Ed. Thanks to my village's-worth of writing groups, who have read versions of these stories and others over the years, in a timeline that goes back more than twenty years: Barbara Lorie, Ralph Earle, Nancy Peacock, Tony Peacock, Virginia Holman, Janet Ray Edwards, Ronnie Lynton, Alice Johnson, Walter Bennett, and many

many others—you know who you are. Thanks to those who read or listened to snatches of late drafts, especially Doris Betts, Janet Lembke, Louise Hawes, Karen Pullen, Sue Farlow, Lisa Dellwo, Dee Reid, Susan Ketchin, Mary Frantz, and Pat Riviere-Seel, friends who keep the faith even when I forget to.

Thanks to Louis Rubin, who by hiring me to copyedit at Algonquin Books gave a Yankee the dream job of reading Southern fiction for a living, which made me want to try my hand at it. To Shannon Ravenel and Max Steele, who kindly reviewed one of these stories years ago. Thanks to Lois Rosenthal of *Story* magazine, for calling me on a Sunday afternoon, and making my day for the rest of my life. And thanks to Paula Closson Buck of *West Branch*, who, in accepting "The Clearing," wrote "Thanks for sending this beautiful story. It arrived (or I read it, finally) just when I was despairing of seeing another story I could really be excited about." Little did she know that I was despairing of finding a home for this story of my heart.

To Emily Herring Wilson and Coastal Carolina Press, who gave my first book its wings. Emily was a perfect editor, providing all the courage I needed to do something different and stand by it.

To Kevin Watson, the cheeriest publisher and editor I ever met, and the most fun, thank you for keeping my books in print and in your heart.

To the people at the Doris Betts Prize, the Novello Literary Award, the Pushcart Prize, the North Carolina Writers' Network Fiction Syndicate, the Blumenthal Foundation, and the Sherwood Anderson Foundation, for providing encouragement. Thank you to the North Carolina Arts Council, the Durham Arts Council, and ChathamArts, for providing support and the pleasure of good company, especially to Debbie McGill, Banu Valladares, Cathy Holt, Dona Dowling, Regina Bridgman, Mary Simpson, and Molly Matlock. Thanks to Weymouth Center for the Arts, Phoebe Walsh, Sam Ragan, Cos Barnes, and Hope Wood Price, for providing a lovely place to retreat to and revise for twenty years. Thanks to Headlands Center for the Arts and Hedgebrook Retreat for Women Writers, for hosting retreats that were exquisite in their comradeship, beauty, and care. And thanks to the North Carolina Writers' Network, which has been a base of support and encouragement for many years, especially Marsha Warren, Linda Hobson, Cynthia

Barnett, Virginia Freedman, Jim Sheedy, Nicki Leone, and Ed Southern, and to the North Carolina Writers Conference, a new cadre of fellow travelers. Thanks to Paul Mihas, Bridgette Lacy, Peggy Payne, and the folks at Creative Capital for keeping me focused and making it fun.

Thanks to my many students, who teach me every time I teach them. You're the best.

Thanks to my mom, Sarah Anne, who reads my work with interest and pride, to my sister, Kathleen, who keeps the faith alive with her undying enthusiasm, to my brother, Steve, and to Silvana, Gabriella, Jonathan, and Clara, who are a sweetness worth waiting for. To my dad, Jack, who let me spy on him when he wrote books. And to my daughter Darah, another sweetness in my life.

Last, and best, forever thanks to Sam, who keeps me in clean laundry, fresh vegetables, loving and laughter every day.

Marjorie Hudson
March 2011

A NOTE ON POETRY

The following poems provided fodder for my characters and my imagination:

Walt Whitman's "Out of the Cradle Endlessly Rocking," "A Song of Joys," and "Dalliance of the Eagles," all from *Leaves of Grass*.

Henry David Thoreau's "All Things are Current Found," from *A Week on the Concord and Merrimack Rivers*.

Emily Dickinson's "XVI. Apocalypse," from *Poems, First Series*; XXXVII; "A Thunder-Storm," from *Poems, Second Series*; and, from *The Complete Poems of Emily Dickinson*: "Split the lark and you'll find music" Part Three: Love. XLI; "God bless his suddenness," Part Two: Nature. VIII; "And now I'm different from before," Part Three: Love. LII; "I never lost as much but twice," Part Four: Time and Eternity. XL; "Has it feet like waterlilies?" LXXXIII. Out of the Morning.

MARJORIE HUDSON was born in a small town in Illinois, grew up in Washington, D.C., and now lives in Chatham County, North Carolina. *Accidental Birds of the Carolinas*, a Novello Literary Award Finalist, is her first book of fiction. Hudson is author of *Searching for Virginia Dare*, a North Carolina Arts Council Notable Book, and her fiction, poetry, and personal essays have been collected in five anthologies. She has contributed to many magazines and journals, including *Story*, *Storytelling Magazine*, *Garden & Gun*, *Yankee*, *West Branch*, *National Parks*, *American Land Forum*, and *North Carolina Literary Review*. Her honors and awards include a Fiction Syndicate Prize, two Pushcart Special Mentions, Writer in Residence at Headlands Center for the Arts, a Blumenthal Award, and Sarah Belk Gambrell / NC Artist Educator of the Year. She is a graduate of American University and holds an MFA in Creative Writing from Warren Wilson College.

Cover Artist **EMMA SKURINCK** lives on the banks of the Haw River in Bynum, North Carolina. After taking rambling walks beside that shallow body of water, she returns to her studio to paint—often creating portraits of the plants and animals she has encountered. Trained as a scientific illustrator, she has lately drifted towards infusing her art with a bit of wry storytelling. By granting her portrait subjects personality and humor, she hopes to impel the viewer to slow down and consider the beings with whom we share our space. To see more of Emma's work, visit web.mac.com/emmaskurnick.

CPSIA information can be obtained at www.ICGtesting.com
Printed in the USA
LVOW061147010413

327010LV00005B/333/P